When Sophia and Ray move from South Florida to Tennessee, they do not expect to be entering a different world. Yet, the differences are so extreme, they feel as if they've taken on a whole new existence. Ray begins his new job as the lone detective of the local police, and Sophia begins her shifts in the ER of the hospital, both looking forward to the peace and quiet of country living. However, on an outing to enjoy nature, everything changes—a human hand tumbles down on Sophia. From there, they learn that the laws are the same, but the criminals can be different. As the case develops in front of him, Ray struggles to keep Sophia out of the investigation—good-luck with that. An exciting adventure awaits them and the reader as they adjust to the pace of country living—and, along the way, solve a major crime.

Randy Rawls
Saving Dabba, Dating Death, Best Defense, Hot Rocks featuring Beth Bowman, FL PI
Jingle and the Magnificent Seven
Justice Secured
Thorns On Roses featuring Tom Jeffries

Previous Titles by the Author:

**Sophia Burgess and Ray Stone
Imperfect Mysteries:**
Imperfect Defense
Imperfect Daddy
Imperfect Contract

Tony Conte Mysteries:
Illegal Intent
Illegally Dead

Stand-alone mysteries:
She Learned to Die
Plan to Kill

GREGG E. BRICKMAN

IMPERFECT ESCAPE

Imperfect Escape ©2019 by Gregg E. Brickman.
All rights reserved.
No part of this book may be used or reproduced in any manner whatsoever, including Internet usage, without permission from the author, except in the case of brief quotations embodied to critical articles and reviews.

FIRST EDITION
First Printing 2019

Book Format by Gregg Brickman
Cover Design by Victoria Landis

Published by:
Gregg E. Brickman
Monterey, TN 38574

This is a work of fiction. Names, characters, places, and incidents are either the product of the author's imagination or are used fictitiously, and any resemblance to actual persons, living or dead, business establishments, events, or locales is entirely coincidental.

ISBN: ISBN: 9781793123459
Imprint: Independently published

For Mark and Laurie, in memory of Jack

Chapter 1

Sophia

Sophia limped off the hiking trail at Bluff Overlook Park and settled on a log. She indicated a space next to her, encouraging Ray to pause a minute. "I need to rest. My leg and hip are screaming." It was the same hip that stopped a bullet when she was on the police force.

Middle Tennessee's Cumberland Plateau's thick green woods closed in around her and trapped the mid-July heat and humidity. She wiped her brow, brushed her short brown hair from her forehead, and pulled her sticky tee shirt away from her skin.

"In a minute." Ray walked around the area, little more than a wide spot in the trail, then stooped to inspect the undergrowth as well as the underside of Sophia's downed tree.

Sophia watched, curious. She knew Ray possessed the normal suspicions of any police detective, but they were in the middle of nowhere. "Looking for gold?"

"Snakes."

"Yikes." Sophia jumped to her feet, knocking her shoulder into a spindly oak. Something thumped her shoulder and slid down her back. She sprang forward. "A snake. Oh my God. A snake slid down my back."

Spinning, she stared at the ground, focusing, not on a snake, but on a blood-stained, severed hand at her feet. "Ray."

Her voice, just above a whisper, cracked. "It's a hand. Oh my God, it's a human hand. A hand went down my back"

"Don't move," Ray said. "Where?"

"There." She pointed a finger, using all her strength to hold it steady.

"Damn." Ray bent his tall frame to inspect the hand. He scanned the area, tilting his head to look into the trees. "I don't see anyone or anything else."

"Good." Her voice quivered.

"The log is clean. Sit." His touch was gentle as he eased her down onto the fallen tree.

Ray crouched close, pulling her against his chest. "It's okay. Relax. Concentrate on me. It'll help." He, in his gentle non-cop mode, kissed her forehead and continued to hold her. "Now breathe."

Sophia's slight body shook. As an emergency department nurse, she wasn't a stranger to violence, but she'd never had body parts drop out of trees before either. Those things didn't happen in her world.

While keeping an arm around her back, he settled onto the log next to her and offered his water bottle. "Take a drink." He held it until she accepted and drank.

"I don't understand. How can a hand just fall from a tree? Bird crap, yes. Human hand, no." She regained her strength and composure, wiggled out of his embrace, and stared at the hideous appendage. It was a man's left hand, complete with shining wedding band. A waxy whiteness showed through dirt and grime. "No wrinkles. He is, maybe was, young. White. It looks like there's no blood left in the hand. Maybe a newlywed."

"Based on what?"

"The wedding band."

"Ah." He studied the hand, but didn't touch it. Instead, he snapped an image with his phone. "This may be one of several pieces of some guy." Standing straight and taking his time, he turned a slow circle, fixing his gaze on the trees and surrounding area. "We're in the center of a crime scene, but I don't see any other parts."

"Look again at the hand. It looks like it was in a fire." Sophia leaned to get a better view. She felt more settled, almost clinical, her nursing experience kicking in.

Again, he bent close to the hand. He frowned in apparent concentration, his cheeks tugging at the edges of his dark-brown goatee. "You're right. Looks like the ends of the fingers got the worst of it."

"What do you think happened?"

"The obvious thing that is someone wanted to get rid of the hand—and maybe more. I need to call it in." He pulled his cell phone from his pocket, tapped the screen, then stared at it. "No signal. Check yours."

"None," Sophia said.

"You'll have to go to the parking lot. It's about fifty yards from here and is a gentle incline. I'll stay and monitor the scene."

"I made it down. Guess I'll make it back up." Sophia bounced to her feet, ignoring the cramping in her hip and leg. "If I can't get a connection, I'll go to the house east of the park. I saw some activity on their deck when we went through the clearing a ways down." She pointed down the trail.

"Good plan."

***

Within a few steps, Sophia learned Ray's definition of *gentle incline* was contrary to hers. Though in his mid-forties and six years her senior, he'd grown up in the foothills of the Blue Ridge Mountains, she in North Dakota—where both hills and trees were the exception. He navigated the trails with practiced ease.

She dug her trekking poles into the path and used them to help haul herself upward toward the northern rim of the bluff. She wished she could measure the distance. Ray's fifty-yard estimate seemed to be straight up.

Feeling a sense of urgency and trying to hurry, she slipped

and stumbled toward the downward slope and the left edge. She grabbed at a sapling to stop her fall, losing one of her brand-new trekking poles in the process.

"Damn it. Son of a bitch." The pole slid down the hill, out of reach, and a tear, born in frustration, rolled down her cheek. She righted herself, paused a moment, and decided a later arrival in the parking lot was preferable to no arrival at all.

With one pole, progress was slower. Within a few yards, the pain in her right hip returned, searing into the bone. She stopped and rubbed the spot, stretching to ease the hurt. Following the climb, rest, rub pattern, she huffed into the lot twenty minutes later, but without another near fall.

Sophia pulled her cell phone from her pocket and noted one dot. Ray had told her to go the 9-1-1 route, since he didn't have the local department's information programmed into his phone yet.

"You've reached 9-1-1. What is your emergency?" a woman's voice said.

"We were hiking out of the bluff on the south edge of Plateauville and a human hand fell from a tree and hit me in the back." Her voice cracked as she shuddered at the memory.

"Ah, ma'am, are you sure it's a human hand, not an animal part?"

"Yes, I'm sure."

"You got a good look at it?"

"I did. And it was wearing a wedding ring."

After several seconds, the operator said, "Noted. Where exactly are you now?"

"I'm in the parking area north of the trailhead. We couldn't get a cell signal down the trail. Um, it's Bluff Overlook Park in the subdivision called the Cove. I think there is only one parking lot."

"What's your name?"

"Sophia Burgess. My number is . . ." She gave her number.

"Thank you. You said we. Who are you with?"

"Ray Stone. He'll be the new detective at Plateauville Police Department starting Monday, ah . . . tomorrow."

"Put him on the line please."

"I can't. He's more than fifty yards down the hill securing the crime scene. He sent me to make the call."

"What else can you tell me?"

"Can't you just send someone?" Sophia's voice shook. She tried to steady herself, but couldn't. The panic she'd tried to bury poked to the surface.

"Ma'am, both the deputy sheriff and the Plateauville patrol are en route to the scene. I put out the call. I want you to stay where you are and await their arrival."

"I just need to tell Ray people are coming."

"No. Stay where you are. You'll need to direct the officers to the correct trail."

Sophia shook her head to clear it. The dispatcher was right. "Yes. Of course. How long will it take them to arrive?"

"The deputy's ETA is twenty minutes. The Plateauville patrol officer should arrive in three minutes. He's in the area."

The lady on the phone said some other things, but Sophia didn't listen. She pushed END, then climbed into Ray's new Ram truck—it didn't feel like it belonged to her sports-car-loving fiancé. Even so, she sunk into the leather seat and reached for a bottle of water from the door panel. Wishing for something stronger, she took a drink while keeping her eyes on the entrance.

A black and white patrol vehicle with lights flashing, but no siren, approached. The front of the car dipped as the officer braked for the turn. The vehicle slowed to a crawl as the driver negotiated a curvy path around multiple potholes and tree debris. Finally, he stopped beside the truck and exited his vehicle.

The officer was built like Ray, tall and lean, and appeared to be almost old enough to shave—maybe twice a week. His blue uniform shirt and dark blue pants looked new, as did the backpack slung over his shoulder.

Sophia slid out of the truck.

"What's your name, ma'am?" Officer Johnson—she read his name tag—said.

She answered the question. "Can I show you the trail you need to take?"

"In a minute. I understand Detective Stone is here. Where is he?"

"He's down the hill with the hand. He said he needed to stay and make sure no one disturbed the scene."

"Lots of hikers out today, huh?" Officer Johnson's voice rang with Tennessee twang.

"No, sir. Just us, I think. But, still, he wanted to secure the scene."

"Is the detective armed?"

"I didn't see a gun." Sophia shrugged.

"You don't know?"

"I didn't strip search him. But he's a cop and carries most of the time, but I didn't see a weapon."

"Sorry, ma'am." Johnson looked offended. "I guess that sounded rude."

"No, I'm sorry. I was rude. I'm stressed."

"That's understandable, ma'am. Please, show me the trail. I'll take care not to startle him."

Realizing the reason for the gun question, Sophia smiled, then limped across the lot to the trailhead. From the website she viewed before they moved to Tennessee from Florida, she knew the local PD handled about two suspicious deaths a year, which explained the young officer's reaction. Her suspicion was he wanted the sheriff's deputy to arrive before he went to the scene. "You coming?"

"Right behind you. I don't want you going back down the trail, ma'am."

"Don't worry about that. I'm not into raining body parts. I'll just show you which one we took—it's the Falls Overlook Trail. I'll wait here for the rest of the troops."

Officer Johnson laughed. "Troops? It's me, Sheriff's Deputy Krantz—who will likely not stay around—and my chief, who's on his way into the department. He'll meet us there when we're ready."

"Okay." She quickened her step, using her pole to help her

negotiate the slight decline. After about twenty yards, she pointed. "There. Ray—and the hand—are down there."
"Did you see any more of the body?"
"No. But, I didn't look very hard either."
Officer Johnson grinned. "I get that, ma'am."
Sophia shuddered as she watched the officer approach the trailhead, hesitate for a long moment, then continue round the first curve of the trail and disappear from sight. She thought she had escaped to Tennessee to avoid finding bodies—and the repercussions that followed.

Chapter 2

Ray

Ray waited until Officer Johnson was close enough to hear him. "Jim, I was hoping you'd catch the call." Ray had met Jimmy Joe Johnson when he interviewed for the detective position at Plateauville Police Department. It was evident to Ray at the time that Johnson wanted the job—the first detective slot in the city. It was also obvious he was not prepared to assume it. As the small department grew, Ray hoped Johnson would be ready to take the next opening through the testing and promotion route, which Ray was assigned to create.

"Who else? I'm the only man on duty this morning, sir."

"Slim scheduling."

"Yes, sir. We schedule light in the mornings when not much is happenin', and double or triple up in the evenings and nights when there's more activity around town. Sometimes it doesn't work out. Chief Mullins is callin' in another man to cover the town so I can handle this."

"Good thing."

"Yes, sir, it is. Another thing. Chief Mullins told me to tell you'uns, you're sworn in today rather than tomorrow morning. You can pick up your shield when we go into town."

Ray laughed. "Is that so?" Ray had been on the department's payroll for the last two weeks, opting to attend

IMPERFECT ESCAPE

the criminal investigation school offered by the Tennessee Bureau of Investigation, TBI, in Nashville. He'd welcomed the refresher on crime scene techniques since detectives in the area handled their own scenes.

"Yes, sir."

"Jim, before we get started. You've called me *sir* four times in under two minutes. My name is Ray. Or you can call me Stone, if you'd rather. If we're with civilians or other departments and on the job, it's Detective Stone, and you're Officer Johnson."

"Okay, sir. I'll try."

Ray resisted the urge to mimic Sophia's annoying eye rolling habit. He satisfied himself with a mental eye roll, something he suspected Sophia had perfected, too.

"I bagged the hand." Ray nodded to where a blue plastic package sat on a stump. "And, I marked off what seems to be a reasonable perimeter for our crime scene." Ray pointed to strips of blue plastic tied to various trees around the area. "What do you think?"

Johnson looked up at the edge of the bluff—a granite cliff with a pronounced overhang. "That overhang has been fenced off for years. The crack on the right side could open at any moment, which don't mean people don't climb the fence. We actually done it when we was kids. Climbed on out and dangled our feet. Tossed our beer cans into the treetops. Got caught once and had to clean up the mess." Johnson appeared thoughtful. "If I climbed out there and pitched body parts, they'd end up in this area. Threw a few rocks a time or two. The result was the same, because of that stand of trees over there." He pointed.

"Yup." Ray nodded.

"I think your area's good. Where'd you get the blue markers?"

"Sophie and I hike with the dog sometimes. I have a roll of bags in my backpack."

Johnson laughed. "City folk."

"I suppose." Ray stepped back a couple of feet onto the

trail. "We contaminated the scene going up and down. We haven't met other hikers on the trail, so maybe we're the only ones who tromped through."

"Most folks are at the church on a Sunday morning and don't walk out their house to do other things until after."

Ray chuckled. "Whoever did this doesn't seem very godly." He pulled his iPhone from the leg pocket on his cargo pants. "Do you have any gear with you?"

"I do. We've all been trained to pick up fingerprints, take photos, that sort of thing. We send everything to the Tennessee Bureau of Investigation lab in Nashville. The District Attorney can call in TBI to handle the crime scene at his discretion. TBI has jurisdiction for drugs—which this could be. Oh, you know the sheriff has authority and can take over any case he wants?"

Ray was pleased with the young cop's knowledge and his desire to share it. He'd covered the same territory with the chief during his initial visit, but Ray was glad to know he and Johnson were on the same page and Johnson was serious about progressing up the ladder.

"I don't want to get out of line, sir."

"You're not. Keep talking."

"You know Tennessee is the meth capital of the world."

"So they say."

"If this is a murder."

"I'd say. Natural causes don't generally lead to body parts dropping from the trees and sliding down people's backs."

Johnson didn't smile. "Anyway, it's likely drug connected. That's when we get our really crazy shit. Pardon."

"And?"

"And it's meth in most cases. Those suckers go off the edge, and I don't mean off this here cliff."

Ray held up his cell phone. "Let's hike the perimeter, take some shots, and see what we can. Then we'll walk a grid. On my first pass, I didn't see any more body parts."

"Animal could have hauled 'em off."

"Could be." He tapped on his phone and held up an image

IMPERFECT ESCAPE

of the hand. "I looked at this. I don't see any evidence of it being gnawed or chewed."

Johnson took the cell phone and studied the picture. "I agree. Let's go up to the left first, then circle around. We should be able to see the trail from there and can watch for Krantz."

"Who is he?"

"Bobby Krantz. He's the sheriff's deputy for the area. I talked to him on the way over. He knows you're here, too."

Ray followed Johnson around the upper edge of the crime scene, allowing the younger man to blaze the trail and take the initial brunt of the thorny brambles. "Hold up," Ray said. "I want to take a few shots as we go to document that there is nothing here." He took the pictures. "Let's continue."

They proceeded around the marked area in the same manner and found nothing of interest.

***

Deputy Krantz, a slightly built, clean-shaven man in his midthirties, was sitting on a tree stump when Ray and Johnson returned to their starting point. His casual presence caused Ray to wonder why the deputy hadn't called out or joined them.

"Sorry to keep you waiting." Ray stepped close and extended his hand. "Ray Stone. Officer Johnson told me I'm officially working at Plateauville PD as of today."

"Stone, you're the new detective I heard about."

"That I am."

Krantz scowled. "Don't know for sure why Mullins thought he needed a detective. We've always provided investigative services throughout the county." He took Ray's offered hand and shook it. "But, welcome."

"Thanks." Ray didn't feel very welcome. He made a mental note to ask Johnson about the deputy's cool reception.

"You new to this area?"

"I am. But I was born, raised, and worked patrol near Roanoke on the Virginia side of the Blue Ridge. I'm no stranger to the terrain or the issues of policing in small towns and rural areas."

"Good to know. By the way, I met your lady in the parking lot. At my suggestion, she took your truck and went home since you'll be here awhile."

"Thanks."

Johnson said, "You can ride with me into town to see Chief Mullins, then he'll assign you a department car."

"Flexible bunch," Ray said.

Johnson laughed. "We have to be."

"Okay, Krantz, I'll bring you into the loop." Ray held up the package containing the hand. "This is all we found. We need to move it to a paper evidence bag as soon as we can."

Krantz nodded. "Nothing else?"

"No, just the hand. Which, by the way, slid down Sophie's back."

"Bet that made her day." Krantz laughed. "City girl . . . and all."

"Not exactly." Ray thought better of explaining Sophia's background—first a police officer, then an ED, emergency department, nurse. He'd leave that to her, if and when she decided to share it.

A confused look crossed Krantz's face. "If you say so. Have you searched the entire area?"

"We did. Walked a grid and took pictures of a lot of nothing. I'll go over it again after I've looked around up there," he pointed, "I want to see down into the trees from the overhang."

Krantz glanced up at the projection of granite.

Ray said, "Johnson, you can stay here and protect the scene while I go up to the trailhead. After I look around, I'll also interview the neighbors. Maybe that will give us reason to expand the search area."

"That would be the only close neighbor, though there are a bunch more houses down the road a little ways." Johnson raised his head to indicate the house on the cliff overlooking the bluff. "The Samuels are the only ones that live close to the park. Fact is they used to own this whole area. They deeded the park and trailhead over to the city when they couldn't keep people out and didn't want the liability."

"Interesting," Ray said.

Krantz stood, dusted off the back of his tan uniform pants, tucked his brown shirt deeper into them, and stepped back onto the trail. "I'm out of here."

"Officer Johnson," Ray said, "I'll not be long." He handed the evidence bag containing the hand to Johnson. "Keep this here. It'll be cooler than putting it in the car."

After Johnson nodded, Ray followed Krantz. They hiked up single file with no conversation. When the trail widened, Ray caught up. "Does the sheriff's office maintain any crime scene facilities in the county at all? I got the idea in Nashville that TBI was the whole show."

Krantz pressed his lips tight for a moment. "We have two coroners, who happen to be local physicians. One runs EMS. The other runs the emergency room at County. They handle the initial examination of bodies at the crime scene and supervise transport to the medical examiner in Nashville. Beyond that we have no crime scene facilities or personnel. The investigators work it themselves, then all the evidence goes to the TBI lab in Nashville."

"Sounds about like what I did in Virginia. How would this have been handled before I arrived?"

"One of the investigators from Crestville would take over and handle the case. But since Mullins hired a big shot detective, you'll have to ask for the support you think you need. Of course, the sheriff may take it away from you anyway. You being new and all."

"Fair enough."

They reached the parking lot. Ray motioned toward the outcrop overlooking the crime scene. "I'd like to have a look from the top. Do you have a pair of shoe covers and some evidence markers in case there is anything of interest?"

Krantz opened the rear hatch of his department-issued Ford Interceptor SUV and handed Ray the items.

"Nice ride." Ray ran his hand over the rear fender of the

white and yellow vehicle.

"We are issued new ones about every five years. I've had this about two months."

"Like it?"

"That I do. It works well for me, and the four-wheel drive is a plus on the country roads." Krantz said. "Need a notebook?"

"Thanks." He accepted the small spiral notebook—which was similar to the ones he preferred—and the accompanying pen.

"Careful you don't end up on the bottom. Stay clear of the crack."

***

Ray approached the rusty chain barrier near the overlook. A weathered sign warned against crossing due to the risk of falling. He took images of the area with his cell phone, then put on the shoe covers and stepped over the chain.

As he approached the rim, he studied the ground in hopes of finding something pointing to the person who tossed the hand. As suspected, the only things he spotted on the grey granite outcrop were bird droppings and a single cigarette butt, which he marked with a numbered yellow flag, photographed, bagged, and labeled.

He moved a few steps closer to the fractured overhang. There he found a single footprint in a dirt-filled depression. Again, he placed a numbered marker, laid a tape measure adjacent to the mark, and took several pictures from varying angles. He stopped to note the tag numbers and details.

Two more strides and he neared the edge. First, he tested the area with partial weight and heard a faint crackle. He lay down on his belly, saying a silent prayer for his own safety, and crawled forward.

The view was breathtaking. The many shades of green canopy shimmered and glowed in the bright sunshine. Focusing on the area directly below the edge, he scanned the

IMPERFECT ESCAPE

treetops and down as far as he could see through the woods. Nothing of note was visible. He wondered if there were more pieces of the victim elsewhere.

He heard the cracking sound again and wondered if he'd soon be among the body parts.

Johnson, having spotted him, motioned for Ray to back away, which he did.

Ray breathed a sigh, feeling relieved, when he was once again on solid granite.

After walking back through the lot and noting Krantz was gone, he headed east on a narrow trail toward the Samuels' house. He passed a private property sign on the left and a metal sculpture of a bear on the right.

The house looked magnificent, appearing to be suspended over the bluff. As he drew closer, he noted that only the deck extended out into space, and the cypress house seemed to be on solid footing—granite he presumed.

An older, dark-haired woman waved from the patio. "This is not part of the park." Her voice was friendly, not hinting at a silent *go away* command.

Ray continued a few steps until he stood within comfortable talking distance. "I'm Detective Stone of the Plateauville PD. I need to ask you a couple of questions."

"I didn't know you'd arrived." She smiled. "There was a big article in the paper, you know."

"No, ma'am, I wasn't aware."

"My name is Jennifer Samuels, by the way. My husband, Steve, is out front washing his car. Come on up the stairs. Watch your step."

The *stairs* were slabs of cut granite fashioned into rough steps, which had settled at varying angles.

"Yes, ma'am." He joined her on the wooden deck and accepted the seat she offered. The spectacular view was higher than the park, clearing the tree line. The cliff on the far side of the bluff was visible—a rock climber's paradise—as well as the valley and small mountains to the west. Ray glanced over his shoulder, noting the two-story wall of glass and the living room and balcony beyond.

"What's going on over at the park?" Mrs. Samuels said. "I saw Jimmy Johnson arrive, then the sheriff's deputy."

"My fiancée and I found a bit of something on the trail." He imagined what she'd think of that response when the news of the find circulated through the small town's grapevine. "We're checking it out."

"What did you find?"

"I'd rather not go into detail at the moment, if you don't mind."

Mrs. Samuels grimaced, then nodded. "I suppose. We import a big city detective and get big city answers. What do you want to know?"

"Other than the official vehicles, what else did you see today?" Ray pulled the notebook out of his pocket and flipped it open to the fourth page, the one after his meager evidence list. He'd fill in the first couple of pages later.

"I've been outside since, let me think, eight this morning. We had breakfast here, then I stayed to relax and knit. The light is good." She motioned to a blue and red work in progress. "I saw a dark pickup around eight-thirty, maybe."

"That was mine."

"Two people got out, wandered around like they were lost, then picked a trail and took off."

"Us. Lost, but learning." Ray smiled. "Anyone else?"

"No, not today."

"Yesterday?"

"A couple of kids parked their bicycles in the rack next to the trails and went down. I saw them come back late in the afternoon."

"Anyone else?"

"Not that I saw. I did go into Crestville in the middle of the day for a luncheon."

"How about Friday?"

"It rained all day." Mrs. Samuels paused. "Now that you ask, I saw lights in the park that night, maybe around twelve. We were standing on the deck looking over there." She pointed

IMPERFECT ESCAPE

west. "There was a big explosion and a fire—just after dark. Probably one of those mobile homes. Fire trucks, police cars, everywhere. We stayed up to watch because we were concerned about fire, even though the woods were wet from the rain. Anyway, Steve thought the lights near the overlook were pickup lights. They stopped, then circled around and left about ten minutes later."

A thick stand of oak trees blocked that part of the park from view. Mrs. Samuels wouldn't have been able to see the activity.

Ray asked several follow-up questions, eliciting no additional information. Then he walked around to the front of the house and introduced himself to Steve Samuels.

"'Morning, Detective," Mr. Samuels said. "Give me a minute."

While Ray waited for him to shut off the hose, he looked around the front of the property. A long driveway disappeared into the trees in a northwesterly direction. Nothing else was visible in any direction except thick woods.

"Nice property," Ray said when Mr. Samuels approached.

"We like it."

"How long is the driveway, may I ask?"

"Eight hundred feet, or thereabouts. The whole point of buying this lot was to be on the bluff, which has its positives and negatives."

"How so?" Ray raised a questioning brow.

"We have a beautiful view."

"I noticed," Ray said.

"But also strong winds, and we get the brunt of the storms as they move over the Plateau. Also, it's a long way to the main road to plug into services like water and electric."

"Well, it's a nice property. Did you see any of the activity at the park this morning?"

"No sir, I didn't. I've been here all morning. I enjoy working outside. That keeps me in the front and side yards mostly. Sorry."

"On Friday night, your wife said you and she saw a truck

pull into the park, stay near the edge about ten minutes, then leave."

"That's right, we did."

"Can you add anything?"

"The truck was a Ford pickup. I recognized the tail lights when it left the park."

"Helpful."

"Probably not." Samuels laughed. "There are more of those in this area than dogs and cats combined."

"Mrs. Samuels said you were watching a fire to the west that evening."

"We were. If you go west on the main road, Dripping Springs Drive is about a quarter of a mile away. It snakes down into the bluff a bit. Lots of old trailers, squatters' cabins, tiny houses. It's a real mess. Some of it was annexed by Plateauville a few years back, about the same time the Cove was, but the town mostly ignores it, except to go out on emergency calls now and then."

"Why'd they annex this area? Seems more rural to me."

"The residents wanted the city services, and the city wanted the expanded tax base. Now we're a sub-division." Samuels shrugged.

"Where, exactly, is the city limits?"

"Right at the bottom of the bluff. That means that some of the park is within the city, but all of the trails aren't. Same with Dripping Springs Drive. It becomes county road at the point it reaches the base of the hill."

Chapter 3

Ray

Ray and Johnson stayed at the park until mid-afternoon. They'd found the singed left hand of a youngish male, a cigarette butt, one athletic shoe tread mark—a partial one—and a generic-looking truck tire track.

As they were finishing, Sandy Lauffer, an investigator from the Sheriff's Department, stopped by to lend a hand and answer questions. "The sheriff thought you might need some help." She wore jeans, a long-sleeved white shirt, and boots.

"I appreciate it." Ray nodded. "Does that mean you're taking over?"

"No. I'm primarily a training officer. The sheriff is happy to have you on board."

"Good to know." Ray took a few minutes to review the case and the evidence. "How long does it take to get preliminary results from TBI?"

"It'll be a while. I recommend you go on with your investigation. Can I see the hand?"

Ray put on gloves, opened the bag, and held out the hand. "I tried to get prints, that would be a fast turnaround, but the tips of the fingers are singed. I did get a few partials. May be enough. What do you think about the damage? It looks deliberate to me."

"I'm thinking someone took a torch to them to obscure

the prints, but they didn't take the time to do a thorough job. You can see where the ends are burnt but some places look okay. The damage is less severe as you move up the hand." Lauffer pointed to the areas.

"My thoughts as well."

"Is there anything you need from me?"

"I don't think so. Thanks for your help."

Lauffer smiled. "Welcome to Middle Tennessee, Detective Stone." She headed toward her vehicle.

Ray stood next to Johnson and watched her walk away. She seemed all legs. "She's dressed warm for August," Ray said.

"Dressed smart." He scratched his upper arm under the short sleeve of his uniform shirt. "I know better. Have a long-sleeved shirt in the car. Cover up or be eaten alive by the bugs in these here woods this time of year."

As Ray climbed into the passenger side of the police car, he thought he was learning and remembering fast. Two hours on the job and already he knew that he'd never really be off duty, he needed to equip his personal and official vehicles with everything from bug spray and long sleeve shirts to writing pads and investigative supplies, and he'd better buy some extra boots. All familiar routines from his time in Virginia.

The eight-mile ride downtown to the Plateauville Police Department was quick. The single-story structure looked like a prefab storage facility, right down to the curved metal roof. The sign in front announced it was the police department as well as the home of the court, the magistrate, and the clerk. There was a second sign restricting parking on court days—Tuesdays and Thursdays.

Johnson pulled through an open gate in the chain link fence enclosing three sides of the building and the adjacent yards and parked in a spot marked *Police Vehicle Only*.

Ray noted three such spaces, plus one marked *Chief of Police*. A new-looking sign read *Detective*. A late model white Taurus sat in front of the sign. "Got my own parking space. That's a first. Is that my assigned vehicle."

"Yup. Believe so."

IMPERFECT ESCAPE

"Different color than my last one." Ray grinned. "Where do the court employees park?"

"On the other side. They have their entrance, we have ours. Inside it's all connected, though. Guess someone wanted to make it look bigger than it is."

Several more parking spaces abutted the fence and were labeled *Police Department Employee Parking*.

Ray chuckled, slid out of the car, and followed Johnson inside. Lots of land and not many people, he thought.

Chief Marvin Mullins, a muscular, capable-looking man in his late fifties, met them at the door.

"Chief," Ray said, in greeting. He'd met with the chief twice during the hiring process, which had been expedited by a referral from a mutual colleague, the chief in Coral Bay. "What a way to start."

"You could say that." Mullins pointed to a glass-fronted conference room next to a closed door marked *Chief*. "We can meet in there. Step into my office first."

Ray followed him and stood in front of the scarred oak desk.

Mullins didn't sit. "Glad to have you here, Stone."

"Thanks. Glad to be here."

Mullins retrieved a shiny badge from the desk drawer and laid it on the table. Then he added a Glock—still in the packaging—and a box of ammo. "Will this work for you?"

"Yes, sir."

Last, he handed Ray a set of keys. Pointing, he said, "Side door. Lock up. Taurus out yonder. Office next door. Most of the men drive here in their own vehicles. That way we have some flexibility. You can take yours home or leave it here since no one else is likely to use it."

"Today I need it to get home. Then we'll see." He picked up the badge, slipped it into his pocket, and took the Glock. "Do I have an assigned desk?"

"You have the office next door." He pointed to the Glock. "You can leave that on the desk in there until we're finished."

"Let's get to it, then." Ray went next door, deposited the

Gregg E. Brickman

gun on his desk chair, and glanced around at the spartan office, noting a computer and a couple of stacks of files. He locked the office and joined Mullins and Johnson in the conference room. He selected a chair next to Johnson and across the table from Mullins, who was rubbing the top of his balding head and messing the few black and gray strands of hair in the process. Through the glass, Ray saw a middle-aged woman wearing a headset sitting at a computer station in the far corner. He motioned in her direction.

"Dispatch. Our 9-1-1 service is integrated with County. Communication is online."

Ray nodded. "Let me bring you up to date on what happened today and what we found." He took a few minutes doing that. "Jim, do you have anything to add?"

"No, sir."

Mullins leaned back. "During your interview, we discussed the meth issues in Middle Tennessee. A large part of our theft and crime relates to drugs, either their manufacture or their acquisition. I put a pile of reports on the credenza in your office to bring you up to date. When something strange happens, our first thought is meth."

Ray said, "Have you had incidents with stray body parts flying around before?"

"Not quite the way it happened today, but when a lab blows, sometimes people are burned and killed. It takes a while to gather all the related parts."

"Any lab explosions in the last couple of days?"

"A huge one out on Dripping Springs Drive at LeRoy Vast's place, beyond the west side of the park. Happened Friday night around nine. Two burn victims were taken to the hospital in Crestville, then airlifted to Vanderbilt. Two were taken to the morgue. One of them in pieces. He was scattered across the yard. Those at the scene said they didn't have a chance. They were in the kitchen doing the cooking. Too far away from the park to be the source of the hand, however."

"Did they find all the pieces of the scattered victim?"

"They were out there all night with search lights and again

IMPERFECT ESCAPE

on Saturday. It's a county case because you weren't here yet. Krantz responded to the scene. He said there were still a couple of pieces missing. Figures the critters got them. Maybe that hand of yours is one of them. Give the medical examiner in Nashville a call tomorrow. We'll run your evidence and the hand to Nashville by courier tonight."

✳✳✳

Ray took his time driving home. He put the Taurus through its paces, getting the feel of the vehicle and leading him to the conclusion it was well maintained. He'd already checked the tires, looked under the hood, and into the trunk—which was stocked with a box of evidence-gathering supplies, protective gear, body armor—in his size—a shovel, flares, two flashlights, a first aid kit, bolt cutters, crow bar, Taser, three pairs of handcuffs, and various other pieces of equipment. What he found satisfied him. It also spoke to a rather broad definition of detective duties.

He turned into the golf course property on the eastern edge of the Cove, where he and Sophia rented a small furnished cabin—the lease called it a villa, but she called it a hut—and followed a bumpy gravel road past the driving range to the row of six buildings. They were of similar design, dark wood with a bit of stone trim, open front and rear decks, and wood-burning fireplaces. Theirs was the second in line and the only one with thick foliage around the front entrance. Good for privacy, but of questionable value for safety. He elected to park next to the storage bin across the gravel drive—his Ram and her MINI were lined up in their assigned space.

The door on cabin five opened. An older man with an unkempt beard stepped onto his porch. "Can I help you?"

"No, sir. I live here." Ray pointed to his place.

The man grunted. "Taking more than your fair share of parking spaces."

"Just for tonight." *Guess that decision is made,* Ray thought.

"Good."

Ray walked over to the man and extended his hand. "Ray Stone."

"Chester Clap. You the new detective?"

"Yes, sir. We moved in a few days ago."

"Know that."

"Well, I'm pleased to meet you."

Clap nodded, turned, and went inside.

"So much for southern hospitality," Ray muttered under his breath while walking the short distance across the yard to his cabin. As he passed their immediate neighbor, he heard yelling. It seemed the couple fought most of the day and half the night.

Inside, he found Sophia asleep on the ugly rust-colored futon, computer in her lap, and Mischief snuggled against her thigh. Mischief stirred, shook her little round head, then hopped down.

He squatted to pet her. The seventeen-pound brown—really brindle—and white Boston Terrier was a recent addition to their family. Sunshine, Sophia's King Charles Cavalier, had died a few months earlier of mitral valve disease. Sophia said Mischief filled the hole in her heart.

He bent to awaken Sophia and kiss her hello. When he jarred the computer, it awakened from sleep mode. He noticed it displayed an article declaring Tennessee was the center of the meth belt, which ran from Oklahoma to the Carolinas.

He touched her shoulder. When she opened her eyes, he said, "We need to talk."

"Why? What happened?"

"Nothing out of the ordinary, given we found a hand, I started work a day early, the neighbor down in cabin five borders on rude, and you're already poking around where you don't belong." He pointed to her computer screen.

Sophia closed the lid on her Mac, placed it on the battered coffee table, and stood. Facing him, she said, "Seems I have every right to look up whatever I want on my own computer. And, I'm not poking into your case, but the thought does occur

IMPERFECT ESCAPE

to me I need to be versed on the subject. I am working in the ED in the drug-infested area you moved me to."

"This area is probably less drug-infested than where we lived in Florida, however, here meth is a major issue."

She rolled her brown eyes.

"I hate it when you do that. How can I argue with an eye roll?"

"I don't want to argue. What I want is some faith and trust on your part."

"Sophia, you promised you'd not get involved in my cases again. Does that promise still hold? Because if it doesn't, I need to know now." Sophia had a history of poking into Ray's cases, leading to suspects threatening her life on two separate occasions.

"Or what?"

"Don't push it. I want to be able to discuss cases with you when I need to talk something out, but I don't want you in danger. I don't want you interfering. I just want a normal, rational, somewhat quiet existence here in the hills."

"Bully, bully. You're acting like one, and I don't like it."

He watched as she raked her fingers through her short dark hair, picked up Mischief, and stormed out of the house.

Rather than follow, he headed into the small master bedroom, then into the bathroom to shower. Though he could turn around in the room, he thought he'd never been in a smaller bathroom, not even in his college dorm in Virginia.

By the time he finished, he decided that he jumped the gun. Of course, she'd be interested in the topic. He found her in the kitchen starting dinner.

"Sophie, listen—"

"I . . . Don't . . . Want . . . To discuss it."

"Fine by me." Ray helped himself to a beer and went out onto the deck overlooking the lake—pond in Sophia's vernacular.

A few minutes later she joined him, glass of red wine—he assumed Chianti—in hand.

"Sorry. Let's move on."

"Okay. It's been a stressful day."

"Yes, it has. How'd it go after I left?"

"Well, I'm officially sworn in starting today."

"I figured."

"We didn't find any more litter."

"Cute. Very cute. I'm sure the victim—if he's alive—will appreciate having his body parts called litter."

"Interesting thought. Why would someone's hand be tossed if he was alive?"

"Um. Maybe it's a gang thing. Is there a mob here? Maybe he was being punished, like I read about with the Chinese triads. Or maybe he's a thief and stole from someone from the mid-east, who then applied old-fashioned justice."

Ray laughed. "Making it up on the fly, I see. But like I said, interesting thought. There *is* an organization surrounding the local meth industry." Ray paused. "In any event, Jim and I did the crime scene investigation bit, then went into town and met with the chief. Lots of questions at this point, but no answers."

"What kind of support is he giving you for your first case? I assume it is your case."

"Until and unless the sheriff or the state comes in and declares it drug related—which it is—and takes over. They have the authority. Anyway, the only manpower available is Jim, and then only when the patrol shifts are covered."

"Means you'll be out and about alone in most cases."

"Yup. I'll be able to get backup when necessary. I'm impressed with Jim so far. He talks easily about the department and the area and doesn't seem angry that I got the job and he didn't."

"Did he apply?"

"He told me he did. There were three applicants after the initial screening was finished, him, me, and Deputy Krantz—who bordered on rude when I met him."

Sophia laughed. "I noticed Krantz had an itch somewhere personal when I pointed him to the path. Wanted to know where Officer Johnson and the hotshot new detective were."

"Did he say anything more?"

IMPERFECT ESCAPE

"No, the good ol' boy told me to be a good little woman and go home." Sophia laughed. "He even asked if I could drive the Ram."

"Hey, I warned you, and you said you'd be able to put up with the *southern male shit*—I think that was how you put it—which, by the way, is a sign of caring and respect."

She rolled her eyes in an exaggerated manner. "I'll tell you a couple of things. First, I've been living with the *southern male shit* for a while. Second, it's easier to think about being treated like that than it is to actually swallow the condescending manner."

"I mean it with respect. And I am not condescending."

"So, you say."

Chapter 4

Sophia

At six-fifteen Monday morning, Sophia drove west towards Crestville. The sun rose from behind the Upper Cumberland Plateau as she made her way down the mountain. Tree-covered hills framed I-40, providing a view she couldn't have imagined when she grew up in North Dakota or during her years in Florida. The varying shades of green highlighted individual trees, which then disappeared into the woods.

She felt unsettled. The whole *falling-body-parts* thing unnerved her, as did the prospect of being involved, even peripherally, in another murder. However, she reasoned, an amputated hand wasn't definitely a murder. "Who am I kidding?" she said to the car. Her mind drifted to the day of her kidnapping in Florida, the day she couldn't fight off her attacker. She doubted her ability to withstand an assault. "Woman up," she said, continuing her conversation with the car.

Ray was emphatic she not poke into his cases again, and she understood his reasoning. In a small town and a small county, anything she became involved in could endanger Ray's position on the police force or carry over, at least politically, to her workplace. She'd gotten a good recommendation from her last job, even though her boss had suggested she move on. The reference letter didn't mention her involvement with the

IMPERFECT ESCAPE

dethroning of a powerful board member and the backlash that resulted or Sophia's refusal to follow orders.

Sophia's one-month orientation period was complete, and it was the first day she was part of the patient-care schedule. She liked the hospital and employees, though they tended to treat her as an outsider. However, the Emergency Department was state-of-the-art and staffed for the needs of the county, which included surrounding rural areas, small towns, and state parks. She looked forward to the variety of clinical challenges the ED and the geographic area would provide.

She opted for the first Crestville exit, zoomed down Spring Street, turned north, and arrived in the employee parking lot with time to spare. Emerging from her car, she took a moment to enjoy the cool morning. It would be hot later, but not as hot as Florida. By the time she finished the twelve-hour shift, it would be cool again.

After arriving in the ED's lounge, she grabbed a cup of coffee and sat at a table with two other nurses, Ricardo Tondo and Katina Cassia.

Ricky, as he preferred to be called, was a short, thin, light-skinned black Cuban American from Miami, who, according to several co-workers, tended to misunderstand and misstate things on purpose. Katina was a thirty-something, Texas-born Mexican American with long black hair and a medium-height, slender build. She had moved to Crestville with her Italian American husband, then divorced him.

"So, this is your first day off orientation," Katina said. "You'll be assigned to the trauma rooms with me."

"Sara is sticking her right in the fire, I see." Ricky's smile rose higher on the left and looked more like a sneer.

Sophia shifted to face him. "Do you see that as a problem?"

"Do you see it as a problem? Seems like you do or you wouldn't ask."

Sophia smiled. "No. I've got trauma experience."

"And you believe it prepares you for what you'll see here?"

"Listen, Ricky." Sophia's voice was firm. "Not that you

give a damn, but I was a police officer before becoming a nurse. I can handle lots of things. Nursing is a more predictable life—even here."

Ricky's wide-eyed stare and dropped jaw showed his surprise.

"I'll get by, and I'm sure Katina will show me the ropes."

"I will," Katina said. She picked up her coffee cup, stood, and dumped it in the trash. "Let's go get report. I just heard the crackle of the radio in our area."

"Good luck." Ricky didn't move. He raised one bushy brow and delivered his sneer-smile. The fact that the brow and the smile both elevated on the same side turned an expression, probably meant to convey a challenge, into a somewhat comical look.

While thinking *asshole*, Sophia followed Katina into the empty trauma section.

Sara Gudgeon, the Director of the Emergency Department, came down the hall toward them. She was a short, plump redhead who walked with a sway of her hips, which, perhaps, signaled her body image. "Katina, Sophia, two units are en route with burn victims from another meth lab explosion."

"From where?" Katina asked.

"Crestville Station, but a ways out."

Facing Sophia, Katina said, "EMS has three stations, one in Crestville, one in Baxter, and one in Plateauville. Crestville is the biggest and covers the most area." She looked at Sara. "Details?"

"Sketchy at the moment. Dr. Gold said they're stable at present."

"Sophia, get into your protective gear. Hold off on the mask until we see what comes in the door. Set out basins since we need to bathe the patients as soon as possible to get rid of the chemical residue. Have you handled meth lab explosion patients before?"

"No. Lots of vehicular trauma, knife and gun club stuff, fire, cardiac incidents, drownings—lots of those in my part of

IMPERFECT ESCAPE

Florida. They did cover it in orientation, though."

"Two things. One, the victims may be contaminated with the chemicals they use. I like to wash the non-burned spots as soon as I can to protect myself and others. If there is a strong odor, we wear masks. At the scene, the paramedics wear respirators. The second thing is that a lot of the meth lab workers—if you will—are also users. Their behavior can be erratic and often violent. Because of that, the police officers or sheriff's deputies stick around—oh, and they want to arrest them, too."

"Alright, then." Sophia tied her gown. "Bring 'em on."

Sophia, Katina, and Dr. Gold, a clean-shaven, nice-looking man of about forty, met the ambulances under the canopy.

When the vehicle doors opened, one of the victims, a scrubby-looking huge man—maybe six-four and three hundred pounds—reclined on the gurney with his head elevated. He'd pulled his oxygen mask to the side and was bantering with the medics. "Pepper, my friend, why don't you just let me out of this here bus, and I'll be on my way?"

Pepper, an almost as large woman in a paramedic uniform, said, "That's what the deputy is afraid of."

"But, Pepper, sweetie, you might as well just kill me and tell the Lord I died."

"Why is that?" Pepper said.

"'Cause if they lock me up, my mama will kill me, sure."

Pepper nodded to her coworker and unloaded the stretcher.

Katina said, "Sophia, Bubba is yours. I'll take the other one."

***

Sophia helped guide Bubba Flocker's stretcher into Trauma Room One, where he moved to the hospital stretcher under his own power.

A deputy sheriff followed them into the room and

stationed himself near the door. "I'll be staying here."

"Is that necessary?" Sophia said.

"It is, ma'am. Bubba is agile for a man his size. Last time he was here, he escaped, and it took us three weeks to bring him in."

Sophia grinned. "I'll keep that in mind." She went through her admission routine, taking his vital signs, performing a physical assessment, and asking basic health status questions. In the process, she noted a chemical odor and identified several minor burns on his face, hands, and forearms. "Do you have any headache or nausea?"

"A bit of a headache. Not much."

"Any dizziness?"

"No, ma'am." Sophia decided that Flocker's exposure to the chemicals was not excessive. "I'm going to bathe you to get rid of the residue. Meanwhile, you can tell me what happened."

"I like this part of coming in here. Make sure you get all of me clean, now."

"Looks to me like your hands function just fine, sir." As she worked, she asked him, "What happened?"

"My barbecue blew up." Flocker coughed, then put a hand on his chest.

"You don't say?"

The officer stepped forward. "Bubba, you might as well be honest. The nurse knows your meth lab blew and that you were there. Cut the bullshit. Sorry, ma'am."

"Now, Mr. Deputy, you'uns are just making sup-po-si-tions. That's no lab of mine." Flocker coughed again.

The deputy stared him down.

"Mr. Flocker, do you have pain anywhere besides your headache? I saw you put a hand on your chest when you coughed."

"Call me Bubba." He pointed at the left side of his rib cage. "Just here in my heart, ma'am. Pining for how I'll miss your pretty face whilst I'm in-car-cer-ated. The deputy is fixin' to frame me."

"Do you feel short of breath?"

IMPERFECT ESCAPE

"No."

"Were you wearing eye protection when the explosion occurred?"

Flocker laughed, a big hearty rumble that seemed to originate in his toes. "No one done ever asked me that before. No, ma'am, I wasn't."

"We'll wash out your eyes, and the doctor will check them." Sophia performed the eyewash, then bathed him. Though Sophia asked more questions related to the explosion, Flocker refused to answer. No wonder, she thought, with the deputy in the room. When she finished, she pulled a stool up to the side of the stretcher.

"So, Bubba, just in general, tell me about meth labs and meth lab explosions. I just moved to Tennessee, so this stuff is new to me."

Flocker looked at the deputy, who had pulled a rolling stool near the door and sat. "Oh, what the hell." He lowered his voice. "I got a friend who cooks the stuff, so I knows a bit about it. What are your questions?" He stared at the deputy.

"Okay." Sophia paused a moment. "What's the process in a meth lab?"

"There's a bunch of ways to cook meth, sugar. They need to cook the pseudoephedrine to turn it into methamphetamine."

Sophia raised a brow at his accurate pronunciation of the drug names.

"How do they do that?"

He explained the process *his friend* used, mentioning the use of red phosphorus and hydroiodic acid. "Then he neutralizes the shit with lye, and runs it through a coffee filter."

"And that's it?"

"Nah, we, I mean he, cuts the meth with some other shit so he makes more money."

"When does an explosion usually occur?"

"When the chemicals are heated. Boom." Flocker laughed. "There was a bitch of an explosion down the road from us the other night. Rattled the cups in the cupboard. Had my mama cussin' like a snake-bit coon hunter."

"Was that explosion in Crestville?"

"No, ma'am, it was up the mountain in Plateauville, out on old Dripping Springs Drive. You should-a saw the cops and stuff."

"You were there?"

"No, ma'am. I rode down there on my Harley when I heard the boom."

Sophia raised a hand to prompt him to continue.

Flocker didn't take the hint.

"Ah." Knowing it was the explosion that may have generated the mysterious dropping hand, Sophia continued. "Did you know the people there?"

"Sure do. Plateauville is small. We all know each other, but I can't keep with them. Them being criminals and all."

"I get that." Sophia thought a moment. "We live in Plateauville, on the other side of the neighborhood from Dripping Springs Drive. Was anyone hurt?"

"Two guys was killed. They say LeRoy Vast, he owned the place, was blown to smithereens." Bubba laughed. "The damn deputies spent the whole of the next day looking for his parts around the damn place. Serves 'um right. I heard they didn't find all the pieces."

"Serves who right?"

Flocker squinted, then frowned. "Now that you mention it, both that asshole Vast and the deputies."

Sophia shook her head. "I can't understand why anyone would want to put themselves at such risk."

"It's this way, ma'am. My friend—the one we been speakin' about—does it for the money. Vast though. He be different. He used the shit, too. Got crazy from the shit, paranoid. I remember one time, I heard he threatened to kill everyone who worked in that there lab. Thought they was telling secrets to the big man."

"Who's that?"

"My eyes burn. Can you flush them out again?"

Chapter 5

Ray

At seven on Monday morning, Ray pulled his Ram into the first empty slot in the Plateauville PD employee parking lot. Since his Taurus—which he'd returned the evening before—was the only official vehicle in the lot, he assumed the patrol units stayed on the road. Five trucks sat in employee parking.

Ray fumbled with the keys for the entrance to the PD side of the building. As he stepped inside, he heard a quiet tenor voice.

Instead of going directly to his office, Ray walked past a scattering of desks in the good-sized squad room, some clean, some cluttered. He stopped at one in the corner, which was occupied by a grey-haired man of about sixty-five. "Morning." Ray extended his arm. "Ray Stone."

"You're the new detective. Ted Ope is my name." He shook Ray's hand.

"It's a pleasure." Ray pulled up a chair and sat. "How long have you worked here?"

"Going on thirty-five years. I was born and raised in this town. I was the only police officer for a good twenty years."

Ray raised a questioning brow.

"Took the job when I got out of the Army. Was an MP. I retired about five years ago after I took a slug during a raid on a meth lab. Then, I asked to come back and do dispatch to keep busy. The wife died, so what's a man to do?"

"I understand. How long has Mullins been chief?"

"Ah, maybe three years. His predecessor got hisself fired." Ope paused, looking thoughtful. "When the city council asked me to take the position, I told them to hire themselves a proper department head. I never wanted to be one. That was about ten years ago, I reckon. Anyways, they brought Mullins in from Nashville. Had a reputation there for being strong and honest. He was a lieutenant."

"Good to know."

Ope's headset buzzed loud enough for Ray to hear. "Plateauville PD Dispatch."

As Ope went about handling the call, which sounded routine, Ray went to his office, stopping to look at the bulletin boards along the way. He saw on the duty board that the chief had assigned Jim Johnson to him. Good news.

After spending an hour reviewing the stack of files on the meth situation, Ray called the county sheriff's office and asked to be patched through to Deputy Krantz. When Krantz answered, Ray said, "Good morning, deputy. This is Ray Stone in Plateauville."

"I know who you are, detective. What do you want?"

Ray noted the snide edge on Krantz's voice, but elected to ignore it. "Who's the investigator in the sheriff's office assigned to the meth lab explosion from Friday night? Mullins said you were one of the first responders."

"Deputy Shim, Erik Shim, caught the case, I think."

"He work days?"

"He works everything."

"Got his number?"

"Hang on a second." There was a momentary pause. "Here's his direct number. You'll find him at his desk most days around noon. You plan on taking his case, too?"

"Don't plan to, no. Thanks again for the info." Ray hung up wondering about Krantz's attitude. He was, in Ray's opinion, taking his grievance over not getting the detective position a bit far.

IMPERFECT ESCAPE

Ray looked up in response to a tapping on his door frame.

Chief Mullins said, "Grab a cup of coffee and come next door. It's time I finish bringing you up to speed on the meth situation here."

"Yes, sir." Two minutes later, coffee in hand, Ray sat in front of Mullins' desk. "Tell me."

"You know from your interview that meth is our biggest challenge. Sure, we have our pot smokers, prescription drug abusers, even one heroin addict—where he gets the stuff, I don't have a clue—but meth is our biggest deal."

"Where are the labs?"

"We are watching a few properties out on Dripping Springs Drive. It wasn't part of the city until a few years back, and, given its remote location, it's largely ignored by the county."

"Was that the only explosion out there?"

"No. There was another one this morning, but it was just outside the city limits in the unincorporated area. County is handling it. We've had three others blow in that area in the last couple of years."

"Anywhere else?"

"Sure. Scattered across the countryside. Mostly County territory. We shut down several labs in town, old houses mostly, and a couple in mobile homes. They were small, personal-use size."

"Sounds like a lot for a small town."

"It's a major problem."

"Is there any central coordination of the enterprise—a drug lord figure?"

"Don't know for sure, but I think so—"

"Who—"

Mullins held up his hand. "Every time we arrest someone, they claim to be cooking for their own personal use, but the quantities don't support that. And, I believe they are making much more than they are selling locally. Everyone so far has been very good about keeping their mouths shut." Mullins paused a moment. "Oh, by the way, the sheriff wants you to take over the investigation of the explosion from Friday night. Erik Shim is the detective assigned. He'll meet with you, bring you up to speed, and tell you his thoughts about the big rat in this hunk of stinky cheese. Shim also touched base with TBI, who at this point wants it handled locally. You can call them if you think the issue goes beyond our immediate vicinity."

Ray nodded. "Well, at least I won't be bored during my orientation."

Mullins laughed with a rumble from deep down. "Speaking of orientation. Johnson can ride with you for the next couple of weeks. If we don't get a load of sickouts, that should work. He's a good man, raised locally, has family ties, and wants to be a detective."

"He told me. Doesn't seem to be bothered by not gettin' the job."

"I think he's relieved. Unlike Deputy Krantz, by the way. Krantz is not happy with the hiring decision and has been vocal."

"Thanks for the warning. He bordered on rude yesterday and was downright snide on the phone this morning."

"Watch your back."

***

In the late morning, Johnson shifted to patrol duties to cover for another officer with a personal emergency. Ray took the opportunity to head into Crestville to the Sheriff's Department. He wanted to find his way around the department without company.

His first stop, however, was at the site of Vast's meth lab explosion. His tour of the crime scene didn't take long. Nothing much remained of what had once been a dilapidated mobile home sitting well away from the road behind a stand of red oak. Debris littered the large open area surrounding the explosion site, tire tracks marred every patch of exposed dirt, and a distinct chemical odor hung in the air. The only remaining intact structure was a new-looking outhouse,

IMPERFECT ESCAPE

complete with a half-moon door and sturdy latch.

Ray took several digital images with his cell phone, knowing they were of no real use. He took one last look around and resumed his trip to Crestville.

As Krantz predicted, Ray found Detective Erik Shim behind his desk in the investigator's office at noon.

"Glad to have you on board." Shim stuck out his hand, which Ray shook. A reedy thin, balding, black man, Shim was a seasoned deputy and major crime investigator in the narcotics section. "What brings you to Tennessee anyway?" Ray noted Shim said Tennessee with a slight lisp.

"My parents and son moved to Knoxville. My daughter's in school in Virginia. This is closer. And to tell the truth, the Florida heat got to me."

"I can relate. I was on the job in Ft. Lauderdale for twenty years. Took retirement, moved here, and couldn't stay away."

"I thought your name sounded familiar. I recall reading about you busting a jewel thief a couple of years back."

"That was quite a case." Shim chuckled, then filled Ray in on some succinct details.

They spent a few minutes talking about South Florida, then about Ray's background as an officer and detective in Parkview, Virginia.

"What can I do for you today?" Shim said.

"The Chief told me you needed to pass off Friday night's meth lab explosion."

"Yeah, I do. Sheriff wants me free to chase after more of the same. In fact, I caught the one on the same road this morning, only it's on the county side of the line."

"What can you tell me?" Ray said.

"Not a hell of a lot, I'm afraid." Shim handed Ray a slim folder. "I copied all the initial reports for you. I sent a box of evidence to Nashville, but truthfully, there is nothing there."

"Mullins said Friday's incident was at LeRoy Vast's place." Ray opened the folder and read for a minute. "Two killed, one thought to be Vast but burned and scattered beyond recognition. The other victim, Vast's cousin, Harold Kramer. I see a note here that Vast had another cousin working for him—Richie Vast. Where is he?"

"We don't know. He was at the scene as far as we know, but he hasn't turned up. I'm thinking he's running fast."

"The other burn victims are in Nashville?"

"Vanderbilt, in the burn center."

"What did they have to say for themselves?"

"Krantz talked to one, Dylan Glad, at the scene and again in the emergency department here in town. Glad refused to answer questions. Ashley Beach, the other living victim, was unconscious at the scene."

"How the hell did five people fit into that trailer?" Ray shook his head. "Did Glad ask for a lawyer?"

"Not yet."

"Guess I'll stop by and see if I can have a chat with him tomorrow when I'm in Nashville to talk with the ME."

Shim leaned forward in his chair. "What I think, make that believe, is we have an escalating war in the methamphetamine market on the Plateau in and around Plateauville. We had two labs blow up, Friday and this morning. We had three blow last month. Another two the month before. That's a lot, especially for here. These are the first deaths, however."

"Were they all in the county, versus Plateauville?"

"Yup, except the one. Listen, location doesn't matter much. Our department and the local PDs work together on these big cases."

Ray hadn't gotten that idea from Deputy Krantz.

"I agreed to give Friday's case to you to pull you into the situation. We need a fresh outlook, another point of view."

Ray nodded. "Sounds okay. Tell me about this war."

"A new guy appeared on the scene up your way about five years ago. Carl Silken is his name. Out of Miami, actually—though I never heard of him when I was there. He moved into town and opened a business, Silken's Dry Goods, on the far end of Commercial Boulevard."

"I've been in the store. The guy who waited on me was slicked-out in pressed jeans and button-down shirt. Looked a

IMPERFECT ESCAPE

bit out of place, if you get my meaning."

"That would be Silken. The thing is, we can't get anything on him, beyond the occasional drug-induced rant from some meth head." Shim looked thoughtful for a moment. "Which is what put us onto him in the first place. He came into town with no visible means, yet he set himself up in a nice house, bought the store outright, and financed his wife's entry into polite society. Which isn't easy, I might add, since it's fairly closed to outsiders. Folks are friendly, helpful, and skilled at keeping outsiders out—where they belong, I'm told."

"What was different about her? They can't be the only people with money who ever moved into town."

"In truth, there aren't very many. An up and coming dentist or physician, maybe. Not much other reason to move into Plateauville."

"Sounds like I should turn tail and run."

"Don't. We need you here."

Ray paused a moment, liking the welcoming sound of Shim's comment. "What makes her different, besides the money I mean?"

"She's Southern, with a capital S. Word has it, her accent thickened every day she lived in town. Second, she joined every woman's group and function that would have her. Her approach worked. And, she's been generous with her time, her baked goods, and her money."

"Here I thought buying your way into society only worked in the city." Ray thought of all the nouveau riche mansions along the New River in Ft. Lauderdale and in the concrete and glass ghettos of Parkland and similar towns.

Shim chuckled. "Money and visibility work everywhere, I suppose."

"What else do you know about Carl Silken?"

"He has no criminal record, however, our friends in Miami tell us he's a known associate in their drug scene. They think he's well placed in the organization and is charged with market expansion, but he always manages to stay out of the way and out of trouble."

"Slick son of a bitch, sounds like."

Shim laughed. "Hell, they even call him Silky to his face around town." Shim tapped his pen on the desk, then tightened his face, giving himself an aged look. "What we think, but can't prove, is that Silken has financed many of the bigger, fancier labs. If the rantings are on target, he takes his cut of product and profits and supplies the necessary protection."

"Protection against whom?"

"The local competition. Maybe law enforcement."

"Is Mullins involved?"

"We don't think so. He's fairly new to the area. His predecessor, however, turned a blind eye to the meth labs, much to the chagrin of the town residents."

"Are others in the department involved?"

"Don't know. Could be. What I do know is I can't remember the last time the Plateauville PD busted a lab that wasn't actively burning. There have been several scheduled raids, but they always came up empty."

"Tipped off?"

"Perhaps. Or maybe, like they try to tell me, it's bad intelligence going in."

"How about here?" Ray waved his hand around the surrounding area.

"That's a tough one. I can tell you *I'm* not on the Silky payroll."

Ray nodded.

"Another thing I don't think I mentioned. The Vast explosion, unlike the others, was definitely arson. Someone wanted it to blow."

Chapter 6

Sophia

Monday evening, Sophia arrived home from work to find Mischief wagging her stub of a tail and waiting at the door, a pizza warming in the oven, and an Italian salad on the table. Ray had stopped at the convenience store on the corner, acquired the main course, and made a salad. A bottle of Chianti sat open on the table. In the short time they'd lived in the cabin on the golf course, they'd learned to love the pizza. And, it was the only food or store of any kind available within five miles.

They devoured the meal with little conversation. Sophia was starved, having taken an early lunch, and missing her afternoon break.

She sipped her warm Chianti. "Thanks for dinner. That was so good. Exceptional. I spent the entire drive home wondering what magic I could do to get food on the table. This is better." She stood and planted a big kiss on his lips, then smacked hers. "Tastes like pizza."

Ray laughed. "You're welcome. Are you working tomorrow?"

Sophia worked twelve hours shifts, which meant she had four days a week off. "Nope. I plan to go into Crossville to get groceries and look around some. It's only eighteen or so miles east of here, and I've never been there."

"You'll find a nice little southern town, about a third the

size of Crestville."

"Nice. I heard there is an outlet mall east of town. I have stuff to get at Walmart, too."

"I need a couple of things from hardware. Walmart should have them."

"Text them to me. Then I won't forget."

Ray fiddled with his phone for a minute. Sophia's message alert dinged.

"I have three days off in a row next week—Tuesday, Wednesday, Thursday. I'd like to fly into Ft. Lauderdale and spend a couple of days with Connie," Sophia said.

"Missing your friend?"

"Yeah, I am. But, more importantly, she asked me to come. There's a baby shower for one of the nurses on Wednesday, and I'll get to see everyone."

"It'll be hard, but Mischief and I will get along without you." He grinned. "By the way, I told the folks we'd go into Knoxville Sunday. Kerri will be there for the week-end, and Branden has the day off from work."

"Sounds wonderful. I miss your kids, Branden especially. He and I spent a lot of time together while I stayed with them."

After dinner, Sophia and Ray took Mischief for a walk. The dirt and gravel road in front of their rental connected to the cart paths for the golf course surrounding the cabins and the lake.

"This is the part I love about coming back north," Ray said.

"We're still in the *South*." She smiled.

"Hell, you know what I mean, woman."

Sophia laughed. "I do. What is it you like so much?"

"The day cools off. The damn heat is gone, even though I know it'll be here mid-day tomorrow."

"Mischief agrees with you—the temperatures here agree with her." Sophia rubbed the Boston Terrier's head. "I like the hills and the trees. It's so different from flat Florida or treeless North Dakota." She continued down the road, urging Mischief onto the grass borders. "The people at work talk about all the

IMPERFECT ESCAPE

half-backs who live around here, especially on the Plateau." She grinned. "I told them I was a *one-third*-back."

"How so?"

"Well, if someone who moves from New York, say, to Florida, then to Tennessee is *half*, then I must be a *third*—North Dakota to Florida to Tennessee." She paused. "I suppose I could compute the mileage and be more accurate about it."

"Very cute." He grimaced.

"They thought so."

"Let's walk to the far side of the lake, then around the hill." Ray turned to the right and followed the paved path leading past the putting green and connecting to the hole beyond and edging the east side of the pond.

A flock of Canadian geese fought amongst themselves, honking, splashing, and taking short flights. A goose with a broken wing kept her distance as if ostracized, but still longing to join in the fun.

"I feel sorry for that goose. She seems lonely." Sophia pointed.

"The couple next door feed her. He said a coyote attacked a bunch of goslings. She is the only survivor."

"Poor thing." Sophia scratched her arm. "We didn't spray ourselves for ticks and chiggers."

He grinned. "We'll do a full-body search and check for ticks when we get home."

"Just like the country song." She tugged the dog away from something disgusting in the grass. "How is your case going?"

"I inherited Friday's explosion at the meth lab, too. I went into Crestville to discuss it with the detective—Shim is his name—who had the case. Helpful guy. He's out of the Ft. Lauderdale PD." Ray paused a moment. "Anyway, the thinking is the fire and subsequent explosion—"

"Isn't it explosion, then fire?" She stepped off the cart path and onto the grass rough south of the pond, stopping to let Mischief sniff the ground.

"Not this time. It was probably arson. I'm waiting on the

final report from Crestville."

"No shit? Which makes the deaths murder."

"Right you are." He filled Sophia in on the possible drug war. "Shim said Carl Silken may be the force behind it all."

"The fancied-up dude from the dry goods store?"

Ray nodded.

"Funny thing. I had a patient today who was singed a bit in an early morning explosion on Dripping Springs Drive—out in the unincorporated area."

"And?" Ray said.

"Anyway, his name is Bubba Flocker. I don't know if he has a *real* name or if his parents were dumb enough to name him Bubba."

"No worse than Boomer, I suppose."

"Anyway, Bubba seemed happy Vast's lab blew up and seemed convinced the exploded body was Vast's." Sophia repeated the remainder of the conversation with Flocker.

"I'll look him up and see what he knows."

"Won't have any trouble finding him. The doctor admitted him to routine care under the watchful eye of a deputy."

Ray stopped and faced her. "Remember, I don't want you getting involved. These meth guys are unpredictable and dangerous."

"Hey, I'm just listening when they talk. Bubba said Vast, the dead guy, was a heavy user of his own product. Said he was a crazy bastard—I think that was his phrase."

"You don't say." Ray looked thoughtful. "If you hear anything else around the hospital, let me know."

She rolled her eyes. *First, he wants me to stay out, then he wants me to report it.* "Will do." He meant for her to listen, not probe, but if the opportunity arose, he's the one who issued the invitation.

Chapter 7

Ray

The note on Ray's desk on Tuesday morning said the autopsies on the Friday night explosion victims would commence at ten o'clock. He called the ME's office to say he was coming, tagged Johnson, and picked him up in front of his house.

During the drive, Ray updated Johnson on what little he'd learned the day before, including the fact he'd picked up the Friday night meth lab explosion case.

"Guess they dumped the sucker on you, huh?" Johnson said.

"I don't feel that way. Detective Shim wants to work the two explosions together. A fresh outlook's good for him, he said. Good for me, too, I figure, since it will be more exposure to the Sheriff's Department. Fast track orientation."

"I guess." Johnson paused, then continued. "Krantz tracked me down at church Sunday morning. He lives outside the city limits a ways north of town. Guess that's why he's assigned to our end of the county. Anyways, he shot off his mouth some about you being the big city detective. I'm thinkin' he's going to be more trouble than I reckoned at first."

"Mullins agrees with you."

"I'm glad I didn't get your job."

Ray nodded.

"But I appreciate being assigned to you. If and when we

get a second opening, I'll apply again."

"Good to hear."

They arrived at the Davidson County Medical Examiner's office a few minutes early. The modern glass and brick building sat, surrounded by parking lots, on R.S. Gas Boulevard. Ray swung into the partially-filled lot and parked near the entrance.

"Have you been to an autopsy before?" Ray raised an eyebrow and glanced at Johnson.

"No, sir, I haven't." Johnson turned a bit pale. "I wouldn't have eaten breakfast if I'd known."

"In my opinion, it's better to eat first. You're less likely to faint." Ray grinned.

Johnson grunted. "I'll get by."

"I'm sure. Typically, we'll get gowns to cover our clothing—and masks." He fished a small blue bottle out of his shirt pocket. "Then we can put a bit of Vicks in our noses to hide the smell, though Sophie tells me to just not inhale."

Johnson started to say something, stopped, then laughed. "Took me a minute. Guess I'm more nervous than I thought."

"Also, remember you can leave and take a breather if you need to." Ray climbed out of the Taurus.

When they got inside, the receptionist greeted them, indicated they were expected, and called a tech to escort them to the autopsy suite. Once they were gowned and given masks, they entered the suite, becoming engulfed in a world filled with stainless steel, white porcelain, and dangerous-appearing implements. Even in the state-of-the-art facility, with what he presumed was modern ventilation equipment, the stench emanating from the table in the center of the room was overpowering. It was a combination of scorched flesh, decay, and chemicals. He opened his Vicks, offered some to Johnson, then took a dab himself.

"Gentlemen." A man dressed in green scrubs covered by a surgical gown turned away from his papers on the counter and stepped forward. "I'm Kevin Smith. I'm one of the forensic pathologists."

IMPERFECT ESCAPE

Ray introduced himself and Johnson.

Dr. Smith indicated the remains on the table with a nod. "Shall we begin?" He pulled up his mask and motioned for Ray and Johnson to do the same. "Stand on the far side, if you will." He pointed, then looked at Johnson. "Officer Johnson, if you need to step out during the procedure, it's fine. Come back in when you're ready."

"Yes, sir. I'll stay."

Ray smiled, thinking Johnson's light green color was obvious to Smith, too.

"We've already washed the body to reduce our own exposure to the chemicals used to manufacture methamphetamine. In this case, based on the odor alone, there is no doubt in my mind this man died in a meth lab explosion. You're aware, I'm sure, that ephedrine, pseudoephedrine, mercury, and lead are also common findings. We've taken swabs to test for those substances and several others as well."

Ray noted the body, with its blown away and recovered parts, was placed in what approximated the original anatomical locations. The right hand was missing. The space for the left hand was occupied by the one that slid down Sophia's back Saturday morning—he recognized the wedding ring. The right forearm appeared to be badly damaged, but was still attached to the upper arm. The left forearm was similarly injured and lay in position with a one-inch gap. The face looked as if it had been beaten with a fiery hot sledgehammer. Ray's eyes slid down the rest of the body, noting everything seemed attached, though there were numerous areas of severe injury, especially the chest and upper belly.

"Lots of damage," he said.

Smith held his arms forward at counter height. "It appears the victim was working over the stove when it blew, hence the injuries to the upper extremities."

"Do you think the left hand is his?"

"Well now, that's the question of the hour, isn't it?" Smith picked up the hand and abutted it to the forearm. "It seems to fit. However," he said, pointing to a spot, "this bone seems too long on the hand. Without the other one for comparison, it's hard to say exactly. The partial prints most likely belong to LeRoy Vast, but it's not a hundred percent. We'll send samples out today for DNA analysis, then we'll know for sure. Vast has a record, so there is DNA on file. I have a friend in the lab who owes me a favor, so he'll jump it in the queue if he can."

"Good to know. Dental?"

"We got the records from Vast's dentist, but the mouth is so badly damaged they will be of little use."

Ray and Johnson observed as Smith completed his examination.

When he finished, he motioned for Ray and Johnson to follow him into the hall. "Let's step outside." After they removed their personal protective equipment, Smith said, "Any questions?"

"So, what I gather is the cause of death, given the arson evidence, will be ruled a homicide," Ray said.

"Correct."

"This victim may or may not be LeRoy Vast, and the left hand is probably Vast's, but may not be."

"Also correct."

Ray thanked Smith, and he and Johnson headed out. Ray felt no smarter than when he walked in.

***

After leaving the medical examiner's office, Ray plugged Vanderbilt University Medical Center into the GPS, dropped the Taurus into gear, and headed to the main road. "It's almost twelve-thirty. Want to find a place to stop for lunch?"

Johnson, who had not regained his normal coloring, shook his head. "Maybe after we're done at the hospital."

"That might not be better. I visited a burn unit a few years back, and some of what I saw wasn't pretty."

"I'm good with the seein' part, I reckon. It's the smellin' part that has my stomach flip-flopping."

Ray chuckled, knowing the smell wasn't always sweet in a

IMPERFECT ESCAPE

burn unit. He didn't admit to feeling a bit queasy himself. "I spoke with the physician yesterday afternoon. He has cleared us to speak with Dylan Glad. Glad's injuries involved his legs and torso and were less severe than the other surviving burn victim's. Her name is Ashley Beach. She's on a ventilator and sedated."

"I went to high school with her," Johnson said.

"Did you now?"

"She was a wild one. Left town after graduation, then showed up again with lots of tats and troubles. Her family threw her out of the house after about three weeks."

"Do you know any of the others?"

"From around town. Glad was a few years ahead of me in school."

As directed by the GPS, Ray pulled onto US 31 and was relieved to see the traffic was light for midday in a city. "Were you involved in any of the arrests? I saw they all had sheets—mostly minor shit."

Johnson exhaled in a loud whoosh. "That's the thing. Anytime we conduct a raid—keep in mind because of our staffing we need to plan it and get the sheriff's help—we don't find a damn thing that will support a case in court for manufacturing and sale of meth. We find traces, sure, but they always claim it's for personal use. Then they get slapped on the wrist and are back in business."

"The chief said a few labs were shut down."

"That's true, but in my opinion, it was small stuff. In fact, the last one in town was like catchin' a runt in a pig litter."

Ray chuckled. "Why do you suppose that is?"

"I think someone is tipping off the big labs and setting up the little ones to take the fall. Has to be."

"Yup. Sounds like."

Fifteen minutes later, Ray parked in the Medical Center East's above-ground parking. He'd lucked into an open space and was able to avoid the garages. They made their way to the eleventh floor's burn center critical care unit.

A phone hung on the wall next to the double door

entrance. Johnson picked it up and stated their business. "They're expecting us."

A buzz followed, and the doors swung open.

Ray led the way.

A tall heavyset nurse in blue scrubs stopped them near the nurses' desk. "Mr. Glad is in room five. The doctor said you can have ten minutes, providing Mr. Glad doesn't get stressed." She escorted them to the glassed-in room and gave them gowns and masks. "Please don't touch the patient or anything in the room."

"We'll keep that in mind," Ray said.

Ray and Johnson found Glad amid a sea of white bandages and white linens. Compared to the adjacent rooms, the amount of equipment was minimal.

"How are you doing?" Ray said after introductions.

"I'll live, they tell me. What do you want?"

"We came to talk to you about the meth lab explosion that injured you."

"Wasn't no lab explosion. Was a gas grill blew up. We had it too close to the house."

"Interesting." Ray leaned in. "Let me tell you the facts. Vast's little cookhouse blew up because of arson. There was a fire, then the explosion. Someone wanted the lab gone and didn't care what happened to the people working inside."

Glad grunted. "I'll find the bastard when I get out of here."

"After you get out of jail?" Ray said.

"Whatever it takes."

"Who was working that day? We know of two dead and two injured. You're the one who got off easy."

"Son of a bitch. Pisses me off. No one was supposed to get hurt."

"Give us some help here. Who was working with you?"

"My girlfriend, Ashley. Is she alive? No one will tell me anything."

"She's bad burnt," Johnson said. "She's on a breathing machine."

IMPERFECT ESCAPE

"The doctor is hopeful," Ray said.

Glad raised his eyes to the ceiling. "Praise the Lord."

"Who else was there?" Ray said. "You might as well tell us. We'll find out anyway."

Glad set his jaw and turned his gaze toward the window.

"Glad, now's the time to speak up. It could help you later on," Johnson said.

"You gonna make me a deal?"

Ray kept his expression impassive. "I don't have the authority. However, I can make a recommendation, say you were cooperative."

"Okay." A long moment passed. "LeRoy, and his cousins, Richie and Harold."

"That's Harold Kramer, right?" Johnson said. "He's the body the ME identified."

"Who else is dead? You said two. Who else?" Glad's voice cracked. He sounded distressed.

"That's what we're trying to figure out. Who was doing the cooking when it exploded?" Ray said.

"I'd gone outside the front door to take a piss. Ashley was going to follow me out in a minute or two, and we were going to take a break—if you get my drift." Glad frowned. "Richie, Harold, and LeRoy were in the kitchen. Someone could have gone out back to take a hit, maybe. Richie and LeRoy use product."

"Is that so? Tell me about it," Ray said.

"Richie is like the rest of us, uses every now and then. LeRoy, though, he's high all the time. He can be a crazy sucker, if you know what I mean."

Ray nodded.

"Another thing. When I went outside, I saw someone in the yard."

"Can you identify him?"

"No, it was fogging in some."

The nurse stepped into the room. "Time's up, officers. I'll help you out of your gowns."

Chapter 8

Sophia

After Ray left for the day, Sophia tidied the cabin—a daily job because of its compact size—grabbed the laundry basket, and drove into Crossville—about eighteen miles southeast. The biggest inconvenience of their rental was the lack of laundry facilities. She planned to catch up with the drudgery, do a little shopping, and check out the town.

She found the laundromat on one of the main drags. It was clean—and seemed expensive. It had been years since she'd ventured into such a place, and she wasn't aware of the huge increase in price. Three young women with children in tow gathered in the seating area in front of the windows. Sophia put her things into three adjacent washers—an advantage, she supposed, of doing her wash at a laundry—and joined the group.

When two of the women smiled, she introduced herself and included the fact she was a nurse working in Crestville. "I'm new to the area. We live in Plateauville."

"Good choice to come to this place," a petite blonde with a babe in arms said.

"Why's that?"

"I live in Plateauville, too. The laundry there is monitored by a guy who is usually hyped up on meth. Kinda scary, if you ask me."

IMPERFECT ESCAPE

"Tell me about his behavior. This whole meth thing is new to me. In South Florida, opioids are more of an issue. Sure, I'd read about meth in the paper, but we didn't get much in the emergency department where I worked."

"Jasper, that's his name, is hyperactive, like a kid off his Ritalin. He's thin. Looks like he's starving to death. I guess in a way he is. And he seems, sometimes, very anxious. Talks to himself like he's seeing things. Paces around. I haven't seen it myself, but my friend who goes there, says she thinks he's paranoid, too. She saw him having a fight with himself—at least she didn't see anyone else there."

"Why do the owners of the place let him work there?" Sophia leaned forward, signaling her interest.

"He's local. He's a vet," the blonde said.

"And," a heavy-set woman said, "there is no one else who will take the job. Stop and look at the place. It's horrid. Half the machines don't work. Then there is a pool table in the back that attracts guys who are sometimes flying high, too." She frowned and touched the shoulder of the toddler playing at her feet. "I'm saving up to buy my own machines. Soon, very soon."

"Do you know anything about the meth labs in the area? They tell me at work home-cooked meth is a big issue. We get lots of burn victims every time one of them blows up."

The heavy-set woman looked thoughtful. "To me, it's like there are two layers of society. There are us regular folks, then there's the whole drug thing. I try my best to ignore that part of our community. If you know what I mean?"

"I do," Sophia said.

"But, you can't ignore it entirely," the blonde said. "You need to lock things up and pay attention to what's going on. Out in the Cove, that's the area by the golf course south of town—"

"That's where we rent one of the cabins," Sophia said.

"Anyway, they've had several break-ins. Some of the people are seasonal residents, and their houses have been almost destroyed by meth heads looking for stuff to sell, money, and drugs."

"I didn't know that," Sophia said.

"My husband installs security systems, and lately, his best customers are out there."

The conversation drifted to more pleasant things. Sophia listened, enjoying the Middle Tennessee cultural lesson. As soon as her clothes were finished, she left, thinking the visit to the laundry for the ladies was social as well as a necessity of life—like going to the hair dresser in Florida.

She turned in the direction she thought would take her to the mall, got lost, and stumbled upon the Cumberland County Library. She parked and went inside, vowing to make better use of the GPS on her phone.

The conversation while doing her wash raised questions. She sought out the computers, picked one, and went on the Internet for some private browsing. She sought to avoid another clash with Ray over the issue.

The first thing she did was look at several sites discussing the issue of methamphetamine use and the characteristic behaviors of chronic users. The same words kept appearing—skinny, malnourished, anxious, sleepless, paranoid, and violent. She learned ingested meth led to a prolonged, less extreme high, while, when smoked or injected, the high was intense, as was the crash afterward.

There were descriptions of users with dilated pupils, elevated blood pressure, and intense sexual excitement. They became hot and sweaty with physical activity. She made notes and sent several links to her work email address. Her overriding thought was that meth was a vehicle of self-abuse, maybe the modern devil's curse right there in Middle Tennessee.

She moved on and Googled the Friday night fire and explosion. A link took her to the Crestville paper, which ran a sanitized version of the incident. What she found most interesting was a statement that explosions leading to death of the workers were not rare. She surfed around and found several examples.

Lastly, she Googled Carl Silken in Plateauville. The results

IMPERFECT ESCAPE

were several links about his store and his wife's community service. One link, however, mentioned that he moved to Tennessee from Miami. It didn't take long for her to find news articles linking him to the drug trade in Florida. She couldn't find any record of his being arrested, much less convicted. Ray, of course, would know all that—even if he hadn't shared the information.

She thought she'd ask a few questions when she visited Connie in Florida. What could it hurt?

Chapter 9

Ray

Ray signed in with the sheriff's deputy guarding Flocker's hospital room door. "I won't be long."

"Take all the time you need, Detective." The deputy returned to whatever he was reading on his smart phone.

When Ray entered the room, he was surprised at the sheer size of Bubba Flocker. His three hundred-pound girth filled the bed from side to side, and his length did the same from top to bottom. Bubba's wounds on his face and hands were open to air, and seemed, to Ray, to be healing.

"Detective Stone, Plateauville PD." Ray stood near the head of the bed and flashed his badge. "I have a few questions."

"Didn't know the big town of Plateauville had its very own de-tec-tive. No sir, I didn't." Flocker laughed, then coughed.

"What's your full name?"

"Bubba Flocker."

"Tell me your real, legal name."

"Charles Malcolm Flocker, but everybody always called me Bubba—except Ma that is." He laughed again. "Seems to fit some better, you understand."

"Why are you still in the hospital? Your wounds look fine to me."

IMPERFECT ESCAPE

Bubba pointed to the oxygen tubing draped over the head of his bed and the IV in his arm. "Can't catch my breath sometime. Doctor thinks I have pneumonia, too. I need the medicine."

Ray motioned to the oxygen tubing. "Why don't you have the oxygen in your nose then?"

"It blows and dries things out. I take it off to let my nose rest a spell."

"Where do you work?"

"I live with Ma on the farm. That's where I work."

Ray absorbed the information, thinking Bubba had issues on all fronts. "Tell me about the explosion in your lab."

"It wasn't my lab. My friend asked to put it on the back of my property where it would be safer. I have lots of space. He has family at his place and doesn't want them exposed to the shit he cooks up. Since I help him out sometime, I said he might could put it out back my land. Ma's pissed about it."

"Who's your friend?"

"Can't tell you that. No, sir." Bubba shook his head.

"Why not?"

"Wouldn't be gentlemanly of me."

"You're telling me you are willing to do the time for *your friend?* That's very neighborly of you."

Flocker glared at Ray. "What's it to you? My land and the explosion were in the county. You have no jurisdiction there. Why are you here?" Bubba coughed several times and reached for the oxygen, pulling the tubing over his head and fitting the plastic prongs into his nostrils.

While Ray waited for Flocker to catch his breath, he marveled at the man's ability to turn off the good-old-boy accent with no apparent effort. "Someone saw you at Vast's place before the fire and explosion on Friday night." Though Glad hadn't described anyone, Ray didn't feel any compunction about stretching the facts.

"Don't you mean explosion and fire?"

"No, I don't."

Flocker looked thoughtful. "Bullshit. I was there, alright?

I rode my bike over when I heard the boom."

Flocker's property was less than a mile down Dripping Springs Drive from Vast's. Ray brought up a mental image of the map he'd looked at earlier. Flocker lived right outside the city limits in the unincorporated area. He would have heard the blast—even clearer if he caused it. But, if he did, why would he admit to being there?

Flocker said, "You expect me to believe someone set a fire and blew the lab on purpose?"

Ray nodded. "That I do."

"And you're here because you think I did it?"

Ray deduced that Flocker was smarter than he looked or acted. "It's a possibility. You are on my list."

"Well, shit. I didn't do that. Just went over to have a look."

"I heard you say that. Did you see anyone around?"

"No. I heard LeRoy Vast bought it. Is it true?"

"Maybe, maybe not. It might not be Vast's body. The ME is working on identification."

"My buddy said Ashley is hurt bad, and so is Dylan."

Ray nodded.

"Said Harold's dead. Said Vast's dead. Said Richie's missing. No one has seen him."

Ray waited for Flocker to continue.

"Bet everyone over at the Vast place is off the friggin' wall."

"Tell me about your relationship with Carl Silken."

Flocker blinked, then took a moment to adjust his bedsheets. "Needed work. He has stuff to unload. I don't talk to him much. He doesn't cotton to my kind, I don't reckon."

"What is your kind, Flocker?"

"You know. A working man."

"I heard you're cooking for Silky, and he buys your product," Ray said, leaning a bit closer.

"Listen, my man. Pay attention. I don't have any product. I help my friend sometime. He pays me. That's why I do it. Money's not good on the farm, so I need it to help out."

Flocker's voice was emphatic, too emphatic in Ray's view.

IMPERFECT ESCAPE

"Do you know anything about Silken being connected to the meth labs in the area?"

Flocker seemed to be puzzling something out. "Well now," Flocker said, "I have heard some around town. I don't reckon I know if it's true or not, but it's been said. Fact is, I heard Vast's big operation was financed by Silky. Don't know if it's true."

"What's the source of your information?"

"Can't say. Just talk," Flocker said.

"What else do you know about Vast's business?" Ray said.

"Nothin'."

Ray asked several more questions along the same lines, which Flocker refused to answer. Ray wondered about Flocker's motivation for commenting on the alleged Silken and Vast relationship at all.

Ray glanced toward the door when he heard it open. A shadow of concern crossed Flocker's face when Deputy Krantz stepped into the room and left the door ajar behind him.

"What you doing here, Stone?" Krantz said, scowling at Ray.

"My job."

"Shim told me to stop by and ask Bubba some questions."

"Shim must be a busy man," Ray said, hoping to push Krantz a bit off center.

"I don't know how it was where you were before, but here, we all help out. Best you figure it out sooner rather than later."

"You're telling me you're working Flocker's case with Shim?"

"I'm telling you, I have questions. If you're done, I'll get to them."

Ray debated about making an issue of the whole thing with Krantz, but decided to check with Shim first. Ray knew Krantz was out to discredit him and didn't want to give him more material to use—especially with another deputy in earshot outside of the room.

"I'm done. Hope you have better luck than I did." Ray

stepped close to Krantz and continued in a quiet voice. "If you ever publicly disrespect me again, there will be consequences."
"Is that a threat?"
"No. Not a threat."

Chapter 10

Ray

On Wednesday morning, Ray, Jim Johnson, and Eric Shim convened at the Plateauville PD. Ray sat behind his desk and the other men occupied the mismatched chairs he'd pulled in from the squad room a couple of days earlier.

"I talked to the ME in Nashville this morning," Ray said. "He hasn't established an ID on the unidentified victim, but is leaning toward—unofficially, of course—the hand not belonging to the body. The DNA results will take several days, even with the rush request."

Johnson laughed. "So much for hittin' up his friend for a favor."

"The ME implied that was the favor." Ray looked from Shim to Johnson. "As far as I'm concerned, we don't have a verified body for Vast—don't know where he is if he's not on the slab—and are missing his cousin Richie, too."

Shim sat straighter in his chair. "I went to Vast's place with Krantz the night of the explosion to talk to the wife."

"I saw the report," Ray said.

"What's not in the report is she knew about the meth lab, though they don't live on the same property."

Ray nodded, remembering his brief tour of the crime scene.

Shim shifted his weight, scowled, then slouched a bit.

"Kelly Ann is her name. Who, by the way, looks to be near the end of her pregnancy. She said she and LeRoy met in rehab. When I asked, she said she's not using meth anymore, implied it was mostly about the baby."

"Did you ask her about Vast's drug habits?"

"She clammed up. All she wanted to know was if her baby was going to be born an orphan."

"The chief sent me to check on her Sunday." Johnson looked at Ray. "That's why I was near the park. She told me she was fine, said Krantz had been by to check on her, and I should leave her alone."

"Any evidence she wasn't alone?" Ray said.

"No. She looked like she'd been crying. That was all."

"I think we should talk to her again, look around if we can. It's been a couple of days, so maybe she'll be more forthcoming," Ray said. "You game?"

The others nodded their agreement and, by mutual consent, went out and loaded into Shim's SUV. Fifteen minutes later, Shim pulled into the rutted driveway leading to Vast's home.

The shoddy mobile home needed paint and general repairs, but it seemed to be intact enough to repel the elements. Ray guessed it had once been white with green trim, but it was now chipped grey. "Charming place to raise a kid."

Johnson said, "It's newer than the other place was. When they got married a couple of years ago, they lived in the other dump first—the one with the lab. When Kelly Ann got pregnant, she insisted they move."

"You're well informed," Shim said.

"Small town," Johnson said.

"Suppose so." Shim opened his door and slid out. "Stone, you take the lead. I'll jump in if I have anything to add."

"Works."

Johnson climbed the three steps to the porch and tapped on the jam.

Kelly Ann Vast opened the door, then cradled her swollen belly with both hands. "What in the hell do you guys want now?

IMPERFECT ESCAPE

Did you come to tell me you identified my husband's body? Is that why you're here?" Her face reddened and tears appeared.

"No, ma'am." Ray stepped forward and introduced himself. "You know Officer Johnson and Detective Shim, I believe. Can we come in? I have a few questions."

"No, you can't come in. I don't know nothing about LeRoy's business, and I know nothing about the explosion that killed him."

"You seemed convinced he's dead."

"Well, he's not here." She waved her hand around the room behind her. "Do you'uns see him? I haven't heard from him—or about him. What am I supposed to think?" She pushed her stringy blond hair off her puffy pock-marked face.

"Don't know, ma'am." Ray held his place at the top of the stairs, putting a hand on the knob to prevent her from slamming the door in his face. "Was LeRoy using meth again?"

"Don't know for sure. Some I guess, 'cuz of his behavior."

"How about you?"

"I'm pregnant. I don't want to friggin' kill the kid, though if my asshole husband doesn't show up, I don't know how I'll feed it." She wiped at a tear.

"Have you seen Richie since the explosion?"

"That creep. No. I heard he's missin'. I suspect he ran off." She looked resentful. "You'uns know he's on probation, don't you? I think he hightailed it to avoid going back inside. Just my opinion, mind you." She tugged on the door. "Now get the hell away from my house and off my property."

Ray didn't release the knob. "We'd like to take a look around the place, if you don't mind."

"I mind. You got a warrant?"

"No, but we'll get one."

"You do that." She jerked the door. Ray released the handle, making sure it didn't slam against her.

After returning to the vehicle, Shim took his time easing down the driveway. Ray studied the view. There was nothing of interest.

"I'll get a warrant to search the place. Seems to me if Vast's alive, this is where he'd be hiding," Ray said. "Otherwise, why didn't she cooperate?"

"Maybe he stored his raw materials somewheres on the property," Johnson said. "Everyone knew where his lab was. You'd not want to leave things around to be ripped off by the competition."

"That's another reason. Or, maybe Richie is hiding here? What I do know is she's hiding something."

***

Shim pulled onto Dripping Springs Drive and turned toward the unincorporated area. "If you two don't mind, I'd like to stop at Flocker's place and have another look around. His mother was cooperative Monday morning, so I'm hoping she'll agree to a more complete search today."

Ray, smarting about their eviction from Vast's place, frowned. "Fine with me. They're tied together at some level. When I talked to Flocker this morning, he sounded well-versed on the details of Vast's explosion."

"Everyone in town knows the details," Johnson said. "Once again, small town."

"Right," Ray said.

The properties along the pot-holed, curvy road seemed to claim an average of about three hundred feet of frontage. Most of the dwellings were set away from the narrow road, some obscured by trees. Others appeared stark and unattended, save for the old cars parked on rutted dirt driveways and an occasional lawn chair or battered swing set. A couple were well-maintained newer houses sitting on beautiful lots, surrounded by outbuildings, lush plantings, and newer vehicles. The sights were a mixed hodgepodge, causing Ray to wonder why people of means chose to build on such a road. The mobile homes were the worst of the lot, many seeming to have crashed there forty years ago without a lick of maintenance in the interim.

Shim shifted to the right twice along the way to allow oncoming cars to pass. The narrow road couldn't

IMPERFECT ESCAPE

accommodate two normal-sized vehicles going at decent speeds.

"Lots of traffic today." Johnson laughed. "I've been down this road many times and never saw another living thing, except for deer or wild turkey, maybe."

"Rural living at its finest," Ray said. "Shim, are you comfortable with living here? It's a big change from Ft. Lauderdale."

"Sure. I grew up in the country outside of Memphis. The road I lived on looked like this—except all of the faces were black and there weren't any new, fine structures. Didn't move into the city until I started college—thank God for sports scholarships." Shim turned into an almost hidden driveway. Trees encroached on both sides, and he slowed to a crawl.

The ride out of the city limits had lasted three minutes. Another five minutes at twenty-five miles per hour brought them to Flocker's place.

"Flocker could have easily heard the explosion, jumped on his Harley, and made it to the scene while people were still moving around," Ray said. "He would have made it in half the time—knowing the road and speeding a bit."

"I'd say so." Shim pulled to a stop in front of a small wood-frame house.

The place had a fresh coat of paint and recent repairs stood out from the older wood, the finish looking smooth in those places.

A thin, tiny woman, who wore a housedress and appeared to be pushing seventy, stood in front of a wooden porch bench. With shaking hands, she set aside a knitting basket and shuffled to the steps. "What can I do for you, officers?"

"Mrs. Flocker," Shim said, "we'd like to have a look around inside, especially in your son's room. Then we'll be going to the explosion site."

Ray watched the woman consider her response.

"Come ahead. If I say no, you'll just get a damn warrant anyway."

"True," Shim said.

Gregg E. Brickman

Mrs. Flocker stepped aside and motioned them inside the home. "Please don't tear things up like the other deputy did."

"Who did that, ma'am?" Shim said

"Deputy Krantz."

A cloud of anger crossed Shim's face. "We'll be careful."

The men entered the tidy home through the living room. The kitchen and dining areas were to the right. The spotless fireplace sported a new screen and shiny implements. Ray thought the place shared construction plans with the little house he and Sophia rented. The floor plan was identical.

The master bedroom, obviously belonging to the woman, had a handmade quilt covering the bed. A sewing machine sat open in one corner. A cutting table blocked access to the single window.

Bubba Flocker's room appeared tidy as well. There was nothing hidden in or below any of the drawers, in the closet, or under the mattress. A modest sum of cash filled a glass mason jar on the dresser. A note sitting against the jar read, *Help Yourself, Ma.*

They returned to the porch.

Shim addressed Mrs. Flocker. "We found nothing unusual, except the jar of money in his bedroom."

"Charles—Bubba as you call him—is my sole support, has been ever since the cancer took my husband. I'm not well myself, so I can't work no more. My son's all I got."

"Does he have a source of income beyond the meth lab?" Ray asked.

Anger flashed in her tired-looking eyes. "He rented that building to his friend. Got a good rent, too, before the idiot blew it up."

"Employment, ma'am?" Ray wanted to verify the statements Flocker made a day earlier.

"He works part-time for Silken in the dry goods store in town."

"What does he do there?"

"Unloads trucks, hauls the trash. That sort of thing. Mr. Silken likes to talk to the customers, but doesn't like to get his

IMPERFECT ESCAPE

hands dirty. No sir. And, my son's strong."

"How long has he worked for Silken?" Ray said.

Mrs. Flocker looked thoughtful. "Three, four years. He started there right before my man died. Now he does that to bring in consistent money, then he works the garden, sells the produce at the fresh market, and takes care of the cows and chickens."

The men thanked Mrs. Flocker and walked away from the house.

Shim pointed to a path curling behind a small barn and a chicken coop. A well-maintained garden, surrounded by high fencing, sat off to the right. "That way."

The path led through the trees toward the rear of the property. They passed a granite rock formation dripping water between the layers.

Johnson pointed. "Hence the name of the road. Dripping Springs Drive."

Once they reached the site, there was little to see. The destroyed structure had been a camping trailer, which lent some credence to the mother's story that the site was a rental. Only a section of outside wall remained, along with the underlying metal structure of the trailer. The camper-sized plumbing and other less-flammable pieces sat at odd angles on the undercarriage.

"Looks like it exploded and burned," Johnson said.

"Nope." Shim scowled. "Burned, then exploded. Or so the arson investigator says."

Shim's cell phone beeped, and he answered. After listening a full minute, he said, "I'm on my way."

"I need to go to County Medical. There's a problem with Flocker."

"What is it?" Ray asked.

"Don't know for sure. I'll let you know when I do. The deputy calling it into the department didn't say. "

Ten minutes later, Ray and Johnson stood on the curb in front of the Plateauville PD and watched Shim's taillights in the distance.

Chapter 11

Sophia

On Wednesday morning, Sophia's manager assigned her to work with Ricky Tondo in the main ED. Sophia held her comments, wishing she'd been assigned to the trauma unit with Katina Cassia, but that wasn't to be. Sara Grudgeon, the ED director, explained that even though Sophia's official orientation period was complete, she wanted to rotate her through all of the services again before throwing her into the fray without support. Sophia decided it wasn't the assignment she didn't like but, rather, Ricky as her resource person.

After listening to report on Ricky's two assigned patients, Sophia said, "Ricky, I guess it's you and me today." She swallowed her chagrin, stuck a big smile on her face, and stood tall. "Where do we start?"

Ricky unleashed his lopsided sneer-smile. "Seems to me you should have been with me on Monday." He shook his head. "What can you do? Sara is the boss lady. Follow me."

"Okay."

She followed Ricky into each room. First, he checked each of the patients, introducing himself and Sophia. Ricky claimed the first patient for himself and gave the second one to Sophia. He continued through the next rooms checking supplies and making things precise. She noted his preferences and followed suit. "Where did you work in Miami?"

IMPERFECT ESCAPE

"Jackson ED."

"Busy place. This must seem calm to you."

"Yes and no. There we had a lot more activity, however we had more staff, more resources, and more residents. Here we adapt to less."

She nodded.

"Why'd you move to Tennessee?"

"I followed my partner. He's the manager of a bank downtown."

"Do you like it here?"

"Yes . . . and no. I miss . . ." He paused. "What we'll do today is alternate admissions. I'll keep up with yours, too, so I can answer any questions."

"Sounds good." Sophia wondered what he missed and why he didn't finish his sentence. If she had to guess, she'd say he missed being accepted without regard to his lifestyle. With the conservative Christian culture, being gay had to be a tougher reality in Middle Tennessee.

"You're aware we take a few minutes every shift to visit the patients we admitted to the hospital. Sara is hot about it. You do an ED satisfaction survey, then make sure everything is going well for them."

"That's new to me."

"Did you admit anyone on Monday?"

"I did. Bubba Flocker. I assume he's still upstairs with his police guard."

Ricky laughed. "Bubba. I've had him a time or two. Okay. I didn't know he was part of Monday's admissions. You can visit Bubba, and I'll see the two I admitted yesterday."

About half-way through the morning, Ricky tracked her down in the clean utility room where the medical and surgical supplies were stored. "Let's go upstairs now. Your rooms are empty, but they won't be for long. My patients are both in X-ray and will be there for a while."

Sophia dropped off a handful of supplies in one of her rooms and followed Ricky to the elevator.

When they got to Intermediate Care, he said, "Go in and

see Bubba. I'll be in five-thirteen or fifteen." He stopped. "I forgot." He handed her a form with the required interview questions.

Sophia nodded to the sheriff's deputy sitting outside room five-eleven. "Is it okay if I go in? I'm from the ED and have questions to ask Mr. Flocker."

The deputy grinned, then looked at her ID badge.

"I need to sign you in."

Sophia watched as he added her name to his list. She saw Ray's name, then Krantz's. "Thanks." Sophia tapped on the door and entered when she heard him respond. "Hi, Bubba. I'm Sophia. Remember me from Monday?"

He smiled. "I do."

"I would have warned you on Monday, except I just found out that the ED nurses visit patients upstairs and see how things went."

"Yeah, I know how it works. Just mark a five on all your questions. You treated me just fine."

Sophia marked the questions, then took a moment to inspect the IV infusion pump, tubing, and medications. She noted an antibiotic was dripping from a small bag and the pump was set to automatically switch back to the large, main IV. It all looked good. She pulled over a chair. "So, how are you doing?"

"Okay. I'm thinkin' you have more to ask me."

"I do, if you don't mind." She decided to charge ahead. "I got the idea on Monday that you'd have told me more about the meth labs around Plateauville if the deputy hadn't been so close."

"Might have. Why do you want to know about those doin's?"

"I work in the ED, and I'm new to the area. I also live in Plateauville now. I need to know what goes on because of my job."

Bubba looked thoughtful.

"For example, you seemed to be happy the lab blew up and some guys were hurt."

IMPERFECT ESCAPE

Bubba looked around the room, then his gaze rested on the door. "It's not that I want people to be hurt, it's just that Vast—it was his lab—be a problem. He uses product, acts like a crazy asshole, and draws attention. That's bad for everyone's business."

"Couldn't someone just rat him out to the cops."

"Hell no. We got to take care of stuff ourselves. Know what I mean?"

"I thought you were your own boss, and you're just talking about a friend."

"I am. It takes a lot of stuff to make good product." Bubba's speech slurred.

Sophia shook her head, trying to act confused. "I heard in town that—"

Bubba's eyes rolled back, he struggled for breath.

Sophia grabbed the oxygen tubing and put it in place around his face. "Breathe, Bubba."

Sophia picked up the phone, dialed the code number. "Code Assist, room five-eleven."

He stopped breathing.

She lowered the head of the bed, then pulled the bed out from the wall. When she did, she noticed a syringe on the floor. As she extended Bubba's neck to open his airway, she saw that the main IV was infusing. The timing of the breathing problem, coupled with the unlabeled syringe on the floor and the IV switching over, gave her a chill. She reached over and shut off the IV, then snatched an Ambu bag from the wall.

As Sophia fitted the mask over Bubba's face, two nurses, one pushing the emergency cart, crashed into the room.

Chapter 12

Sophia

Sophia handed Ray a beer and motioned to the deck behind the little house. She grabbed her glass of Pinot Grigio. "Come on Mischief. Let's go out and harass the geese."

Ray followed Sophia outside.

Mischief stared through the pickets at the gaggle of geese on the grass between the deck and the pond. She didn't bark, so the geese went about their business but seemed to keep watch on the humans and dog.

"I feel sorry for broken wing. She just watches the others, but they ignore her." Sophia pointed to a lone goose standing ten feet away from the group.

"I don't know a lot about geese society," Ray said, "but she didn't fly in with them and won't leave with them either. Chances are she won't survive the winter. When the pond freezes, she won't have anywhere to escape predators."

"That's horrible." Sophia felt a wave of sympathy for the animal.

"That's life." Ray raised his Sam Adams. "Thanks for buying the beer."

"I aim to please." She swirled the wine in her glass, then sipped. "I talked to Bubba Flocker today."

"Ah, I thought you were staying out of things?"

Sophia sat in one of the four chairs surrounding the glass-

IMPERFECT ESCAPE

topped table, then set her drink in front of her. "Ray Stone, we need to talk about that."

"I thought it was settled. You're a nurse. You nurse. I'm a detective. I detect. Seems simple to me."

"Well, I know I agreed, but it's not as simple as you make it." Even though his expression turned angry, she continued. "In the ED, I'm going to come into contact with people in your cases, and I'll learn things. Either I tell you what I find out or I don't, but I will find out things. I'm not stupid, you know."

"Sophie, sweetie. It's not that I think you're not capable. You get into trouble."

"I don't always get in trouble. I've helped you before. No one was the wiser."

"Sophia, this is not what we agreed."

When he called her *Sophia,* she knew he was pissed in a major way. "It's not working out for me. You said you wanted to discuss cases because it helps with your analysis. When you do, and I have a thought, I'd like to share it. You can ignore me. As you said, you're the freaking detective." She glared at him. "It's your choice. Either I tell you what I think and hear, or I don't."

Ray let loose a loud, exasperated-sounding sigh. "Damn it, Sophia. I love you, and I worry about your safety. You didn't want to stay a cop. Why do you want to poke around?"

"It's not that I didn't want to be a cop so much as I didn't want to be shot again. Nursing allows me to investigate things—albeit people's health, not crimes—but a lot of the thought process is the same. Please let me help when I can. I'll be careful."

"Will you keep up your shooting skills and carry your Sig when I tell you to? No questions asked?"

"Yes, sir. I will."

"Okay. We'll give it a try again. You will, however, stay away from areas when I tell you to."

She nodded.

"Your Florida carry permit will cover you for six months, but we'll get you an application and start the process."

Gregg E. Brickman

Damn, she thought. She hated carrying a weapon.

"Now, what is it you're itching to tell me?" He didn't smile, but the pure anger wasn't visible on his face.

"After you saw Bubba this morning, I went to his room to do an ED satisfaction survey." She told Ray about the conversation with Flocker and his comments about Vast.

He nodded. "Flocker denied knowing anything solid about Silken's connection to the meth issue or being a drug boss. He wouldn't even confirm there was a drug boss. Danced around the issue. I suspect his answers change like the Tennessee weather. Go on."

"Anyway, he quit breathing while I was in the room. There was an unmarked syringe on the floor. And he had his problem right when the IV switched from the little bag of antibiotics to the main IV. I turned off the IV and called a code. I told the doctor about it."

"First, what happened with Flocker?"

"He started breathing on his own. They sent him to ICU for observation for a day or so." She paused. "The doctor said the patient acted like he was recovering from anesthesia. He speculated that maybe something had been added to the IV. Then we called in the deputy who was guarding the door. He called Detective Shim who works for the sheriff."

"I know Shim. In fact, I might have been with Shim—we were out at Flocker's place—at the time."

"Anyway, Shim came in and took all the tubing and syringe with him. I heard him tell the deputy they'd find out if the IV was contaminated and what was in the syringe. He said he'd have it checked for prints, too."

"Sounds like you turned off the murder weapon and saved Flocker's life."

"That's what the doctor said, too," Sophia said.

"Do you have any idea how the IV got contaminated?"

"No. What I do know is that the staff nurse hung the antibiotic a little after nine. She wrote it on the drug label. The drug couldn't have been in the main IV before then. She set the bag of antibiotics to run for forty-five minutes. I was there

IMPERFECT ESCAPE

when the pump changed back to the main line. The other thing is, when I went into the room, I saw on the deputy's log that Krantz went into the room after you did."

"I was there when Krantz arrived. As usual, he was rude." Ray looked thoughtful. "He implied he was on a mission from Shim, but Shim denied sending him to interview Flocker. Besides, Shim seems to be the kind of man who gets into the cases himself, asks his own questions."

"Well, I do know when Shim came into Bubba's room—I was still there writing up the notes from the event—he had a very take-charge attitude. Also, it seemed odd to me, but he was surprised to see Krantz's name was on the visitor's list."

"I'll need to ask him about that."

Sophia nodded, then took a sip of her wine.

"The other thing not adding up for me is Flocker says he works his mother's farm—which she confirmed," Ray said. "She also said he works at the dry goods store for Silken—which Flocker mentioned in an off-hand, ah-shucks way."

Chapter 13

Ray

Ray started Thursday morning by following up with the uniformed officers on a robbery they'd handled during the previous night at Silken's Dry Goods. Their work had been thorough. They gave him a report detailing the stolen goods, and they had taken fingerprints.

"You say here," Ray pointed to the report, "that the mess you encountered suggested the thieves were looking for something. Do you have any idea what that might be?"

"Silken didn't know," the taller, younger officer, Al Crag, said. "I think somebody may have been looking for product—methamphetamine or maybe pseudoephedrine—and took other stuff."

"Interesting. Talk to me about why you think that."

"Well, it's just rumor, but I hear it a lot—saying Silken is involved in our drug problem, maybe even heading it up."

"When does Silken's open?"

"Not until nine," Crag said. "He said he'd go into the store early this morning and clean things up. The thieves damaged the register and took the cash."

"Given Silken is a mature businessman, I would have thought he was smarter than to leave cash in a closed store." Ray asked a few more questions of the officers, then decided he needed a meeting with the chief to see what he thought of

IMPERFECT ESCAPE

Silken.

"Chief?" Ray tapped on the frame of the open office door.

"Come in, Stone. What's on your mind?" The chief didn't look up until he finished writing on the paper on his desk. "Have a seat."

Ray sat. "Carl Silken."

Chief Mullins nodded.

"I've heard from several people that he is behind our high-end drug channels."

"Why do you say high-end?"

"Because the labs that exploded here and in the county aren't just make-some-for-me and sell-a-bit-to-my-friend operations. And there are too many rumors to discount."

"I hear you."

"Why didn't you mention Silken when we talked on Monday?"

"I wanted to see if you'd pick up the same thread." Mullins looked back at his paper, then glanced up. "I suggest you tug the thread, Detective."

"Did we get the search warrant for Vast's place?"

"It's on your desk."

Ray didn't like the feeling that Mullins was toying with him, or perhaps testing him, but he could see the point. Both the sheriff and Shim wanted Ray's fresh perspective. Perhaps that was Mullins' agenda, too.

Ray stopped by his office, then headed out of the department. Silken's store was about three blocks west, but he took his vehicle, planning to head out to Dripping Springs Drive and Vast's trailer next.

After Ray parked in front of the store, he called Johnson. "When I'm done with Silken, do you want to meet me and have a go at Vast's property?"

"Sure thing. I've been covering the school zones. I'm clear to join you at nine."

"Works." Ray checked the time. It was eight-fifteen.

The lights were on inside the store, and Ray could see

Silken working in the first row of merchandise. Ray exited his car and headed toward the store. The view through the front window revealed goods cluttering the floor. The place looked messed up but not ransacked. When Ray knocked on the door, Silken looked his way and motioned him in.

"Good morning, Detective Stone. You here about the robbery?" Silken stepped away from the row of shelving.

"Yes, sir." He produced a copy of the officers' report from the scene. "It says you lost several small kitchen appliances, two power drills, two radios, a laptop computer, several small knives, and two thousand dollars in cash. Have you noted anything else missing?"

"No."

"Seems like a lot of cash to have available." Ray walked around, inspecting the merchandise and wondering why other valuable things were still on the shelves. "Are you in the habit of leaving cash in the store?"

"I'm not."

Ray waited. After several moments when Silken did not volunteer more information, he said, "Why was there so much money in the store?"

"Sheila, that's my wife, brought it in just before closing. She had been to a fundraiser and thought to put the cash in my safe here until this morning when the bank opens. I was busy so I stuck it in the register and then forgot to lock it up."

"What fundraiser?"

"The Plateauville Women's Club has a charity program that provides lunches for kids in the summer. Yesterday they had a craft sale. All the items are donated, so it's total profit."

"Who is the chairperson of the club—in case I want to talk to them?" Ray said.

"That would be Sheila."

Ray made a note. Maybe he'd have a talk with her. He suspected the insurance company would be getting a claim in a few days for money that wasn't actually stolen. "What else you can tell me about the robbery?"

"Nothing."

IMPERFECT ESCAPE

"It's not the kind of haul the thieves will fence," Ray said. "More likely, their wives, mothers, girlfriends, and sisters will get gifts, and they'll keep the rest."

"Is that all?"

"No. I have another issue to ask you about. Can we sit in the back for a few minutes?"

Silken looked at the remaining mess, shrugged, and headed toward the rear office, which was actually a wide spot in the hallway that was closed off with a door. He sat in one of two chairs, motioning Ray to the other.

Ray sat, made himself comfortable, and looked around the area. A window opened onto the back alley. He assumed the door on the back wall was the service door. "Mr. Silken, I've been on the job since Sunday. That's four days. I've been told as many times that you are the power behind the methamphetamine problem in this community."

Silken didn't flinch. "Now, Detective, that's the biggest line of bullshit I've heard in a long time."

"You deny the allegations?"

"Not only do I deny them, I take particular exception. I am an upstanding businessman." Silken's face reddened as he plunged into the topic. "How dare you? Do you know who I am? I'm a respected member of the community."

"If you say so, sir." Ray decided to push a bit harder. "However, I've learned that where there's a trace of smoke, there's often a flicker of flame. Why do you think so many people would tell me that?" Ray rubbed at his goatee as if puzzled by the notion.

"Know what I think, Stone? I think you came in here to jack me up because you know you'll never solve the robbery. I think you're a small-time dick who couldn't cut it in the big leagues and came up here because it was the only job you could get. Now, get the hell out of my store. I'll be talking to the mayor and have your ass fired within the hour."

Ray stood and ambled toward the door, taking his time. "Have a good day, Mr. Silken. I'll be pulling on this string a bit more." He headed into the street thinking he'd baited a bear

Gregg E. Brickman

and vowing to make Sophia carry her gun.

***

Ray crossed the street and walked a couple of doors down to the Plateau Cafe. He parked himself on a stool in front of the counter. The place was small and somewhat ragged looking. A half-dozen tables of various sizes filled the space between the counter and booths on the far wall.

"Mornin', Detective." The older lady smiled. "I'm Elma May Bib. My husband and I own the place."

"Nice to meet you, ma'am."

"Folks call me Elma May." She reached for the coffee pot. "You drinkin'?"

"I am." Ray thought that only in a small town would the mayor's wife be working behind the counter at the cafe.

After she set the coffee in front of him, Ray tasted it. They made an excellent brew. The nearby pastry box enticed him, and he ordered a Danish.

"I hear that Silken's was busted into again last night."

It was the first Ray heard of multiple break-ins. "How many times has it happened before?"

"Fairly often, really. Maybe every couple of months. It's only his place that gets hit. Mine? Never. And, as far as I know, none other on the street neither."

"Interesting. Do you know why?"

"Well, his is the only place with that kind of merchandise. You know what I mean?"

"Tell me."

"Said enough. Maybe you should talk to my husband about it. Enjoy your coffee."

He did. Officer Johnson walked in the door just as he was finishing and ordered a coffee to go.

"Where's your vehicle?" Ray asked.

"I saw yours across the street. Figured you were here. I parked at the department and walked a spell."

A couple of minutes later, they were in Ray's unmarked

IMPERFECT ESCAPE

with Johnson behind the wheel. Johnson zipped across town, taking side streets. They headed toward the park and Dripping Springs Drive.

Johnson sped along, taking the curves and missing potholes like a pro. He swung into Vast's driveway.

Kelly Ann stepped out of the chipped gray trailer a second after Johnson put on the brakes. Again, she held her hand under her swollen belly as if holding up the baby.

"I told you officers you can't be on this here property." She zeroed in on Johnson. "Jim, you know better than to keep comin' on out."

While Ray collected a bag of crime scene supplies from the trunk of the vehicle, Johnson approached the house.

"Ma'am, we have a search warrant. Step aside," Johnson said.

Her face reddened, but she did as Johnson directed. She looked cleaner than on the earlier visit, and there were no tears.

"Stay on your porch, please. We'll give you a receipt for anything we take with us," Ray said, then nodded to Johnson to step inside. Ray followed. "Jim, don't make a mess. Let's just get this done."

The search yielded a couple of small baggies of what looked like meth hidden inside the cap on a can of shaving cream. They found a stack of cash, mostly fives and tens, in a battered tool box. A ledger book that seemed to be written in code was wedged behind the commode. There was a stack of wound care supplies on the counter.

"Vast needs to be more creative in his hiding places." Ray put the cash on the kitchen counter. He stood a moment writing out a receipt for the book and the bags of white crystals.

"You're leaving the cash?" Johnson said.

"We don't need it to make our case, and she certainly needs it. We have enough with the other items—if we find him alive."

Back on the porch, Ray handed Mrs. Vast a receipt.

She studied the paper. "Don't know nothing about that

book." She pointed to it. "If I'd found the crank, I'd have flushed it with the rest." Crank was a slang term for methamphetamine.

"You sound like you don't approve of him using?"

"I don't. He was good for so long."

"Have you seen your husband?" Ray asked, staring into her eyes.

"No, sir." She averted her gaze a bit, then stared back at Ray.

He suspected she lied. "You're sure now. I see you have groceries inside and no car around. Who's been helping you?"

"My friend."

"Who might that be?" Ray asked.

"None of your business, Detective."

Ray knew she wouldn't say more. "Call us if LeRoy shows up."

She glared at him.

Ray started down the steps, then turned back. "Why do you have all of those medical supplies on the counter in the bathroom?"

"We run a farm here. People get hurt. If you looked around some, you'd see there ain't a lot of places to put things."

Ray shouldered the bag with crime scene supplies, then joined Johnson in the yard. "How big is this property?" He waved his arm around to indicate the wooded area behind the house.

"Thirty acres or so."

A dilapidated barn stood off to the left, but the roof looked to be in decent repair. A small fenced area contained a couple of goats and a cow. A chicken coop, in better condition than the house, sat a bit further back in the yards. Several pieces of farm equipment filled a lean-to. "Maybe they do farm."

"They do. Personal use, mostly."

Ray and Johnson checked the outbuildings, netting a crate of pseudoephedrine, several other chemicals, and a stash of various filters.

After they hauled the goods to the car, they handed Mrs.

IMPERFECT ESCAPE

Vast another receipt. This time she said nothing.

Next, the men avoided the vegetable gardens and walked the woods. Thorns and stickers stuck to their clothing and poked the exposed skin on their arms. Several growths of Poison Ivy required detours, as did a stand of thorny wild blackberry bushes.

"Ray, look." Johnson pointed.

A small cleared area looked as if someone had camped since the last time it rained, maybe three days ago. Cigarette butts littered the cleared dirt circle surrounding a fire pit. Holes on the perimeter of a raked square seemed to indicate the placement of a tent. Further searching revealed a makeshift latrine trench.

"I'd say Richie Vast was hiding here, or maybe LeRoy really is alive," Ray said.

Johnson pointed to the sky where clouds were rolling in from the west. "Better make it quick." He stepped through the trees to the left of the camp site. "Snake Creek Trail is about thirty feet away."

"So, Mrs. Vast has deniability about knowing someone was living here." Ray pondered the thought. "Looks like a well-worn path," he pointed, "leading in the direction of the house."

"Woods are full of them. I'd say Kelly Ann will tell you about the blackberries if you ask her about the path."

Ray took numerous photos of the site, then he and Johnson collected cigarette butts, excrement samples, and a few other small pieces of potential evidence. Ray packed them all into a larger bag for containment and transport, then took a minute to sketch the property and the location of the campsite on the outside of the bag.

"We need to compare the DNA with both LeRoy Vast and his cousin Richie. Maybe we will finally know who is alive and who is running."

"Well now," Johnson said, "that could be interesting. I don't know if I told you, but I'm sorta related to the Vast boys. My uncle by marriage is a cousin of the Vast brothers."

Ray shook his head. Everyone was related to everyone.

Gregg E. Brickman

"Explain why it should be interesting. I thought LeRoy and Richie were cousins. Shouldn't be a problem"

"Oh, they are. Double-first. Their dads are brothers. Their mothers are sisters. I'm no expert, but I think the DNA analysis won't be cut and dried—not if my biology professor knew what she was talkin' about anyway."

Chapter 14

Sophia

Standing a couple feet from the foot of the stretcher, Sophia observed her patient, Darrell Fealty. Above his head, an electric clock proclaimed the day as Thursday.

He gazed around the small, private ED room with wide eyes, dilated pupils, and a nervous shaking that encompassed his entire body. He'd thrown off the lightweight flannel blanket and sheet the night shift had provided when they admitted him, revealing a gaunt, emaciated body. A couple of minutes earlier, he'd ordered Sophia away from him. Now she waited, hoping he'd calm, so she could do her assessment.

"Sharon, you bitch, get over here." His tone rang nasty, but compelling.

The wife, Sharon Fealty, eased off the rolling stool she had commandeered and placed a safe distance away. She stepped closer to the stretcher, but appeared careful to stay out of arms' reach.

"Closer."

"No, Darrell. You tried to choke me. Remember?" She rubbed at the marks on her neck.

"I'm sorry about that, Shar. I thought you was trying to take my stash."

"Darrell, I don't want, nor have I ever wanted your damned crank." Sharon looked disgusted.

"Shush. Don't tell them about that, baby. They don't have to know. They just have to take that thing out of me."

Fealty tried to get out of bed, but before Sophia could get closer, he collapsed against the pillows. "I need to sleep. Just let me sleep."

"Mrs. Fealty, how long has it been since your husband slept?"

"Don't know for sure. A few days. He got fired, then started binging. Taking one hit after another. I took the kids to Ma's 'cause he gets mean, but I went back home to make sure he didn't hurt hisself."

"Did you tell the cops he tried to choke you?"

"Yeah. They didn't care. Said I should take my kids and leave."

"Should you?"

"Yes, I guess. But it's not that easy. If I went to Ma's, he'd just tear up her house again. He doesn't care about the kids when he's like this, but he wants me around."

"You've been through this before?"

"Yes. Darrell and I met in rehab. I stayed off the meth. He went back to it a few months back, and he keeps getting worse and worse. He's out of control now. Lost all his friends. His pa won't even talk to him no more."

"I need to take his vitals and do his assessment."

"Uh huh. Better get some help. Even though he looks calm now, he'll blast out at any minute."

"What did he mean by 'take that thing out of me'?"

"He gets paranoid when he uses too much. That's when he tries to hurt me or the kids. Thinks we're demons or something and are after him. Today he decided someone—me most likely—put something in his body to kill him. I told him he was the one who put something in his body—meaning the crank. That's when he decided to choke me."

"How long does the behavior last?"

"Until the stuff is out of his system. Then he'll sleep for a week."

"Then what?"

IMPERFECT ESCAPE

"He wakes up and goes looking for another hit. There isn't any in the house. When I find it, I flush it. He almost killed me over that a time or two."

"Where does he buy it? If you don't mind my asking."

"There's a guy in town. Big shot. When it comes to meth, Plateauville is a dirty little town. I wish my kids and I could move away somewheres. I won't say no more." Mrs. Fealty shifted side to side, and she looked through the room door as if afraid.

Sophia excused herself and returned a couple of minutes later with a strong male ED tech and a security guard. She handed Mrs. Fealty a brochure about help for abused women. Then with help from the men, she accomplished most of her care, finally having to stop when Fealty woke up yelling, swinging, and grabbing. In the process, however, she learned that his blood pressure was dangerously high and his heart rate was excessive. She went to get the doctor.

The charge nurse assigned the strong tech to stay in the room with Mr. Fealty and his wife, and the security guard stationed himself near the door.

Feeling confident the situation was under control, Sophia headed toward the nurses' lounge for a much-needed cup of coffee and a brief rest. She'd been on her feet for three hours, and her right hip screamed from the abuse. She rubbed at a huge bruise on her left forearm, the result of Fealty grabbing her, then picked up a blank incident report form to complete during her break.

Ricky Tondo looked up and engaged his sneer-smile when Sophia entered the lounge. "I saw you were having a hard time in there."

Sophia exhaled and dropped into a chair next to Ricky at the big central table.

"Lots of chairs." He swung his hand around the room. "Why are you all cozy all of a sudden?"

"Because other people will come in, and I want to talk to you."

Ricky scowled. "So talk."

Gregg E. Brickman

"First, how often does something like that happen? My patient's behavior, I mean."

"He's fairly typical of an out of control meth abuser. Violent, abusive, paranoid, sleepless. They often don't eat, don't sleep, and maintain an extreme activity level. Some get sexually excited and may assault their girlfriends, wives, or even strangers."

"It's worse to deal with than to read about in the orientation materials."

"You got that right, girl."

"The patient's wife implied there is a big shot dealer in Plateauville."

"There is. We hear about it all the time. Never a name though." He looked thoughtful. "Be careful asking questions. There are also rumors of police involvement or maybe protection. Something along those lines."

Ricky's uncharacteristically friendly answers and forthcoming manner encouraged her to continue. "Did you see a lot of meth abuse at Jackson in Miami?"

"Sure. Big inner-city hospital."

"Do you know anything about the meth scene in Miami?"

"A bit, I suppose. I have a friend who is a social user. Tried to offer me some, but I told him I'd seen the effect too many times."

"I ask because I read that a lot of the supplies come in through Miami, the pseudoephedrine especially."

"I think it's probably true enough. There are some major labs—we got victims from the explosions—and several big suppliers. I know because the meth heads would come in complaining about the supply. That sort of thing."

"Do you know any names?"

"Why are you asking?"

She told him about the explosion on Dripping Springs Drive. "I've been poking around some, just so I can understand where Ray—he's my fiancé and the new detective in Plateauville—is coming from when he talks about his cases."

"Okay. Basically, you're an interfering female who wishes

IMPERFECT ESCAPE

she were still a cop."

Sophia objected to his description, but didn't voice her concerns. Instead, she said, "Maybe so."

"I'll call my friend later."

***

Sophia pulled the MINI off to the right when she saw Ray make the turn past the golf course's clubhouse. She knew she'd leave first in the morning, so she wanted her car to be in the rear. That could backfire, she supposed, if he got called out later. After he parked, she pulled in.

"Hi. How was your day?" She closed the car door and hurried to catch him. She stood on tiptoes and accepted a gentle kiss.

"Had a good day. Maybe making a little progress."

"What did you learn?" Sophia grinned.

"For one thing, everyone is related to everyone in these parts. For example, Jim Johnson is a distant cousin to the Vasts."

"It's no different where I grew up in North Dakota or where you grew up in Virginia for that matter. But it still seems like a conflict to me."

"Maybe, but without it, there would be no deputies at all. He doesn't seem overly impressed by the connection." Ray explained the relationship of Richie and LeRoy Vast as he keyed the door and stepped inside.

Sophia bent and picked up the dog, cuddling her close and accepting her wet licks. "How about you walk Mischief, and I'll hop in the shower and try to think of some miracle to put on the dinner table."

Ray grabbed the leash, took Mischief from Sophia's arms, and headed out the door.

Sophia stripped off her uniform and stuffed it into the laundry bag, then showered, and dressed in worn jeans and an old tee shirt.

When Ray and Mischief returned—they had a long

walk—her head was stuck in the refrigerator. "Okay, this is good. I've got yesterday's grilled chicken, half a jar of pesto, makings of a salad, and pasta. I call that dinner." She set several containers on the counter, pushed them against the back splash, and grabbed a pot and a sauté pan off the open storage shelf next to the fridge.

"Works." He retrieved a bag of kibble from under the sink, filled the dog's dish, and set it near her water bowl. Then he grabbed a cold beer. "Want one?"

"Yuk. I'll take wine. There's an open bottle of Pinot Grigio." While Ray poured her wine, she started her preparations. The one thing she had learned in the short time they'd lived in the little house was that with four total feet of counter space, it was essential to be systematic—and simple—with meal preparation. "When we move again, I want lots of counter space."

Ray laughed. "We'll see to it." He took the salad fixings to the table, sat, and began working.

"Thanks," Sophia said, setting a kettle of water on the stove to boil. "I had a patient today who was whacked-out on meth. That's a clinical term, by the way." She laughed. "Anyway, his wife told me his source is a big shot in Plateauville. She looked scared and refused to tell me more. Then, I was talking to Ricky—"

"That's the guy from Miami that annoys you."

"Yes, Ricky Tondo. Anyway, he said they hear about the Plateauville connection a lot, and the meth heads also claim there's involvement with the police."

"Sorry to say, none of that is new news. I think the big shot's name is Silken, aka. Silky."

"Is there involvement in the department? Ricky said he's gotten wind about people paying protection. And, he told me to watch myself if I kept asking questions."

"That was going to be my next point. I rattled Silken's cage today." He pulled a folded paper from his shirt pocket. "Here's the carry permit application. Fill it out. Meanwhile, your Florida permit will cover you."

IMPERFECT ESCAPE

"Know that already."

"Take the Sig with you, like you did in Florida the last time you pissed someone off. We'll head out to the range Sunday before we go to Knoxville and let you get in some practice."

"Ray, I—"

"Listen, girl. We made a deal. If you play, you pay. You will carry your weapon, or you will not be involved, ever, in my cases. And, you'll transfer out of that damn ED to someplace safe at the first opportunity."

Sophia exhaled, then nodded. "Okay. We did have a deal. I'll do it." She pouted and cooked with no further comments for several minutes. Then, she said, "There is more."

"What?" Ray's voice was gentle. He stepped in behind her and wrapped his arms around her shoulders, resting his bearded chin on her head.

"Ricky called his buddy in Florida this afternoon. I asked him to. I'd been asking him about the meth scene in Miami, admissions to Jackson, that sort of thing. Anyway, his friend told him his supplier was named Krantz. Isn't that the name of the deputy who keeps popping up and is in your face?"

"It is. What I don't understand is why you think it's relevant, or why you would even ask. Or for that matter, how your mind works sometimes."

"I read an article at the library on Tuesday about Silken moving here from Florida. Then I poked around about the meth scene in Florida and found out a lot of the supplies come into the country through Florida from South America. I was just thinking, sorting it out in my mind. Then when Ricky mentioned the guy's name was Krantz, I thought there might be a connection."

"It would explain some things. That's for sure." Ray seemed lost in thought as he sliced five times more onion than the salads needed. "Oh, by the way. You did save Flocker. The IV contained propofol—I think I said it right—probably not enough to kill him, however. Perhaps the purpose was to scare him or send a warning."

"Were there any prints on the tubing or IV bag?"

"A couple as yet unidentified partials on the tubing. None from the nurse who originally started the IV."
"She might have worn gloves." "
"They found lots of prints, yours included, on the pump."
"So, it was someone who knows their way around hospitals and drugs."
"I'd say so. Yes," Ray said.

Chapter 15

Ray

Ray started the Friday workday at seven-thirty with a return visit to the Plateau Cafe, which sat across the street from Silken's Dry Goods. His purpose was twofold. First, he wanted a chance to meet and talk to the locals over coffee. Second, the location provided him an opportunity to see the early morning activity at Silken's.

Five men sat around the six-top table near the large front window.

"Good morning." Ray approached the table and pointed to the empty chair, which had a good view of the street. "May I?"

"You're the new detective." An older man with a dusting of white hair, dress shirt, and tie extended a hand. "Have a seat. I'm Bob Fitz. I run the bank."

"Nice to meet you."

Each of the other men introduced themselves. Sam Sloan owned a small local grocery. George Schmidt was the pharmacist at Plateau Drugs. John Johnson operated an auto body shop and was Officer Jim Johnson's father. Archie Bib was the mayor and the owner of Plateau Cafe.

Bib, who looked to be pushing seventy-five, pointed to a sign on the wall. "I keep hoping to sell this place. I like it just fine, mind you. I'm just ready to retire." He half stood. "Elma, can you bring the detective a cup of coffee, please? Elma May is my wife. She does most of the work around here, truth be."

Elma hurried to the table with the coffee pot. She turned over the cup in front of Ray and poured. "Nice to see you again, Detective."

"Thank you, Elma May." Ray sipped, then ordered eggs, biscuits and gravy, and grits. It wasn't his usual morning choice, but he thought the selections would serve his purpose.

"Southern boy?" Sloan said.

"Born and raised in Virginia."

The men asked questions about his personal and policing background, and he replied, keeping a casual tone and providing the basic information. He knew anything he said would be common knowledge around town by noon.

As the conversation continued, Ray watched a Sheriff's Department yellow and white SUV park across the street and Bobby Krantz emerge from the vehicle. The door to the store opened, and Silken stepped aside to admit him. Ray thought Silken expected Krantz's visit.

The conversation continued around him. Ray wanted to ask about Krantz's history in the town, but thought better of the idea. He'd wait to get the mayor alone, then, perhaps, the conversation would be confidential.

"So, Detective," John Johnson said, "my son tells me you've got yourself a full plate already, what with all the meth lab issues around here."

"He's right. The chief assigning him to me has been very helpful."

"Jim has aspirations to be a detective."

"We'll see what we can do to help him get up to speed."

"I'd appreciate it."

Elma delivered the meals to everyone at the table, and the conversation lagged as the men ate.

Ray finished first, declined a coffee refill, and took his leave after assuring the men he'd join them for breakfast when he could.

He drove the short way to the department and noticed

IMPERFECT ESCAPE

Krantz's vehicle parked to the right of the building in court employees' parking. There wasn't a session scheduled, and, usually, the lot was empty until the clerk arrived at ten. The police section contained two pickup trucks, which Ray knew belonged to the officers on patrol, two patrol cars, Ray's Taurus, and another small pickup belonging to the dispatcher. Mullins wasn't in yet. Neither was Johnson, who was scheduled to meet Ray at nine.

Ray elected to enter the department through the public entrance facing the street. He used a passkey, eased the door open, and stepped down the hall at a quiet, measured pace.

A light glowed under his office door.

When Ray opened the door, Krantz looked up from an open file in the middle of the desk.

"What in the hell are you doing in my office and in my files?"

"Just checking on you, you interfering son of a bitch. Seeing if you know what—"

"Get out of my chair." Ray loomed over Krantz. He pointed to the visitor chair. "Sit there."

Krantz raised an eyebrow. "And, who's going to make me?"

Ray, who towered over Krantz and outweighed him by fifty pounds, grabbed him by the collar. "I'd be happy to." He lifted him without resistance and planted him in a side chair with some force. "Stay."

The color rose in Krantz's face, but he remained in the chair.

Ray perched on the desk at an angle to block Krantz's exit, then looked at the file the deputy had opened. It was a summary of the visits to Vast's and Flocker's homesteads. He pulled his cell phone out, set it to record, and placed it on the desk, then took a moment to set the scene. "You know this information is available at the sheriff's office from Shim."

Krantz said, "He told me to stop by and talk to you. When you weren't here, I thought I'd have a look."

Ray picked up the desk phone and called Shim. "Got

Krantz here. Caught him going through my files. Did you send him to talk to me?" Ray listened. "Thought so. Hang on a minute."

"Krantz, why were you in Bubba Flocker's room the day before yesterday?"

"I wasn't."

"Short memory. You came in as I was leaving. We spoke."

"I forgot."

'What were you doing there?"

"Just my job. Following up on the explosion at Flocker's place."

"Did Shim know you were there?"

"Uh."

Ray picked up the phone. "You getting this?" He listened. "Good. What do you have on the prints from the IV tubing?" Again, he listened. "Let me know when you have something."

Krantz's face changed from angry red to pale.

"Here's the deal. Shim is going to talk to the sheriff about you going rogue. How does that work for you?"

"I'm not going rogue. I live in this community, too. We all want what's best and getting rid of the meth labs is what's best."

"If you say so." Ray shifted forward. "Tell me, why were you at Silken's place an hour ago? Place doesn't open until nine."

"I wasn't there."

"I saw you. In fact, it looked like Silken expected you. Why?"

"Um, I stopped to check on a special order for my wife."

"That's interesting. What did she order?"

"It's none of your business."

"Now it is. What did she order that couldn't wait an hour?"

"Okay. I stopped in to say hello."

"Odd. But it does explain a few things." Ray stood and stepped back. "This is not finished. Stay out of my way. I've got this conversation recorded." He pointed to his cell phone.

IMPERFECT ESCAPE

***

Ray watched Chief Mullins step through the PD entrance, stop and talk with the dispatcher, Netty Casper, then proceed to Ray's office door. He nodded and took a single step into the office.

"Heard you had breakfast with the men at the cafe this morning."

"News travels fast."

"Small town. Archie Bib called me. He was happy you were social. He said it pleased the men to know you have Southern roots. It was a smart move."

"Thanks. I didn't know Bib was the mayor until I sat down. Seems a friendly sort."

"He's owned the cafe for as long as anyone can remember. It won't be the same when he finds someone to buy it."

Ray nodded. "Got a minute?"

"Let me grab a cup of coffee." The chief disappeared and returned a couple of minutes later with two steaming cups. "Black. Right?"

"Yes, sir."

"What's on your mind?"

Ray took a minute to describe Krantz's sneaky parking, his going through Ray's files, and the meeting with Krantz. "Shim denied sending Krantz to see Flocker, or anyone else in the case for that matter. He thinks Krantz is going rogue and will discuss it with the sheriff today. Further, we suspect Silken may be involved with high-level drug trafficking in and around the county."

"True."

"Someone, apparently, is tipping off the labs every time a bust is scheduled by the sheriff or us."

"Largely true."

"Krantz has an inside track on the sheriff's information and ours as well because so many of the operations involve the sheriff and our department."

"Sometimes, but not every time."

"It seems logical we need to consider that Krantz is the leak. Why would he be stopping at Silken's at eight in the morning? Why did he feel like he needed to lie when I asked?"

"Well, for one thing, Carl Silken is Krantz's uncle by marriage," Mullins said. "Krantz's Aunt Sheila, Silken's wife, has been connected to the community for years through her sister and their extended family."

"The soup thickens."

"It doesn't mean he isn't the leak. It also doesn't mean he didn't tamper with Flocker's IV." He looked thoughtful. "When was Shim planning to speak with the sheriff?"

"He was headed that way an hour ago."

"Good. I'll give the sheriff a call and ask him to reassign Krantz to another area of the county."

"Works for me."

"He'll have another reason to hate you."

Ray said, "I've been hated by dirty cops before. Seems like a compliment."

Mullins laughed. "Where you headed today?"

"As soon as Johnson shows, we're going to take another go at Kelly Ann Vast."

***

Ray and Johnson rolled up in front of Vast's mobile home. Ray couldn't help but think it was a horrible environment for an infant, especially with a single mother. He had suspicions Vast was alive. At some point, they'd find him. Then he'd still be gone from his family while he served time.

Mrs. Vast slammed through the trailer door and stomped onto the porch, a series of movements made all the more impressive by her advanced pregnancy. "What in the hell do you want now?"

"That's not very friendly, Kelly Ann." Johnson walked toward the porch and started up the steps.

She looked past Johnson, making eye contact with Ray. "You want to go through my house again? It's the same as

IMPERFECT ESCAPE

yesterday."

"No, ma'am, we don't. I do want to ask you some questions, however," Ray said.

"You've already done that. I don't have any new answers."

"Have a seat. This will only take a few minutes."

She dropped into a metal rocking chair that looked fifty years old and set it in motion with a gentle tap of her foot.

"Tell me about LeRoy. What was he like before he started using so heavily?"

She smiled, but managed to still look sad and angry. "We dated in high school, you know. Then we reconnected in a treatment center. I really thought LeRoy would make it. Stay clean, you know. He wanted to back then, but—I don't know what happened to him. He uses more and more crank."

"Who is behind the lab? Not LeRoy, above LeRoy."

"Don't know. I don't ask. He don't tell." She looked on the verge of tears. Then she stared at her belly while her hands made circular motions. "I'm going to make sure my baby never uses."

Ray gave her a moment. "Have you seen LeRoy's cousin Richie?"

"No."

"How about LeRoy?"

"LeRoy is dead." Tears rolled down her pock-marked cheeks.

"Is Richie dead?" Johnson said.

"Don't know. I expect so. Probably got burned clean up in that fire. I surely haven't seen that boy."

"Someone was camping out back on your property," Johnson said. "We found the site yesterday and gathered some evidence to identify who it was. I expect that later today they'll tell us either LeRoy or Richie. Which one was it, Kelly Ann?"

"Don't know nothing about it. I want you to leave now. Please, just leave."

Ray stepped off the porch and returned to the Taurus. When Johnson joined him, Ray said, "That was informative."

"How? I didn't hear nothing I haven't heard before from

her."

"She spoke about Vast as if he were alive. I'm beginning to believe the corpse is Richie and LeRoy is alive."

"But the hand."

"Oh, I think the prints and the DNA on the hand will match LeRoy. I'm thinking it was LeRoy's hand, but Richie's body."

As he drove, Ray called the ME, filled him in, and asked him to test the DNA from the hand and the body, too. Ray laughed when the ME said he wished he'd thought of that.

Chapter 16

Ray

Ray strolled into the police department a few minutes after nine on Saturday morning. He wasn't scheduled for duty, but Sophia was at the hospital and he had things on his mind. He planned to work on his murder book, hoping the review of information gathered so far would shake loose another avenue to investigate. His gut told him LeRoy Vast was alive. It made sense. But that didn't tell Ray who started the fire and committed murder.

He saw Ted Ope's folded walker leaning against the wall behind the dispatch desk, but Ope was nowhere in sight. Curious, Ray waited until Ope came out of the bathroom.

Ope walked with deliberation, placing each foot with apparent care. Unsteady, he grabbed various desks and rolling chairs for support along the way.

"Why aren't you using your walker? If you fell in the middle of the night, you'd be in deep shit."

"Now you sound like my wife before she died." Ope laughed. "But you're right. After I broke my hip, it was never the same."

"Sorry. I shouldn't flap at you. My fiancée is an emergency nurse, and I hear about the things that happen to people all the time."

"Hell, everyone else gets on me. You might as well join the

fun."

"I'll stand down, but I do have something to ask. You've been in this town a long time. What do you know about the Vast family?"

Ope took a moment to handle the call that buzzed in his headset, then he directed his gaze at Ray. "The family has lived in town or on the outskirts for as long as I can remember. There's a slew of them. They keep to themselves, mostly."

"Not unusual for big country families," Ray said, remembering a similar large family in Parkview, Virginia.

"No, I don't suppose it is. Anyway, the two older Vast brothers were identical twins, JT and TJ—"

"Original."

"Right. Anyway, they married sisters, who were also identical twins. I think JT married Sharon and TJ hooked up with Karon—she spelled it funny, with an o instead of an e."

"Who are LeRoy's parents?"

"TJ and Karon."

"Are they still in town?"

"No, both couples died in a car wreck out yonder on Bended Branch Road a couple of years back."

"JT and Sharon had Richie. Any other children?"

"No, just the one boy."

"How about TJ and Karon?"

"They had two boys. Calvin is the oldest. He's about forty now, I think." Ope paused. "The thing is the two families blended together as if they were one. Most folks couldn't tell the parents apart. And, the boys were cut from the same genes."

"Interesting. Makes me wonder if the ME will ever be able to identify the body he has in his cooler." Ray shifted his weight, then leaned against a desk. "Where did they live? I know LeRoy has a trailer out on Dripping Springs."

"The trailer that blew up last week was originally the family home of JT and Sharon. The place where LeRoy lives or lived is where he grew up. The house wasn't as bad back then. TJ took care of things. He just couldn't make a decent

IMPERFECT ESCAPE

living."

"Do you know why LeRoy didn't move his wife into that place when they got married? Johnson told me they lived in the trailer with the meth lab at first."

"They did. Don't know anyone was aware of the lab back then. It was right after the folks all died, and Richie didn't want to be alone. So, they all lived together. They moved when the wife got pregnant."

"Good choice on her part, I suspect. Is Calvin involved in the meth trade, too?"

"Calvin is different from the rest of the Vast clan. He's a straight arrow. He did good in school. Played sports. Pretty much ignored his family and their troubles, though he worked on the farm for his dad when TJ made him. Calvin got religion. Doesn't drink, smoke, or do drugs. He married young, headed to Nashville, got a degree in something to do with computers—her father footed part of the bill, I hear. Now he's a big'un in some business there. He's kept in contact with LeRoy from a distance. Won't give him any more money or help."

"Would have been nice to know this stuff a few days ago. Getting LeRoy's wife to talk is like pulling teeth from a chicken."

Ope laughed. "I'd have told you if you'd of asked."

Ray resisted the scowl he felt forming. "Do you know where I can find Calvin Vast?"

"I can get his number from my daughter. She stays in touch with Calvin's wife."

"Thanks. Give a yell when you have it. I'll be in my office."

Ray grabbed a cup of coffee from the single-serve machine in the break room and went to his office, where he made notes about the interview with Ope. The most outstanding feature was Ope referred to Vast in the present tense—as if he were alive—during the whole conversation. It could be habit. Or perhaps, he hadn't assimilated the possible death. But still, the man was a cop for years. Ray puzzled on what he learned, why he hadn't heard it sooner, and jotted more notes.

Ten minutes later, his desk phone rang. Ope provided the contact information and address for Calvin, and five minutes later Ray was on the road headed to Nashville for the second time in a week.

***

Ray found Calvin Vast's home in suburban Nashville. Given Vast's affluent job, Ray had expected something upscale, but it was ranch style, small, and rather simple. A pink tricycle decorated the front yard, and a T-Ball tee sat to the side of the door on the front porch. Toys aside, Vast had maintained the yard and house in magazine-cover perfection.

Vast answered the door chime.

Ray introduced himself, displaying his badge.

"Detective, come on in." He guided Ray into the kitchen.

Ray noted the interior, which was also tidy—save a scattering of toys—sported muted tones and top-quality furnishings. He sat on a stool at the counter and waited until Vast pulled one up on the opposite side. "I've come to talk about your missing brother."

"Okay. But he isn't missing. He's dead and in the morgue waiting to be released so his wife and I can put him to rest."

Ray nodded. "I learned today you come from an atypical family."

"In what way?"

"I understand your parents are part of two sets of identical twins who married each other."

"True."

"Were you more closely linked to your parents' twins than to the rest of your relatives?"

"Not exactly. It's true we spent almost all day, every day as one big family. However, all of the cousins are tight." Vast seemed thoughtful for a moment. "Listen, Detective. Richie, LeRoy, I, and the cousins were raised as brothers. Some of them opted for the quick money route. I chose school. Now, I

IMPERFECT ESCAPE

hear my cousin and my double-first cousin also died in that explosion. Pardon me if I'm blunt, but ask your questions, and let me get back to my grief."

"Do you all look the same?" Ray noted his comment about who died.

"Basically, I suppose. LeRoy and Richie are—were—both around five-ten. I'm an inch taller. Their hair was about the same medium brown as yours, and short like yours. Our dads had that coloring. The other cousins look a bit different, but still like Vasts."

Ray noted Calvin Vast's hair was blond and worn longer. "Your mother was blonde?"

"Right."

"Why are you convinced Richie and a cousin died in the fire?"

"Didn't they? Ted Ope called after the explosion and told me they were all dead. He—Ted—thinks LeRoy died in the fire, too."

"I'd believe, in all likelihood, either LeRoy or Richie is missing and maybe on the run and the other is dead. The issue is we haven't identified the body yet."

"Oh." Vast rubbed a thumb under his eye, removing a tear. "I hope one of them survived."

"Have you heard from either?"

Anger flashed in Vast's eyes. "If I'd talked to one of them, I wouldn't think they were both dead. Now would I?"

Ray thanked the man and headed out, deciding to stop at the ME's office on his way home. He pulled into a strip mall and called ahead, learning Dr. Smith, the ME handling the case, was on duty.

He swung onto R.S. Gas Boulevard, then pulled into the parking lot in front of the brick and glass building. Dr. Smith waited in the lobby.

"What can I do for you today, Detective?"

"Have you had any luck with identifying the remains? Deciding if it's Richie or LeRoy Vast in your cooler?"

"No, it's most unusual. After you called about their

relationship, we sent an investigator to get DNA material from both of their homes—they got a used razor from one and a toothbrush from the other."

"Well," Ray said, "the reason I stopped by today is that I learned this morning that their fathers were identical twins, as were their mothers."

"Isn't that the damnedest thing? I'll talk to the lab and see if I can speed things up. We need to see if they can sort out, once and for all, who owned the hand and who owns the body." Smith shook his head, sending thick gray hair flying. "It could be the only way we'll identify the body is for you to find the cousin who's alive. That might be faster than waiting on the lab. We know for certain there wasn't another charred body in that trailer, which means one of them is out there somewhere—dead or alive."

"My thinking, exactly." He paused a beat. "Do you have anything else for me since we talked last?"

"No. Wish I did. Did LeRoy's wife identify the ring from the picture I sent you?"

"Yes and no. The wedding ring LeRoy wore looked like it, but it had been his father's ring. Richie wore the exact same ring, which he got from his own father, even though he wasn't married. The rings were seldom worn and looked new."

Ray took his leave. On the drive home, he contemplated the interview with Calvin Vast. The man's responses were clearly thought out in advance, except for the slip about who died in the fire. Did Calvin know who was in the morgue? Did he have contact with the other cousin? And, what about the damned hand? Then he moved on to considering how a family interlocked to the point the various members couldn't be identified. And was that what the surviving cousin—if he was surviving—was banking on?

***

Ray stopped in Crestville on the off-chance Shim was working on a Saturday afternoon. Ray remembered Shim commenting

IMPERFECT ESCAPE

he often spent time on the weekend going through his active cases while the office was quiet.

Ray pulled his unmarked into the restricted area next to the Sheriff's Department and hung his parking permit from the mirror. As he exited, he heard voices raised in argument. He recognized Shim's slight lisp, made more pronounced by the heat in his words.

As he listened, the conversation floated in his direction. Rather than slamming the door and announcing his presence, he eased it closed, then stepped to the rear to somewhat hide himself but retain his line of sight.

First Krantz's clear unaccented words. "That son of a bitch Stone reported me to the sheriff. The bastard reassigned me. Didn't even ask for my side of the story."

"As I heard it, Mullins reported you and asked you be reassigned. You should be glad you're not suspended."

"What the hell are you talking about? And why do you know about it anyway?" Krantz reddened, then hauled himself up to his full five-foot-six.

"Well, Bobby," Shim said, his voice calm as ice, "I happened to be in the sheriff's office when Stone called me about you rifling his files."

"The son of a bitch lied. I had my own files and grabbed an empty desk to use, which happened to be his."

"Right. Which happened to be in a locked office. You want the man's job. You're looking for something to discredit him."

"That's a lie. I wouldn't want to work for Mullins if he was the last chief in Tennessee."

"Then maybe you finally decided to climb in bed with your scuzzy uncle. Is that it, Krantz?" Ray said as he stepped between Krantz and Shim.

Krantz chambered and let loose a powerful left hook. Ray had expected it and ducked, then decked the younger, shorter deputy with a well-placed punch.

Shim eased his way behind Krantz.

Ray saw Shim's eyes flicker in his direction.

Krantz scrambled to his feet, elbows bent and clenched

fists held high.

Shim took the opportunity to grab Krantz's arms at the elbows and restrain him. "Deputy Krantz, take a breath and calm yourself."

Krantz struggled to get free.

Shim held tight, preventing further aggression from Krantz.

"Thanks, friend," Shim said, "but I was looking forward to decking the boy and you had the pleasure instead."

"What do you mean boy? You black asshole."

"Hey, Krantz, at least you avoided the *N* word." Shim backed off, out of reach. "I called you boy because you are acting the part. Now, are you ready to calm down?"

Krantz nodded.

"Detective Stone, would you kindly step back and out of reach of my coworker?"

Ray did, watching as Shim released his hold on Krantz. Ray said, "Is the sheriff around today? I think he needs to know about this."

"I'll take care of it." Shim stepped close to Krantz. "Bobby, if you ever take a swing at another officer again, you'll never work here or anywhere else in law enforcement."

Krantz's facial color changed from angry red to a sick, bloodless white, causing Ray to wonder if he was about to faint.

Krantz said, "It won't happen again. Don't report me. I need my job. I have family."

Shim nodded. "We'll give it a thought. Go home. Go now."

Ray and Shim stood silent as Krantz sulked away.

"Do you think he'll keep his word?" Ray asked.

"Hell, no. I think he's in cahoots with his uncle. I'm going to talk to the sheriff and suggest we keep him away from Plateauville's PD entirely. You and Mullins need to pull a raid, keep it within your department, and only call the sheriff for support at the last possible minute. Better yet, I'll update the sheriff, then let me know the when and where, and I'll bring support with me."

IMPERFECT ESCAPE

"Then we'll know if Krantz was the leak, or if there is a source at Plateauville who is passing on the information."

"Or someone who is leaking to Krantz."

"There's a point." Ray paused a moment. "What's happening with the investigation into the attempt on Flocker's life?"

"You already know there wasn't enough drug in the IV to kill him. I still think it was a threat. We found Krantz's prints on the IV. He claims Bubba told him to move the pump and he touched it then. What's odd is that the nurse's prints aren't on the IV bag."

"Someone wiped it clean, probably after adding the drug to the bag."

"My thought, too. Krantz admitted going to the room without authorization, but denies trying to harm Bubba."

"It still could have been a murder attempt—someone who didn't know the effective dosage of the drug, maybe. But, the person would need to know their way around medicine to go into a room and inject something into the IV," Ray said.

"Krantz knows. He was an army medic before he joined the department."

Chapter 17

Sophia

At two o'clock Saturday afternoon, Sophia pulled a rolling stool over to Kelly Ann Vast's stretcher. Sophia had admitted the twenty-four-year-old pregnant woman earlier in the shift and had spent a few minutes cleaning the bruises and abrasions that covered her arms and face. The self-inflicted horizontal slash on the patient's left wrist bled minimally, but would require sutures and a dressing.

"Mrs. Vast," Sophia said. "I—"

"Please call me Kelly Ann."

Sophia nodded. "Kelly Ann, I have some questions. Let's start with the pregnancy. How far along are you?"

"Don't know for sure. I figure almost nine months. I haven't had my time for that many months anyway."

"Have you had prenatal care?"

"No, ma'am."

"We'll get an OB doc in here to have a look at you."

"That's good."

"While we wait for her to arrive, one of the nurse clinical specialists from OB will come down and assess your pregnancy. Is that okay with you?"

"Yes."

"Did you feel your baby move today?" Sophia asked as she applied the fetal heart monitor, then heard the reassuring tones

IMPERFECT ESCAPE

of the baby's heartbeat.

Kelly Ann smiled. "Yes, my baby moves all the time, it seems." She paused. "Is that my baby's heart? I never heard it before."

"Yes. We'll keep the monitor on while you're here." Sophia made a note in the chart, then said, "You cut your wrist."

"I . . . I . . . don't know what to do. I'm so alone. I have no money. How am I going to take care of my baby?"

"We can have social service hook you up with some help." Sophia waited a moment. "Was it your plan to solve your problem by taking your own life?"

"Uh-huh, but I got scared. I don't want to die, not really. I just want a normal life. Then I got to thinkin' that if I died, the baby would die slow inside me. And I felt bad for the baby. I mean, the poor thing never did anything to deserve dyin' before it could be born. I couldn't stand that. So, I called 9-1-1."

Based on the shallow nature of the wound and Kelly Ann's comments, Sophia didn't believe the suicide attempt was serious. She asked more questions and learned that it was the patient's first attempt.

"You look like you've been beaten. Did your husband do that to you?"

Kelly Ann's body shook as tears rolled down her battered face. "I could have killed my baby. Oh my God. What a horrible person I've turned into."

Sophia moved to sit on the side of the stretcher and put a comforting hand on her patient's shoulder.

Between sobs, Kelly Ann said, "LeRoy wouldn't hurt me. He loves me. But he's hidin', you see."

"No, I don't. Please tell me."

"Oh, I shouldn't. I have to talk to someone."

Sophia waited. She knew Ray was looking for a man named Vast, or maybe a couple of men named Vast. She wondered if Kelly Ann's LeRoy was one of them.

"He's hurt. Hurt bad, but he can't go to the hospital because people are lookin' for him."

"The police?"

"Them, too, but no. People who want to kill him."

"Kelly Ann, you're not making sense. Start at the beginning, please."

Kelly Ann sniffed, then blew her nose. "LeRoy ran a meth lab for the man. Then it blew up. He got hurt bad, but he ran away. He knew they were tryin' to kill him."

"Who is they?"

"I can't tell you. He might hurt you, too." She rubbed her face and winced. "See how he hurt me. He wanted me to tell where LeRoy is. I said I didn't know. I thought he was dead. Then Krantz said 'No, Richie is the one who's dead.' I don't know how he knows. The cops came to my house and said they didn't know whose body it was."

Sophia sorted through the garble, confirmed for herself it was Ray's case, and that LeRoy was one of the men Ray was looking for. "Krantz? The deputy?"

"He's who beat me up."

"Kelly Ann, I'd like to call the police so they can come in and talk to you. You'll need some protection when you get out of the hospital."

"No. I'm afraid."

Sophia thought about how to approach the problem, then decided head-on was the best way. "I can't talk to him if you won't allow it, but my fiancé is Ray Stone. I think you met him already. I can call Ray and tell him what you told me. He's a good man, and I promise you he isn't working for the meth business here."

"I know there is someone in town at the police station who is, though. I know because LeRoy always got a call if there was going to be a raid. Then they'd strip the lab and hide everything."

"That isn't Ray. He's the new detective at the department in Plateauville. We moved here a couple months ago."

Kelly Ann grimaced, then rubbed her belly.

"What did you feel?"

"A squeezin' sensation. Do you think the baby is coming?"

IMPERFECT ESCAPE

"Could be. I'm going to call upstairs and hurry up the OB nurse, then I'll get the ED doc to fix your wrist."

Sophia made a note of the time of the contraction, then stepped out of the room to place her calls. As she did, the OB clinical specialist walked down the hall and entered the room. A few minutes later, the specialist stepped out and reported the patient was in early labor.

When Sophia returned to the room, Kelly Ann said, "Call Detective Stone. You have my permission."

"Is there someone, family perhaps, I can call to be with you while you have your baby?"

"Maybe my mom will come. She hates that I married LeRoy and the life I lead. Doesn't even know I'm having a baby." The tears returned. "You can call her."

As Kelly Ann recited her mother's name and number, Sophia keyed it in. "Mrs. Hogarth. Your daughter Kelly Ann is okay." Sophia always started a conversation with family by saying the patient was okay—if they were. She found it prevented needless worry. "She's in the emergency department at Crestville Medical Center."

"What's wrong? Is she hurt?"

"There are a number of things going on. She asked that I call you because she is in early labor. She's all alone here."

"Can I talk to my daughter?"

Sophia handed the phone to Kelly Ann.

"Mommy, I need you. I'm so sorry. Please come."

Sophia listened for few minutes, assured herself the mother would come, then stepped out of the room. She had time to get the suturing completed.

Chapter 18

Sophia

Sophia's efforts to contact Ray after transferring Kelly Ann Vast to Labor and Delivery were in vain. She attempted twice, then got busy, deciding it would wait. Ray, after all, could not interview Kelly Ann in her current situation.

Sophia clocked out following her shift and rode the elevator to Labor and Delivery to check on her patient, who had progressed to active labor. The future grandmother, Ella Hogarth, a short, round, tidy-looking lady with greying brown hair, hovered at the patient's bedside and doted on Kelly Ann's every wish.

"Thank you for helping me today," Kelly Ann said. "They did an ultrasound. The doctor said my baby is small. She thinks my daughter is six weeks early and will need to spend time in neonatal ICU."

"Where will she live while the baby is in the hospital?" Sophia looked at Mrs. Hogarth.

"I'll stay in the area with Kelly Ann. My best friend lives just west of here and has room for both of us. When the doctor discharges the baby, we'll all go home. We live outside Lebanon."

"And the daddy?"

"LeRoy is either going to die or is going to jail. I don't much care which." Anger flashed across the older woman's

IMPERFECT ESCAPE

lined face.

"Mama, don't say that. He's my husband."

"For all the good it did you." Mrs. Hogarth's look softened, and she patted her daughter's hand. "Listen baby, you need your step-daddy and me now, and we're here for you."

Kelly Ann's tears ran, streaming over her battered cheeks. "Did you tell the detective about my LeRoy?"

"Not yet. I couldn't get in touch with him. I'll talk to him tonight. You won't be up to an interview for a while anyway." Sophia directed her attention to the mother. "Can I have your friend's contact information? Just in case."

Sophia noted the information, said goodbye, and headed home. She pulled in behind the Ram in the shared parking space just as Ray returned from a walk with Mischief. "Hey, there," she called as she slid out of the MINI.

She scooped Mischief up in her arms and submitted to the requisite face wash. After wiping her sleeve across her face to dry it, she put the dog down and slid into Ray's embrace. "Good to be home. Got lots to tell you."

Ray raised a brow. "Oh?"

"Yup. Had Kelly Ann Vast as my patient for most of the day."

Both Ray and Sophia followed Mischief into the house, conversation on hold until the dog's dish brimmed with kibble. Then, as they started dinner, Ray making a salad and Sophia reheating left-over chicken parmigiana and pasta, she recited the events of the day. "I didn't realize who she was at first. I think she agreed that I could tell you because she is out of options. I mean, it seems like Krantz went out of his way to rough her up. She told me she didn't give up LeRoy."

"That's interesting on several levels. First, it implies that Krantz knows LeRoy's alive. Second, it speaks to his complicity in the whole mess." He took a moment to update her on Krantz's relationship with Silken and on the parking lot squabble. "Third, Krantz has been lying to me, Shim, and everyone else." He went on to tell her about the raid that was in the planning stages. "Mullins, Johnson, and I met today to plan it while no one was around except dispatch. We're hoping it'll bring out the moles. My thinking is that Krantz is dirty, but someone else is, too. I checked the records on previous raids, and I don't think Krantz was close enough to the action to have a lot of detail on all of them."

"It's a mess."

"When do you think I'll be able to interview Kelly Ann?"

"She was in active labor when I left the hospital. She knows you'll be around, but you probably should wait until Monday. I mean really." Sophia dug in her pocket. "Here is her mom's friend's address and phone number and the mom's info as well. The mother thought they'd be safe at the friend's place. LeRoy never met the woman, so it's anonymous."

Ray folded the paper and slipped it into his notebook. "I'll keep this out of my murder book and out of the electronic reports."

"Thanks for that." She carried the plates to the table, poured wine, and sat.

"Give me a minute. I need to update Shim." Ray took out his cell phone and placed the call before joining her at the table.

During dinner, their conversation centered on domestic concerns. They cleaned up, walked hand-in-hand around the lake with Mischief leading the way, and watched the geese.

Ray embraced her. "Do you suppose we can share a shower and not hurt ourselves in the process?"

"We can try." She grinned and cozied further into Ray's arms. "That's a small tub."

"All the better to get close to you, my dear." Ray wiggled an eyebrow.

***

Sunday morning brought the day of their scheduled visit to Ray's family in Knoxville. The cool morning drive down the mountain offered light traffic and beautiful scenery.

"Probably because I was alone in the car, but this seemed a much longer drive when I stayed with your folks and drove it

IMPERFECT ESCAPE

every day," Sophia said.

"I'll bet. It's a good thing that phase only lasted two weeks." They'd had to wait for the little house to be empty and cleaned. Sophia stayed in Knoxville while Ray attended the crime investigation program in Nashville.

"Agreed."

Ray's parents, John and Martha Stone, moved to Knoxville from Parkview, Virginia because of the scandal surrounding Ray's ex-wife's death. The elderly couple wanted the kids to visit and not have to deal with rumors and innuendos. Then Branden, a college freshman, decided to attend the University of Tennessee and moved in with them. Kerri attended nursing school in Virginia and visited her grandparents often. With everyone so close, Sophia hoped to strengthen her relationship with Ray's family.

"Industry." Sophia pointed to a grouping of smoke stacks. "I enjoyed my time with your parents and Branden. He's a good kid. I think he's moving past all the trauma and getting on with his life."

"He is. He's still talking about going into the military as preparation for following in my footsteps. God forbid."

"Not bad footsteps overall."

Ray didn't respond, and Sophia guessed his thoughts had drifted back to the job. "What's on your mind?"

"Thinkin' about all the things that don't add up in this investigation."

"For example."

"Krantz was a medic in the army."

"I didn't know that," Sophia said.

"If he was going to murder Flocker, you'd think he'd get the dose right. Unless the purpose was to scare him."

"Hey, it scared me. What a shock. I was talking to the guy, then he was gone."

"Good response on your part." He paused. "Why would he wipe the bottle, pump, and tubing clean of all prints but his own? Doesn't make sense. That, alone, gives some credence to his claim that Flocker asked him to move the IV contraption."

"It does. Maybe someone was in earlier—or maybe someone tampered with the IV in the medication room or in the pharmacy."

"Why was everything wiped clean?"

"When a pump is in use, it's the nurse's responsibility to keep it clean. That doesn't happen very often, but once in a while, a nurse is very conscientious about it. Someone could have doped the main IV—the big bag—while it was hanging. When I was there, the small one was running at first, then the pump switched to the main. I remember noticing it looked full, so it's possible the nurse hung both at the same time, then set the pump to run the little one first. The chart will have the information."

"That all sounds logical. I suppose Shim can track the handling of the IV from its origin. Tell me how the system works."

"The medications Flocker received were mixed in the pharmacy. Therefore, a tech would break the seals on the bags there. A tech or a courier brings the IVs to the nursing units in batches. There it lays on the counter until it is given—usually. Any number of people could have touched that IV."

"For example."

"The medication room also contains the supply shelves. The room is frequented by nurses, pharmacists, techs, nursing assistants, housekeeping, and central supply staff."

"Isn't it locked?"

"Sure. But the code is standard for the entire hospital—ED aside. The point is to keep out non-hospital folks, not hospital workers."

"Someone who works there and is also aligned with whoever wanted Flocker out of the picture could have fixed the IV."

"That's a cast of hundreds."

"No doubt."

They exited the highway and drove into a residential neighborhood on the west side of Knoxville. The elder Stones had a tidy three-bedroom ranch that reminded Sophia of the

IMPERFECT ESCAPE

house where Ray grew up in Parkview. Ray pulled into the driveway behind Branden's aging Ford.

Sophia said, "It's sad they had to leave their home after all those years."

"True, but I think it's okay with them. When Kathleen moved to Knoxville, they started talking about it. The gossip in Parkview was the push."

"I remember your mom saying she wanted to live close to your sister again."

Sophia and Ray went inside the house and were engulfed in family and activity. The tantalizing scent of fried chicken drifted out of the kitchen. Ray's mother, Martha, and father, John, administered hugs, as did Branden, which surprised Sophia.

"I've missed you. I can't say I miss the daily drive, but the coming back in the evening was good." Sophia returned the hugs with enthusiasm. "This feels like home."

Sophia's cell phone rang. "It's the hospital." She stepped outside.

Ray followed.

"Hello," she said.

"This is Katina."

"Hey, girl. What's going on?"

"You said you wanted to know about your patient from yesterday."

"I did." Sophia tapped the speaker button on her phone so Ray could hear the conversation. "I put you on speaker so my fiancé can hear. I have the patient's permission to talk with him about her case."

"That's fine."

"Now, tell me."

"First, she had a four-pound girl, who is in NICU and holding her own."

"Kelly Ann?"

"She did wonderful with the birth—natural, no drugs. But now she's missing."

"Good God. What is being done about it?"

"Because of the fact she was beaten up before her admission, the hospital and her physicians are *officially* concerned. I get the idea they think she's just another druggie who dropped a baby here and took off."

"But, did they call anyone? Are they doing anything about it?"

"Yes, and no. A deputy came out. My friend in Mother-Baby said he seemed unconcerned and held the druggie opinion himself. Said he'd file a report."

"Do you know who the deputy was?"

"He came through the ED on his way upstairs. He's been in here a time or two before. Krantz is his name."

Chapter 19

Ray

Ray started his Monday morning across the desk from Chief Mullins. He reviewed Sunday's events as related to Kelly Ann Vast and Deputy Krantz.

"The thing is, Stone, we can't prove Krantz is dirty, though I understand and agree with your suspicions. The word of a known meth user won't hold up against a sworn officer. Likewise, her beating could have been administered by her husband, if, in fact, he's alive."

"Based on what Sophia said, it would be a lot of damage to administer with one hand. My thinking is Vast, one of them—Richie or LeRoy, probably LeRoy—lost a hand in the explosion. I believe he's alive, and based on the evidence at the hidey-hole, is not in good condition."

"Makes sense. I don't know why Krantz was sent to the hospital. The sheriff knows about our issues with him."

Ray nodded. "Shim said Krantz wasn't authorized for that visit."

"Well, damn." Mullins paused, looking thoughtful. "The other thing, Stone, you need to be careful when talking about Krantz. You're the new guy on the force, and it's common knowledge Krantz is out to discredit you. It's not a big jump in logic for people to assume you're administering a payback."

"That's a consideration." Ray scratched his goatee,

Gregg E. Brickman

thinking Mullins was right. "I'm headed to Crestville Medical Center to talk to Bubba Flocker this morning."

"Take Jim Johnson. When you're dealing with this case, it's good to have another cop with you."

"Okay." Ray felt it was early in his career at Plateauville to hear such distrust from his chief, but he did see the point. "I'm thinking I'll stop and talk to Shim and see what else I can find out, unofficially, about Krantz's appearance at the hospital on Sunday after Kelly Ann Vast went AWOL. He seems to show up unannounced at all the right—or wrong—times."

"You're sure Shim is clean."

"Very. I did some checking. His reputation in Florida was stellar. And, he was only peripherally connected with the meth problem. He worked straight homicide, never worked Narc."

"Okay, tread carefully."

The men went on to discuss their planned raid, keeping their voices low to avoid being heard by passersby. Then Ray met up with Johnson in the parking lot and headed to Crestville.

Ray updated Johnson as he drove, then grew silent. On one hand, Ray trusted his young associate. On the other hand, Johnson was a long-time resident of Plateauville and had known many of the meth lab operators his whole life. There was no evidence he was connected to Silken in any way, but Johnson could have kept the fact hidden.

A quick conversation with Shim yielded the information that there had never been a call placed to the department about Kelly Ann leaving the hospital. If Krantz went to the hospital, it was on his own initiative. Then there was the question of how Krantz would have known.

Ray decided to visit the OB unit while in the hospital. A reedy-thin woman approaching seventy met with them in the otherwise empty family waiting room.

"I'm Mrs. Marshall. I'm the OB department director."

Ray made introductions, then said, "Tell me about Kelly Ann Vast's leaving the hospital yesterday."

The woman shook her head, causing grey curls to float

IMPERFECT ESCAPE

around her head. "I talked to her nurse this morning. The patient asked to be taken to NICU to see her baby. It was a bit early for that, but she'd done well with the delivery and was stable in all respects. Since the unit was quiet, the staff accommodated her, taking her in to hold the infant. She asked the staff to put the baby's name—Keri Lynn—on her tag, then asked to be taken back to her room. It was not an unusual series of events at all.

"Later, the patient's parents arrived, and the three of them went back to NICU. The nurse got involved with another patient. When she went back to check Mrs. Vast, the room was empty and all her belongings were gone."

"How long did it take for the deputy to arrive after the sheriff was called?" Ray said. He knew, of course, the sheriff had not been called. He asked to get Mrs. Marshall's reaction.

"Oh, we didn't call the sheriff. Mrs. Vast has no insurance, was very stable, and wanted to be discharged later in the day. Technically, she left against medical advice—AMA—but she'd have been gone anyway in a matter of hours."

"Is that unusual?"

"Not with our poorer patients. They want to do everything they can to keep the bills low. Her baby will stay with us until she's big enough to go home in any event."

"What if the mother doesn't return?"

"I expect she will. Most do. But if she doesn't, we'll turn the baby over to relatives or to the foster system, where she might be better off anyway."

Mrs. Marshall excused herself, leaving the two men in the family room.

Ray checked the display on his cell phone, having felt it vibrate earlier. He saw a text from Sophia.

Kelly Ann's mother was here. Told me they took her. Kelly Ann doesn't want you to go there, but you can call her. Use this number. 931-844-7002.

When Ray tapped the number into the phone, a tired-sounding female voice answered.

"Is this Kelly Ann Vast?"

"Who wants to know?"

"Ray Stone. We met at your home."

"This is Kelly Ann."

"The number is different than Sophia gave me yesterday."

"My parents got me a disposable phone. I don't want Krantz to be able to find me."

"Tell me what's going on?"

"I'm so afraid. I'm afraid I'll never be able to take my baby home with me. Krantz came to my house on Saturday morning. He wanted to know where LeRoy is. Said he knew LeRoy is alive."

"What did you tell him?"

"That I didn't know."

"Is LeRoy alive?"

"Yes. He's hiding out. But I'm scared about that, too. His arm, where his hand was cut off, looks all infected. I tried to get him to go to the hospital. I told him the police would protect him. But he's afraid. Said it's the cops he's worried about."

"Did Krantz hurt you?"

"He beat me up a bit around my face and arms. When I fell on the floor, I pretended I was unconscious. He went away. Then after I cut myself, I called 9-1-1. Krantz came with the ambulance and acted all nice."

"Have you seen Krantz since you got to the hospital?"

"He came into my hospital room early Sunday morning. He started to threaten me again. Said he'd make sure I never saw my baby, but a nurse came in, and he got all polite again. Then he left."

"What happened after that?"

"I called Mama. When she and her husband came, we said goodbye to Keri Lynn and left."

"Do you think you're safe where you are?"

"I do. Even LeRoy doesn't know about Mama's friend. Mama will take a different route every time she goes to check on Keri Lynn, wander all around, like you see on TV."

IMPERFECT ESCAPE

***

A bored-looking sheriff's deputy guarded the door of Flocker's private room on the fifth floor of the hospital. The young, dark-haired woman raised her eyes from the book she was reading. "May I help you?"

"Deputy Poore," he said, reading her badge, "I'm Detective Stone from Plateauville PD, and this is Officer Johnson." He motioned to Johnson. "We'd like to spend some time with Mr. Flocker." Ray saw her eyes drop to the shield clipped to his belt.

"Certainly. You're just in time. The physician is discharging Bubba from the hospital, then we'll haul him downtown to the jail."

"Do you happen to know if any arrangements have been made to keep him alive there? His life has been threatened twice that I'm aware of."

"Knowing Bubba—and I do—twice is a conservative estimate." Poore looked thoughtful. "Shim told me Bubba would be in general population. Said he's big enough to take care of himself."

"That's probably a stretch, even for someone who isn't on a hit list." Ray laughed, signed the log she held out for him, and went into the room.

Johnson signed and followed, then took a position against the wall on the far side of the room. He pulled out a notebook and pen.

Flocker looked like a small mountain sitting in the arm chair next to the bed, bigger than he'd looked when Ray saw him in the bed a few days earlier.

Ray reintroduced himself. "Mr. Flocker, I'm here to talk to you about the events at Vast's meth lab."

"I know who you are. I told you to call me Bubba."

Ray nodded.

"So, De-tect-ive, why would I want to talk to you, anyway?"

"I'll put in a good word with the sheriff. Maybe they'll go

easy on you, or at the very least, protect you from whomever it is who wants you dead."

"How do you figure someone wants me dead?" Flocker wore a confused expression.

"Well, this is the story. The lab on your property, the one that blew up, was torched. The arson report is conclusive. There is no doubt."

"Silky, the bastard." Flocker spit out the words,

"You think Silken is behind it."

"Who else? He's behind most of what goes down around here."

"Can you prove that?"

"If I did, I'd really be a dead man."

"Perhaps, but a second attempt was made on your life here as well. Someone added a drug to your IV. It's what caused you to quit breathing. One of the ED nurses saved your fat neck."

Flocker seemed to caress his impressive double chin. "I know Sophia saved me. The nurses in ICU said that. Otherwise I wouldn't of know'd it."

"Lot you don't know, it seems." Ray paused. "Listen, Bubba, it's about time you come clean about everything. If you don't, I can't see how the sheriff can protect you long term. Once everything is out in the open, there is no reason to kill you to keep you quiet."

Flocker reached for his water and took a long drink. Then, he sat quietly, a thoughtful expression on his face. Ray decided, perhaps, Flocker wasn't as dumb as he acted.

"Have you met my mama?"

"I have. She told me you take care of her, the farm, and work in Silken's Dry Goods, too."

"Mama is a good woman. She hasn't been the same since my daddy died. She's got the cancer, too, now."

Ray nodded.

"Do you have any idea how much time I'm looking at? If I'm convicted, that is?"

"Oh, I think you will be, if you live that long. If you're cooperative, maybe it'll be less time."

IMPERFECT ESCAPE

"Maybe I'm better off in jail."

Ray raised a brow. "I'm thinking Silken's reach is long. Why is he pissed at you anyway?"

"The hell with it." Flocker sat up straighter. "I'm just a good old boy. Never was in much trouble until this all happened."

Ray pulled a chair over, sat, and waited.

"It wasn't long after I went to work for Silky that I figured out he was bringing in the fixin's for cooking meth. I didn't say anything at first, just did my job, and went on my way. But, he had more shipments come in and wanted me to work some extra. I did. I needed the money."

"Go on."

"I paid attention when I was there. I know I look big and dumb. People misjudge me. Think I'm stupid." He waited a moment. "Guess I am, huh?"

"Remains to be seen, I think."

"LeRoy came and went a bunch, took boxes of stuff with him. Sometimes LeRoy came in and made a delivery. I saw Silken pay him in cash."

"Bubba, why should I believe you? You ran a meth lab on your property. Maybe you're just trying to eliminate the competition."

Flocker laughed. "Silky isn't the competition. He owned the lab on my property."

"Explain that."

"This is how it is. Silken found out about the camper on my property, probably from LeRoy. He asked about it, then asked to buy it. Secret like. Off the books. He paid me twenty grand, and I still own the land it sits on."

"Did you know what he wanted it for?"

"Of course." Flocker exhaled. "Mama needed an operation on her feet, and we didn't have the money. I thought, why not?"

"How did you end up working there?"

"At first, I ignored it. Then Silky said he'd pay me to supervise the operation. Big money. At least for me."

"You agreed?" Ray said.

"Yeah, but not right off. Then he turned up the pressure. Said there was no record of him owning the cabin, and he'd see to it that it got raided by the sheriff, who would hold me responsible."

"He had you there. Then what happened?"

"I started working the lab more and more and the store in town less and less. Mama thought I went to the store every day, but I just drove out the driveway and took the back way to the cabin."

"She didn't figure that out?"

"No, her hearin' ain't what it used to was. Used to be," Flocker said, correcting himself. "And, she doesn't walk around in the woods nomore."

"Go on."

"Then Silky told me he wanted me to blow up Vast's lab with all the workers in it, especially Vast. I refused. I'm not a killer. A meth cooker, yes, but not a killer. Silky got pissed. Said he owned me. I told him he didn't, and I wanted him off my property."

"If you didn't blow up Vast's operation, who did?"

"Like I've said all along, I don't know. I saw the blast from my place, and rode down there on my bike, circled in the back way. I didn't recognize the man who blew the lab, but I did see a vehicle speeding away."

"What did the guy look like? What can you tell me?"

"I only know he was big as me, maybe bigger."

"What kind of vehicle?"

Flocker laughed. "It was a little Chevy rent-a-car. I recognized the shape of the bumper sticker. Didn't see the plate good enough to read it. It was light colored. Maybe white, even."

"What else did you see?"

"Someone else running away from the scene. Looked like Vast or his cousin Richie. Don't know which one. Can't tell them apart if the light's not good."

"Do you know who blew up your operation?"

IMPERFECT ESCAPE

"Yeah, I do."

"Who?"

"Well now. Without LeRoy's output, Silky was nervous about meeting his production goals—his words. He wanted me to run my lab twenty-four-seven." Flocker laughed. "That pissed me off, and I blew the sucker up. The only problem is I didn't run fast enough and breathed in a bunch of the poison—dumb, fat bastard that I am."

Chapter 20

Sophia

When Sophia stepped out into the concourse at Fort Lauderdale-Hollywood International Airport, a frenetic level of activity slapped her. Though she's left the area less than three months earlier, she'd grown accustomed to the more relaxed, more congenial atmosphere in Middle Tennessee—exploding meth labs aside.

She wove her way around and through the crowd. A variety of languages mixed in a babble—Spanish, Haitian Creole, Bostonian, New Yorker, Canadian English, and a smattering of what she thought was Portuguese, perhaps Brazilian, surrounded her. If she stayed in the airport, she knew she'd encounter a bigger variety. Instead, she hurried to the rental car bus.

Her friend Connie Kuhn had offered to pick Sophia up and loan her a car. But, she preferred to be able to come and go as she pleased, knowing Connie had to maintain her work schedule, and if it was her car, control.

Sophia called Connie at Coral Bay Medical Center, where Sophia had worked until recently. After Connie supplied the address for the shower, Sophia embarked on her own agenda.

Deg Lewis, Ray's former partner, answered on the first ring. "Hey, sweet thing. I've been expecting your call. Ray told me you were coming to town and would probably give me a

IMPERFECT ESCAPE

shout."

"I'm glad you haven't deleted me from your address book. Want to meet me for lunch? I just got off the plane, and I'm starved."

"Where?"

"The deli in Lakeview Plaza." The lunch date served several purposes. First, she was starving, and the location was convenient. Second, she missed having an easily available Jewish-style deli. Third, she wanted to pick Deg's brain.

When she entered the deli, she saw Deg had already commandeered a table near the back of the room. A typical detective, he sat with his back to the wall, facing the door. Ray would have grabbed the booth in the back corner, but Deg hated booths. Deg was six-six, broad-shouldered, muscle-packed, bald, black-skinned, and gentle as a new born lamb. Unless pissed off, that is.

"Hi, sweet thing," Deg said when Sophia approached the table. "How are you?"

"Good. Lovin' Tennessee."

"To each, her own. How's the man?"

"Up to his eyeballs in meth lab explosions, but liking the area—I think. Have you talked to him?"

"A couple of days ago."

"When you do again, please leave most of this conversation out of it."

"We will see."

"Fair enough."

"You're messing in where you don't belong again."

"Maybe a little. Things are different there. I'm working in the ED in the main hospital that serves the county, of which Plateauville is a part. As such, I'm encountering Ray's victims and suspects, sometimes before he does. We've reached a truce of sorts. I can contribute, as long as I carry when he tells me to and stay safe in the process."

Deg raised a questioning brow.

"I think the difference is, there is no way for me to stay deaf, dumb, and blind. And, his resources are slim. He has a young patrol officer assigned to work with him on occasion, and a loose alliance with a sheriff's investigator."

"He called me about Shim. I worked with Shim some years back. He's a good man. Honest. Solid skills. I told Ray as much."

A waitress dressed in black slacks and a white blouse approached the table.

"Good to know." Sophia waved away the menu offered by the waitress. "I'll have the Reuben. Iced tea."

"Same for me." After the waitress left the table, Deg said, "So, what is it you want to poke your nose into?"

"I have the notion—maybe Ray does, too—that there's a direct South Florida connection to the meth problem in Tennessee. One of my coworkers knows a guy at Jackson Memorial who knows a guy named Krantz who's involved with drug sales. Silken, the local drug lord in Plateauville—masquerading as an upstanding businessman—has a South Florida history. I just want to head down to Miami and ask a few questions. Maybe help out while I'm here."

Deg glanced to his left, then leaned away from the table to allow the waitress to set down the sandwiches and drinks. He reached for a packet of sweetener and added it to his tea.

"A new skill I learned in Tennessee is to ask for unsweet tea wherever tea is sold." Sophia laughed. "The first week I was there, I discovered that the default value is sweet—with a capital S. You could almost stand a straw in the stuff."

"My wife likes it that way. She actually boils up the water and adds both sugar and honey to it while it's still hot and brewing. Says it's better that way, never grainy."

"Of course, your wife weighs one hundred pounds in her skivvies. She can use the calories."

Deg laughed. "True enough. If I let you go to Miami and poke at the drug culture, Ray will swoop down and take it out on me, especially if you get hurt."

"I'm not planning on wearing a sign that says I'm investigating the meth trade."

"I know that, sweet thing, but you have a way of pulling

IMPERFECT ESCAPE

the trouble your way." Deg ate a few bites of his sandwich.

"This is really good. Can't get a good Reuben in Plateauville." She finished off the first half, stared at the second portion, then picked it up. "I have to eat this all. Who knows when I'll get another."

After a few minutes of quiet eating, Deg pushed his empty plate next to Sophia's. "How about I pick you up on Thursday morning and go to Miami with you? I have a narc friend who works the precinct closest to Jackson and deals, mostly, with meth. He can tell you the names of the players. Then if there's a connection, you can have Ray contact him for the details."

"That'll work. Ray will be pleased that at least I poked into his case safely."

"I'll bet." Deg sipped his tea and rolled his huge, dark-brown eyes.

Chapter 21

Ray

On Tuesday morning, Ray finished updating Chief Mullins on his Monday meeting with Charles "Bubba" Flocker.

"You believe he blew his own place?" Mullins raised a questioning brow.

"I do." Ray leaned forward a bit in the chair. "First, it's too damn stupid to not be true. Second, Flocker appears to be a reasonably honorable man."

Mullins raised the brow higher this time.

"He takes care of his sick mother, farms, and works part-time for Silken. I think his meth lab involvement was a convenient opportunity to earn money, then Silken sucked him in. His response was to blow up his structure and settle the matter."

"I'm surprised he didn't start a forest fire in the process."

"Could have, I suppose. He called 9-1-1, then started pumping water on the mess. Luckily, he has a generator-powered well and pump close by."

"He probably put that in so the lab had running water."

"That's what he said."

Mullins looked thoughtful. "The county will go after him anyway."

"Maybe not. Shim has it worked out. If Bubba testifies against Silken—and Vast when we get our hands on him—

IMPERFECT ESCAPE

they'll cut him a deal. He'll get minimal time, plus probation."

"Then what? Silken, if I guess right, has the capability of ordering a retaliatory hit—make an example of him."

"My sense is Flocker has no real threat from Vast, who is just a worker in the supply chain—but Silken's a bigger player." Ray paused a moment. "There is a long-standing connection between Silken and the drug traffic in South Florida. He left there some years ago, but has, I think, maintained his connections. He may even be a supplier for them, as well as for product along the meth belt."

"Go on."

"I've contacted my former partner in South Florida, Deg Lewis, and asked him to check things out for me on the quiet. If what I believe is true, then not only the raw supplies but the finished product are moving across county lines and state lines in a big way. The county will then bring in TBI and the DEA."

"The Tennessee Bureau of Investigation and the Drug Enforcement Administration will complicate things."

Ray nodded. "Yup, but for Flocker, it'll make things easier. Likely, Silken would be incarcerated out-of-state, and the Federal Witness Protection Program would then be a possibility for Flocker."

"When do you expect to hear from Lewis?"

"He's going to Miami to ask informal questions tomorrow. If it pans out, Shim can follow with TBI, then the feds. They'll pull all the pieces together."

"Meanwhile, to maintain focus, our piece of the puzzle is the incident in Vast's lab and the resulting deaths. We have an open murder case—more than just a drug case—even though it's all mixed together."

"I know that." Ray felt offended, but understood Mullins need to supervise his activities until he was a known entity. He swallowed the comment he wanted to make. "Flocker saw a huge, unknown person driving away from the explosion at Vast's in what looked like a sub-compact rental, at least based on the Budget logo on the license plate frame. That suggests imported talent. I figure after Flocker refused to blow the place, Silken moved on, but he still needed a certain level of output, so he started muscling Flocker to up production."

"Lots of suppositions on your part."

"Agreed."

"Keep poking at it." Mullins took a sip from the cup on his desk. "Nasty. Cold coffee."

"I'll fix that." Ray picked up Mullins's cup and his own, went to the break room, and refilled both with fresh, hot brew. He returned, pulled the office door closed behind him, offered the cup to Mullins, and sat. "What else is on your mind?"

Mullins stared at the closed door, then nodded. "Deputy Krantz."

"Thought he was out of the picture, at least in this town."

"He's still badmouthing you to anyone who will listen. After the scuffle you two had in the parking lot—bad move on your part, by the way—the sheriff got involved. Krantz has been ordered to stay outside our area in any official capacity and to stay away from the Silken-Vast-Flocker meth lab fiasco. Krantz blames you for his troubles. The concern is he lives in our jurisdiction, so there will always be some interaction. It also makes it likely he'll be yammering in town to anyone who'll listen."

"I'll do my best to stay clear."

"The sheriff called to express his concerns. Now, you need to know that he also discussed you with Shim, who gave you a vote of full confidence. At the moment, Shim's endorsement trumps Krantz's opinion around the Sheriff's Department, but Krantz won't shut up. Believe me."

"Let him talk. In my experience, eventually those types self-destruct anyway." Ray sipped from his mug. "This isn't bad for department coffee."

"Not when it's hot." Mullins set his cup on the desk. "We still have to unravel how our plans for raids got out into the community. In most cases, Krantz—who we now know has a direct connection to Silken—wasn't involved."

"He could be tapping into the plans at any point along the information path. From someone here. During meetings in

IMPERFECT ESCAPE

Crestville. When he's assigned to the raid."

"That's the catch," Mullins said. "He hasn't been assigned to any of the raids. The sheriff checked the last half-dozen joint ventures, and Krantz was not in the loop. The other thing he said was they play things very close, involve the narcs, and only the narcs."

"Which doesn't explain how Krantz always manages to be in the vicinity and involved. I went back to the reports here, and there's always some mention of Deputy Krantz. Usually, he happens on scene after the raid came up empty, sometimes he shows up early to join in. Further, he was involved after the blasts and insinuated himself into the investigations."

"Which means?"

"I think he has an accomplice here, in this office, who is feeding him the information."

"And who might that be?" Mullins turned red. "We keep our information on a need-to-know basis."

Ray nodded in the direction of the dispatch desk where Ope sat busily taking calls. Ray lowered his voice. "The morning Krantz was in my office. Ope knew he was there, but didn't warn me. I've seen them chatting, friendly-like."

"I don't think—well, maybe." Mullins bit his bottom lip and looked past Ray toward where Ope worked.

∗∗∗

Ray drove by Silken's Dry Goods and verified that Silken's Silverado 2500 was in its usual spot in the alley behind the store, then headed to the neighborhood behind the golf course to see if Silken's wife was home. Ray had stopped by the house almost every day since his interview with Silken the previous week, but she was never home.

The Cove subdivision stretched from the main road, where the golf course occupied a prime location, to the bluffs on both the south and west. Over sixty miles of roads spanned the area. Many of the homes on the lots away from the bluff were affordable. He and Sophia planned to buy or build one

Gregg E. Brickman

when the time was right—meaning he knew his job was secure. The homes on the bluff lots were another matter entirely. They were custom built and expensive with designs maximizing the mountain views. They had long curving drives and wooded acreage to the front and dramatic decks to the rear.

As before, Ray eased the Taurus down the long drive, expecting to turn around near the house. This time, however, there was a sleek Mercedes convertible sitting in the drive. The top was up and littered with a scattering of leaves, attesting to the probability it had sat there all night. Ray parked behind the car and made his way to the house and knocked on the door.

Like its invisible neighbors that were hidden by the trees, the house was immense. It looked to be made of cedar and had two levels of open decks encircling the structure. Windows, extending from top to bottom, reflected the morning sun. Though most of the lot was in its natural state, the plantings near the house bloomed with color. Life must be good running a dry goods store, Ray thought.

"Sheila Silken?" Ray said. He studied the stunning tall, slender woman in her mid-fifties who answered the door. She wore pearls with designer jeans. He held up his badge for her to see. "I'm Detective Stone. I have a few questions for you."

The woman smiled. "You must be the new man I read about." Her grammar was perfect, but her accent was syrupy.

"Yes, ma'am." He thought perhaps Carl Silken hadn't mentioned their conversation to her.

"Did something happen in the neighborhood, Detective?"

"Can I come in, please?"

She stepped away from the door and motioned for him to enter. The large room stretched from the front door to a wall of glass. Several cozy seating areas provided views of both the bluff beyond the deck and the large fireplace to the right. No electronics were in view, and Ray assumed there was a family room, and perhaps a theater, elsewhere in the house.

He crossed to the window and looked. "Beautiful view."

"We like it."

"Too bad you can see the properties on Dripping Springs

IMPERFECT ESCAPE

Drive."

"I suppose it is. I rarely look that way, but we live in Tennessee. Places like that are a reality." She pointed to a conversation grouping. "Have a seat, Detective."

He did. "Have you been out of town? I've stopped by a couple of times during the last week."

"I was visiting my parents in Atlanta. I go every couple of weeks. They're elderly, obviously, so I feel it's good to see them. This time my mother had surgery, so I stayed a few days."

"You were raised in Atlanta?"

"I was. Carl and I moved to Miami after we married." Mrs. Silken paused. "What is this visit about, Detective?"

"I'm looking into a concern about the funds from the Women's Club Craft sale." Ray kept his voice casual and friendly.

"Oh, my. Why? Was there a complaint?"

"No, I think just a concern. Your husband told me the money was stolen when the store was robbed last week. Tell me about the money raised at the last sale and what was done with it."

She pursed her lips for a moment, and Ray thought she might deflect the question.

Mrs. Silken said, "The sale was last Wednesday afternoon. We finished around five, so the bank was closed. I stopped by to talk to Carl. He suggested I leave the money in the safe there, and he'd put it in the bank the next day. Then he forgot to move it from under the tray in the register to the safe when he closed up at six."

"How much was involved?"

"We had a good sale. There was two hundred dollars." She looked puzzled. "It's not a problem, though. I just wrote a check and made an online deposit into the club account. It was my responsibility, after all."

Ray thought Silken was taking advantage of the robbery to pad his insurance claim since he'd claimed the club losses were two grand.

"Do you usually take the money from the sales to the store

and have him do the deposits the next day?"

"No. It was because I was headed out of town that evening. That's all."

Ray looked around the room, being obvious about it. "This is a lot of house to afford on income from a small store in a town with a depressed economy. Did you bring private money to the marriage, perhaps?"

"I don't know what this has to do with the money from the club sale. You seem to be making a big deal about it."

"Just go with the questions for a minute, please. I'll make my point."

She half-smiled, her expression curious. "I had a little money set aside from an inheritance. But, not much, not really. Carl does well in the store. That's one of the reasons we moved here from Miami. He wanted a fresh start and a chance to excel before he retired."

"How long were you here before you built the house?"

"Oh, three years, I guess. We struggled a bit at first, but things are good now."

"Do you help in the store?"

I'm not involved at all, but I do see the tax returns. The truth is, I've been surprised about how well he does."

Ray thought Silken did well laundering drug money. "Someone made the allegation your husband is involved in the methamphetamine business in the area, perhaps even running most of it. Do you know anything about that?"

"So that's why you're here." She rose and pointed to the door. "That's the most ridiculous thing I've ever heard. Carl is a good man. A fine citizen. Get out of my house."

Chapter 22

Ray

On Wednesday morning, Ray stood in the front yard outside the little rental house watching Mischief complete her morning's business, part of which included sniffing every blade of grass in the vicinity. Because of her flat Boston terrier face, she tipped her head down in a pronounced fashion to get her nostrils close to the object of her interest.

It was early, not yet six-thirty, so Ray had plenty of time. He sipped his coffee, enjoyed the cool mountain air, and planned his day. His cell phone buzzed, interrupting his thoughts.

"Stone."

"Got a possible car theft. Thought you'd want to be involved, start your Wednesday morning off right." Johnson's voice drifted though the connection's static. "The victim is George Schmidt, friend of the mayor and the chief."

"Okay, I'll head in."

Johnson was involving him at the get-go. The historic limited resources in the department meant officers handled everything that came their way. At one time, they called the county sheriff for big cases. Now, they had a detective on staff, and the victim was well-connected. It made sense to call Ray rather than just write a report.

He interrupted Mischief's sniffing, returned her to the

house, and drove the short distance into town to the address Johnson supplied.

Ray parked on the street in front of a well-kept, older home on North Holly Street. As he walked up the path to the front door, he noted three late-model vehicles in the driveway, a Chevy truck, a Lexus, and a Lincoln. He wondered what was stolen.

A man of about sixty answered the door. "Good morning, Detective."

"Morning, George." Ray had met the man over coffee in the local cafe. He was one of the town's pharmacists in addition to being politically well connected. "I understand you've had a vehicle stolen."

"That I have." Schmidt stepped back and motioned Ray into the entry foyer. He led the way to a modernized kitchen—decked out in stainless steel, black-patterned granite, and rich-looking oak cabinets. "Have a seat." Schmidt produced a mug of coffee.

"Thanks for the hospitality." Ray opened his notebook and poised a pen. "Tell me about the theft. Start with the make and model of the car."

"It's a 2011 Volkswagen. It was gone when I got up this morning."

"Seems odd someone would take that and leave the other vehicles alone."

"Probably not. I confess to leaving it unlocked with a key under the mat." His expression was sheepish. "The others are locked and alarmed."

"Why, may I ask, are you so lax about the Volkswagen?"

"I'm usually not. My grandson called last night and wanted to borrow it. His car is in the shop. I put it out front for him."

"Are you sure he didn't take it?"

"Yes, I'm sure. He woke me when he couldn't find it."

Ray got more details from Schmidt.

As he finished, he received a text from Johnson saying, *I've found the car.* The street name and approximate address followed.

IMPERFECT ESCAPE

Ray stood. "Johnson found your car."
"Where?"
"On a side street about a mile from here."
"I don't know what it's doing there." George looked puzzled.
"I'll let you know what happens."
"Fine." George walked Ray to the door, locking it as Ray stepped onto the porch.

Ray spent the short drive to the stolen vehicle's location marveling at someone who was so careful to lock the door and yet so careless with a vehicle. He supposed the theft heightened Schmidt's awareness.

Johnson stood next to his patrol unit about twenty feet behind a banged-up, white Volkswagen, which sat well away from any of the small houses on the block.

Ray parked his Ram across the street and joined Johnson. "Any idea which house the perp lives it?"

"I'm guessing the second one on the right."

Ray grinned. A path of muddy boot tracks led from the driver's door on the vehicle to the steps of the house. "Good thing crooks aren't too bright. Really increases our solve rates."

Deciding to err on the side of caution, Ray unclipped the strap holding his weapon in place. He put his hand on the weapon and knocked on the door with the other hand.

There was no response.

Ray banged again on the door. "Open up. Police."

This time, there was shuffling behind the door and the sound of the lock being turned. Ray motioned to Johnson to stand on the left of the door, while Ray moved to his right.

When the door opened, a disheveled, bed-headed man opened the door. Ray judged the emaciated male to be in his mid-thirties.

"What's goin' on?" He looked at Johnson. "Jim, why are you here?"

Johnson said, "This is Ken Hinter. He's one of our local meth heads."

"Charming." Ray stepped into the doorway. "Mr. Hinter,

we need to talk about the car you stole."

Hinter looked confused. "Okay, man. Come on in."

The small living room looked like it hadn't seen a vacuum cleaner or dust rag in several years. Every surface held fast food wrappers, trash, and empty soda cans. A glass bong gleamed on the kitchen table. A plastic bag containing white substance sat next to it. Ray thought Hinter's priorities spoke for themselves. A key was close by. He stepped closer and identified it as belonging to a Volkswagen.

Ray said, "We're going to have to arrest you for stealing the vehicle."

Hinter blinked, laughed. "That's Uncle George's car, man. He told me to take it."

"Johnson, go outside and call Schmidt. I'll stay here with Hinter and talk about his pile of meth."

"Hinter, sit down."

He sat.

"Where'd you get the meth?"

"Thought this was about the damn car."

"Started out that way. Now I want to know about the meth. Do you cook it yourself?"

"Hell no. Man can get blowed up that way."

"Where do you buy it?"

"What's it worth to you if I say?"

"I'll talk to the chief about reducing the charges."

"Okay, man, that's fair." Hinter looked thoughtful. "I got the last bag down at the dry goods store."

Ray raised a brow. "You went into the store and bought meth?"

"No, man. I went behind the store, by the loading dock. Supplier is there sometimes."

"Who is the supplier?"

"Skinny guy who worked for LeRoy. Don't know who he works for now."

"When did you buy it?"

"Yesterday around lunch time. I think. I guess. Maybe."

Ray put another pin in his mental map linking Silken with

IMPERFECT ESCAPE

the local meth trade. He reasoned that someone selling by his loading dock during business hours would be doing it with Silken's knowledge—perhaps with his product as well. "You buy your stash there all the time?"

"Sure, man. Right to the source. You know what I mean?"

Ray nodded, then looked past Hinter to the kitchen table, which was stacked with small appliance boxes. "What's with the appliances?"

"I'm keeping them for a friend."

Ray slipped on plastic gloves, then inspected several of the boxes. They were sealed from the factory and had Silken Dry Goods price tags. "These from the heist at Silken's place last week?"

"Don't know. I said I was keeping them for a friend."

Ray moved to face Hinter. "You have the right to remain silent . . ." He finished reading Hinter his rights, "You're under arrest for possession of the methamphetamine and for the stolen goods. We'll add to the charges as we sort things out."

"Ah, man. My ma will be so pissed." Hinter moaned and slumped in the chair.

Johnson opened the door and flagged Ray over. In a low voice, he said, "Schmidt *now* remembers loaning out the car. Says he'd had a few too many beers so he forgot. He's sorry he caused trouble."

Ray shook his head. "Put on gloves and grab an evidence bag. Let's take his stash and pipe and haul him in. There are several stolen appliances in the kitchen, too. Bag them and then dust them for prints when we get to the department."

***

The Plateauville PD was bare bones—two offices, several desks plus dispatch in the large open squad room, a break room, locker room, a small conference room, and a waiting area and reception counter they shared with the court. There was no lockup and no interrogation room. Officers transported suspects to Crestville to the Sheriff's Department.

Ray, however, wanted to talk to Hinter before transporting him to jail. "Officer Johnson," Ray said, "stay with the suspect for a minute while I sanitize my office to use for interrogation."

"Why not use the conference room? That's what we usually do."

"The chief has it set up for a meeting later."

"Got it." Johnson pointed to a chair and motioned Hinter to sit. "You going to cooperate, Kenny, or do I need to put the cuffs on?"

"Jimmy, my man, give me a break. At least, just take me to the slammer and don't make me talk to that there detective. I'll call Ma to bail me out."

"Sorry, Kenny. I told you the last time that your chances ran out. And, your ma told you no more bail money."

Hinter slouched in the designated chair, his expression forlorn.

Ray left Johnson to his guarding task, cleaned off his desk, and locked his file drawers. Then he carried a straight-backed plastic chair from the break room into the office, shoving his two mismatched, yet comfortable, side chairs aside to make room.

After Hinter was situated on the plastic chair in the makeshift interrogation room, Ray left him there to wait and perhaps worry. He opened the blind a crack and stationed Johnson to watch from outside the room.

"Why don't you just talk to him, then I'll run him down to the jail?"

"I'm waiting for him to get in the proper frame of mind and worry a bit. Is he going to ask for a lawyer?"

"Nah. Hinter has been through this before. He thinks he knows the ropes."

Ray chatted with Ope at the dispatch desk for a few minutes, then used a computer in the staff room to pull Hinter's sheet. It was long but not impressive—several busts for possession, jail time for possession with intent to sell, and a couple of busts for petty theft. It read like a meth head supporting his habit.

IMPERFECT ESCAPE

When Mullins arrived about an hour later, Ray briefed him, then invited him to join in the interrogation.

"Thought you had him on the possession and theft."

"We do. I want to see if we can get him to turn on Silken. He already fessed up to buying from a guy behind Silken's store. Maybe there's more."

Mullins nodded and followed Ray in to see Hinter, who jerked awake when the door opened.

"Have a nice nap, Hinter?" Ray sat on one hip on the edge of his desk, positioning himself to loom over the suspect's right shoulder.

"Ah, I guess."

Ray removed a digital recorder from his shirt pocket and placed it on the desk. "We will record our conversation." He handed Hinter a form. "This says I read you your rights and you understand them."

"I never signed one of those before."

"Sign it now."

Hinter straightened himself in his chair, then leaned forward to sign the form on the desk. When he finished, Mullins took the form, looked it over, nodded, then pulled a chair close to the desk and sat to Hinter's left.

"Hinter," Ray kept his voice sharp and hard. "You're going down for possession of meth and possession of stolen goods."

"I had the meth, yeah man, but I don't know how those boxes got into my house. I didn't even know they was there until you saw them. I told you my friend must have left them."

"Not exactly what you said earlier." Ray made a show of checking his notes.

"You woke me up. I was confused."

"Johnson is dusting those boxes for prints at this moment. In a few minutes, we'll know if your prints are on them."

"You haven't taken my prints." Hinter sneered.

"Have them on file."

"We also have prints from the store. If yours are on the shelves where the goods were stored—and I think they are—we'll have you for the theft as well."

Hinter gulped. "I didn't steal nothing."

Ray encroached further into Hinter's space. "Kenny-boy, you're going down big time on these charges." He grabbed Hinter's shoulder and squeezed hard enough to cause Hinter to yelp in pain.

On cue, Mullins intervened. "Detective Stone, there is no reason to get rough."

"Son-of-a-bitch hasn't seen rough yet. I'm going to make sure he gets real prison time. They'll eat his ass alive in there."

"Kenny, Stone has a point. We've got you with solid evidence, and you won't do well in prison. Trust me."

After several more minutes of the same type of interrogation technique, Hinter said, "What can I do? I'll tell you stuff."

"That could work. Depends on what you say and if it checks out."

"It's good. Honest."

"I'm listening." The good cop-bad cop routine had worked. Ray backed up a bit, giving Hinter room, and hoping to imply trust.

"I did rob the store. I was looking for drugs."

"Did you find any?"

"He had a huge plastic container in his back room full of crank. I think it's his shipment to Florida—all ready to go, you know. Someone comes into town to pick it up. I've seen him make the delivery in the alley behind his store a few times. The car is always a big SUV with a Florida plate."

"Did you take any of the meth?"

"Yeah, I did, but only a couple of little baggies. Silken would know it was me if I took a bunch."

"Why would he know that?"

"Because he trusted me. When I go in there to buy some stuff, I see him get it from the back."

"You're saying that Silken sells meth directly from his store?"

"Only to us special people. Other people have to buy it from his dealers on the street."

IMPERFECT ESCAPE

"Was that the stash I found in your house?"
Hinter nodded.
"Answer the question out loud for the tape."
"Yeah."
"Yeah what?"
"Yeah, it is the stash from my house."
Ray and Mullins both continued the questioning, hoping to find a crack in the story, but Hinter stuck to it.
"Did you take cash, too?" Ray asked.
"Yeah, two hundred dollars is all."
Ray filed a mental note about the amount, remembering that Silken had reported a couple of thousand missing.
"Okay, Hinter. Johnson will take you to Crestville for booking." Ray stood. "We'll have this all transcribed for you to sign. You'll be expected to testify against Carl Silken. If you keep your end of the bargain, we'll talk to the DA about amending your charges."

***

Ray and Mullins met in the conference room an hour later. Several files sat on the credenza in preparation for the meeting. A map on a poster board sat on an easel near the head of the table. While they waited for Johnson to get back from Crestville—he was in transit—they discussed the ongoing investigations.

Ray said, "I'd like to send a specimen from Hinter's stash to Nashville. There was residue on a couple of the bodies from the explosion at Vast's. It they can match it, it would tie Vast directly to Silken."

"It's worth a try. Just keep in mind that Hinter is a born and bred liar. We need to take every word he said as a potential lie."

"What's your best guess about Silken?" Ray said. "Is he the drug lord people tell me he is?"

"Well, now that's a mighty good question, isn't it?" Mullins took a sip of coffee. "All the arrows point in that direction.

The issue is, we have no firm evidence to support a warrant—not even enough to make a solid accusation. And a failed raid would tip our hand."

"Hinter . . ."

"And others have accused him, but they are all known meth addicts with a reason to lie—something to trade for a reduced sentence."

Ray laughed. "Guess meth addicts and their suppliers are like birds of a feather."

"You might say that."

A tap on the door interrupted the conversation. Mullins got up and let Johnson in. "How'd it go?" He left the door open a few inches.

"Hinter asked for a lawyer as soon as he was booked, and they led him off to his new accommodations." Johnson took a seat across the table from Ray. "I'm thinking he'll not be turning state's evidence. He was shooting his mouth off about illegal search."

"Did you get the encounter on film?" Ray said.

Johnson tapped his body cam and grinned. "I did at that."

"Does Hinter know?"

"He doesn't. The thought would never occur to him that we had body cams, or that the town would fund them."

The devices were a gift to the department from a local men's club and hadn't been made public yet. They were still in the trial phase.

"Okay, gentlemen, we are here to talk about tomorrow's raid."

Johnson squirmed in his chair, then motioned to the open door.

Mullins mouthed, "I know." Then he got up and walked slowly to the door while talking. "As near as we've been able to tell, that lab on Cherry Lane isn't connected to Vast's and Flocker's operations or, in the same vein, to Silken. We'll hit it tomorrow." He closed the door.

Johnson raised a questioning brow.

Mullins said, "I want to make sure Ope has the

IMPERFECT ESCAPE

information and doesn't think we know he has it."

"Oh." Johnson drew out the word. "I can't believe Ted is the one leaking our plans for raids."

"I think he might be," Ray said. "I went back and researched each failed raid. The commonality is that Ope was scheduled for duty during the planning of each one. For a couple, he was even in the room since he was assigned to call in the team at the last minute."

Johnson's expression registered shock. "But he hired me, trained me."

"We'll know more after this one. If the lab is tipped off, the mole is either Ope or you, Johnson. No one else is around. I wouldn't, and Stone hasn't been here long enough."

Johnson's face reddened. "I'll be damned." He shoved his chair back, stood, and stomped toward the door.

"Sit down, Jim," Mullins said. "We know it wasn't you."

"How do you know that?"

"You were in class for one of them and at your granddaddy's funeral for another. Ope, on the other hand, was here."

Johnson returned to his chair.

Mullins went to the white board on the wall near the head of the table. First, he drew a map of Cherry Lane, showing the intersection with Dripping Springs Drive. "It's about a mile north of the intersection. There's a side road here that's unmarked." He pointed. "You guys need to run down the road and make sure you can find it in the dark tomorrow night."

"I know the place," Johnson said. "We used to party there—in high school, I mean."

Ray said, "I'd like to get the lay of the land anyway. Let's go out that way in my truck after this meeting."

"Fine." Johnson nodded.

Mullins waited a moment, then continued. "I've talked to the sheriff. He's onboard. He won't tell anyone until we start to roll, then he'll send his deputies. We'll use the same approach and same men as for the last raid."

"Krantz?" Ray said.

"No. The Sheriff wants to see if he gets wind of it and shows up uninvited."
"Shim?"
"No." Mullins laughed, then went on to review the plan in detail for Ray's benefit, making notes on the whiteboard as he talked.

When the meeting concluded, Mullins made a show of locking the conference room—which was normally open for anyone's use. "I'll see you two tomorrow."

Ray and Johnson headed toward the door.

Ray nodded a goodbye to Ope on the way out.

Chapter 23

Sophia

Sophia spent Tuesday evening at the baby shower, then enjoyed a late dinner with friends. On Wednesday, she hung out with Connie, then visited the ED at Coral Bay Medical Center, where she used to work.

By Thursday morning, she felt visited out. She returned her rental car at the airport and waited at the exit for Deg Lewis to pick her up. It didn't take long until Deg's personal SUV rolled into view.

"Hey, sweet thing, climb in." Deg reached across the vehicle and pushed the passenger door open. "How was your visit?"

"Wonderful." She climbed in. "Strange though, I'm ready to go back to Tennessee. It's really gotten into my blood. That and the fact Ray and Mischief are there waiting for me to come back."

"Did you tell the man what you're up to?"

"Of course not. He'd have a hissy. Better he should find out when I give him good information—or not find out at all."

"Can't wait for him to get down here and offer to tan my hide for getting involved with you."

Sophia laughed. "He'll be glad I didn't go it alone."

"There is that. We do, however, have a change of plans." He turned toward the Sawgrass Expressway entrance. "My

Narc buddy, Jay, is rolling undercover at the moment. So, he's not available. He did put me onto a dude who has agreed to have a Cuban coffee with us on the condition his name isn't used."

"Is he one of Jay's snitches?"

Deg smiled. "No. He's a crackhead Jay went to high school with. Nick is his name. Jay has pulled the guy out of trouble a time or two, and Nick agreed to meet with us as a favor. Oh, Nick isn't aware Jay is a cop. Don't say anything."

"How did he explain us wanting to ask questions then?"

"Jay told him you're a reporter from Tennessee writing an article about the connection between the meth business here and there. I'm your trusty escort."

"An escort with cop stamped on your head."

"Won't be a problem."

As they drove, Deg peppered Sophia with pointed questions about the meth problem in Tennessee. She responded with as much detail as she could muster.

After taking a couple of different tollways, Deg exited the expressway system, drove down a side street, then parked in a spot a hundred feet or so beyond a Cuban cafe.

Sophia saw the hospital complex in the distance. Jackson Memorial and its associated clinics, the VA, and Cedars all shared the same access road. They, and the restaurant, were surrounded by one of Miami's most infamous slums. She was glad to have her private escort, remembering getting lost in the area a couple of years earlier when she'd attended a seminar at Jackson. She'd taken a wrong turn, missed the expressway entrance, and spent an extra hour finding her way out.

"Stay put for a minute." Deg got out of the SUV, walked around to the sidewalk, and turned both ways. Then he opened the door for her and guided the way to the cafe.

The place was small and smelled of roast pork, onions, and Cuban coffee. Most of the tables were occupied with Hispanics in medical uniforms. A sad-looking specimen of a man sat alone at a table for four along the west wall.

She touched Deg's arm. "Do you think that's Nick?"

IMPERFECT ESCAPE

"Fits the description Jay gave me." In three long steps, Deg stood before the man. "You Nick?"

"What's it to you?"

"I drove Jay's friend down to see you." He tilted his head in Sophia's direction.

"Have a seat."

"Have you eaten?"

"Rather have money." Nick turned over his hand to reveal an empty palm.

"I'll buy food, but I won't give you cash."

Nick nodded. "Pork. Plantains. Please."

Sophia stepped to the table and slid into a seat. "Deg, that sounds delicious. I'll have some, too."

"As will I." He went over to counter and placed the order, paying in advance, as was required. He returned to the table with three paper cups of water. "They'll bring the food out in a few minutes. Meanwhile, Sophia, you can get started."

"Nick, do you mind if I record the conversation? I promise not to ask you any identifying information, and I won't add it later. You're an unnamed source who's familiar with the meth trade in Miami."

"I'll be like one of the White House leakers."

"Pretty much." She took out her phone, set it to record, removed a notebook from her purse, and opened it to a list of preplanned questions.

"Do you have any connection with the manufacturing of methamphetamine in this area or are you a customer?"

Nick looked thoughtful. He started to speak, then stopped as the server placed three heaping plates on the table. After taking several bites of pork in rapid succession, he glanced at Sophia. "I work for a friend some, but the real high-grade meth gets shipped in."

"Where does it come from?"

"That depends on who you buy from. Some comes from Mexico. Some from the Keys. Some local. If you buy from a distributor named Krantz, it comes from Tennessee."

"Just what I'm interested in."

Gregg E. Brickman

"A few years ago, I worked for his operation. Just doing manual work, you know. We'd get packages of supplies in from South America. Sometimes we'd go out in a boat and transfer the goods there. Other times, we went to the Everglades to get the stuff. A lot of it came in through customs, hidden in other stuff."

"What did the packaging look like?"

"Mostly in plain boxes. But inside, the ingredients were in boxes with Chinese writing."

She nodded. "Based on my research, that's what I expected to hear." She looked at Nick. "Who does Krantz work for? Do you know?"

"It's a big organization." Nick glanced away, then stared at Sophia's iPhone.

"Did you ever hear the name Carl Silken?" she said.

"Old Silky."

"You know him?"

"I know of him. He left town a few years back. Still hear his name, though."

"What can you tell me about him?" she said.

"Only that down here he had the reputation for being a mean son of a bitch. Nobody was sad when he left town." Nick shuddered.

Sophia continued with general questions with the hopes of clouding Nick's memory about the questions involving Silken.

Deg ordered three Cuban coffees and grinned when the thick sweet coffee arrived in one-ounce plastic cups.

She sipped and savored the rich taste. The caffeine jolt would last until she landed late that afternoon in Nashville.

Chapter 24

Ray

Ray wanted to stay with Sophia, but if his guess was right, he'd be home by ten. Instead they shared a fast and simple dinner of rotisserie chicken and salad she had bought at Publix in Crestville on her way home from the Nashville airport.

He met Chief Mullins, Johnson, and Al Crag, a younger night-shift officer, in the conference room at the PD a bit after eight on Wednesday evening.

"What's going on, Chief?" Crag said. "Not saying I object to the overtime, mind you."

"We're hitting that meth lab on Cherry Lane. My source said it was going strong this afternoon."

"Just the four of us?" Crag frowned, shifting his weight side to side.

"No, we'll have four deputies. They'll be waiting in two unmarked cars at the turn off to Dripping Springs. The plan is the same as for the last raid, and again, we have a no-knock warrant. We'll roll in quiet, polite-like, lights off. If no one is out and about, three of us will take positions around the perimeter. Stone, backed up by the four deputies, will breach the front door." Mullins continued to review the plan. Then he picked up the landline and dialed. "Sheriff Foster, please."

While he waited, Ray ran through a mental checklist of the equipment he'd moved from his and Johnson's official rides into his Ram. The PD didn't own any unmarked vehicles, so he offered to use the Ram to help ensure an anonymous approach. He was satisfied he had everything they needed. The vests, helmets, and hazmat suits were already on the floor on the back seat, and they would take weapons, including assault rifles, to the truck on their way outside. If there were suspects to transport, they'd go to Crestville with the deputies.

Foster must have responded to the call, because Mullins appeared to be listening.

"That's right, Stretch." Mullins used Sheriff Matthew Foster's nickname. "Putting you on speaker." He punched the button. "We're ready to roll."

At six-eight, Foster had played college basketball, but by his own words, hadn't been drafted by the pros because his singular qualification was height, not skill. "I'm sending the same deputies as last time. They know the plan and the area. They should be arriving at the rendezvous point in a few minutes."

"Good," Mullins said. "Where's Krantz?"

"Off duty and out of the loop. These men have no real use for him, so be assured, there will be no notification."

"You hanging around?"

Foster laughed. "I wouldn't miss it for the world. This is a win, no matter what happens. If we make the bust, we win. If not, we know who our mole is."

Ray agreed with Foster's assessment. He'd thought the exact same thing on his drive to the PD.

Mullins broke the connection. "Let's go." He patted the Glock in the holster on his belt, grabbed a rifle from the cabinet near the door, then led the way to Ray's truck and climbed into the shotgun seat.

Johnson and Crag slid into the back, handed two vests forward for Ray and Mullins, and proceeded to put on their gear.

The ride to the corner of Cherry Lane and Dripping Springs Drive took less than fifteen minutes. Deputies in unmarked SUVs were waiting in a neighboring driveway about

IMPERFECT ESCAPE

fifty feet from the turn. Ray stopped, and Mullins exited and approached them.

When Mullins returned to the Ram, the three-car caravan crept to within a hundred yards of the targeted address, turned off their headlights, and eased down the road and into the drive.

Ray stepped from the truck and waited for the others to exit the vehicles and get into position. He and the deputies formed a tight *V*, aiming at the front steps of the dilapidated mobile home. Ray extended a hand and turned the knob. It wasn't locked. "On three." Ray mouthed the words.

"One. Two. Three." Ray slammed the door open at the same time he dropped into a crouch, allowing the deputies behind him clear shots if necessary.

The house was silent.

"Spread out and search."

It took less than a minute to confirm the place was empty.

"Damn," Ray said. "I hoped for a different result."

Mullins walked in the front door.

"Looks like they cleared out," Ray said.

"They left the door open." Mullins raised a brow. "Guess there's a message in that. Stone and Johnson, suit up in your hazmat gear and have a look around."

"Yes, sir," Ray said.

The smell of an active meth lab filled the building, but, no raw materials were found. The operation appeared to have packed up and moved.

"Then, let's seal it. We'll get decontamination people out here tomorrow. One of the sheriff's deputies will stand guard for the night." Mullins turned and left.

***

Ray found Sophia asleep on the sofa with Mischief in her lap. She wasn't working the next day—good schedule planning on her part—so he poured a couple of glasses of Chianti, then woke her.

"Oh, sweetheart, I must have drifted off." She rubbed an eye.

Ray smiled. She looked as if she'd passed out three hours earlier.

"What time is it?"

"Midnight." He handed her the wine.

"Wake me up to put me to sleep. Just like the hospital." She sipped. "Good. I'll take Mischief out, then join you."

He reached for the dog and put her on the floor. "I'll take her."

When he returned from the short walk, Sophia met him at the door with a glass in each hand. She looked more awake, had combed her hair, and wore a soft pale-pink nightgown that clung to her curves.

He took his wine. "You look delicious." He kissed her. "First a snack. Then dessert."

"You hungry?"

"Ah, yeah."

"I mean for food."

"That too. What do you have in mind?"

"Chicken sandwich and chips. I picked up those big Kaiser rolls you like."

"Bring it on, but be quick about it." He nuzzled her neck.

Sophia pushed him away, then went to the kitchen and made the snack. She set it on the table in front of his chair, refilled the wine glasses, and sat, then reached over and stole a chip. "How was the raid?"

"Failed, as expected. Ope was on duty in dispatch as planned. He's the only possible leak."

"Krantz?"

"The sheriff made sure he was out of the loop."

"Now what happens?"

"Tomorrow, we'll be on Ope like bat shit on a rock in a Tennessee cave." Ray took a bite out of the sandwich. "Good."

Sophia laughed. "Where'd you get that one?"

"Made it up on the fly." Ray grinned, then wiped at his goatee with a napkin. "Tell me about your trip—not the shower

IMPERFECT ESCAPE

part, the poking around in my case part."
"How do you know I poked?"
"Because you're you and I'm me. We have history. See?"
"Have more wine, dear. You're rhyming."
He laughed. "In all seriousness, what did you do?"
"I called Deg, who escorted me to Miami to talk to a meth-head associate of an undercover cop. We were supposed to meet with the cop, but that fell through."
"Now everyone in Miami knows you're poking around." His temper flared for the moment. He'd agreed to her paying attention and reporting to him, but he hadn't agreed to her sticking her nose into trouble.
"Calm down. We claimed I was a reporter looking for a story on the connection between Tennessee's meth problem and the situation in Miami. The guy wanted to be sure he wasn't mentioned by name in the article."
"And Deg?"
"A big, tough, cop-looking escort, helping me out, and keeping me safe."
"You got that right. I thanked him this afternoon. He said you could give me a full report."
"You knew we went to Miami."
"Yup. Made sure Deg was available to take you."
"You son of a bitch." She grinned. "Guess I deserve it."
"Yup. Deg didn't have a lot of time to talk and wants me to call him back."
"He has a bunch of questions about the problem here, most of which I couldn't answer, so be prepared to spend a few minutes. Anyway . . ." Sophia relayed what she'd learned. "Oh, I have a recording, too."
"Good. I'll listen to it tomorrow. Can you send it to my phone, please, so I can share it with the chief? Did the guy know he was being recorded?"
"Yup. I recorded that on my phone, too."
"Were you armed when you went to Miami?"
"Armed with Deg—who was carrying."
"Three weapons, at least, if I know him. But why weren't

you?"

"Ray, I couldn't take my Sig on the airplane."

"True." He grinned, taking another bite of his snack. "I'll give you a pass on that."

"Big of you."

"What else did you learn?"

"That's pretty much it. But it sounds like your friend Silky is a bona fide bad dude. The source, for lack of a better word, Nick's his name, told us about several guys busted up on Silky's orders and at least three forever missing. Said he didn't know for sure what happened, but the word on the street was the guys stole from Silky, and Silky ordered the hits."

"Now all we have to do is figure out how to get him off the streets of Plateauville, Tennessee."

"Do you think he's responsible for Vast's lab blowing up?"

"And, a lot of other things as well. We're thinking that Krantz has been his conduit of evil—being family and all—but we don't know for sure. It could just be Krantz is an asshole and Silken is the asshole's uncle. It has to be tied together in a neat little package."

"Won't the people in town be up in arms—one of their own and all?"

"I don't think so. The Silkens, both of them, have done everything reasonable to fit themselves into local society, but they're still outsiders when it matters. Also, there's a powerful undercurrent in the town that wants the meth trade dealt with, so the chief believes there will be support."

"Some relatives of high-placed locals are bound to be caught up in the mess when Silken goes down."

"There is that, and they won't be happy."

"But, good Southern values will win out."

"Here's hoping." He took the last bite of the sandwich and upended his wine. "Good to the last drop." Then he cleared his dishes to the sink.

"I'll get them in the morning." Sophia slid into his arms, then worked her hands under his shirt. "Take this off."

"Here?"

IMPERFECT ESCAPE

"No," she pointed to the bedroom door, "there. I'll settle Mischief."

He wrapped her in a hug, then kissed her, this time with a measure of heat. "Hurry up, now. I'll jump in the shower. Want to join me?"

"I . . . Oh, what the heck, a second shower is good."

Ray headed toward the bedroom, tugging off his shirt and holster along the way.

"Crate up, Mischief," she said. "Here's a treat for you, little girl." Sophia closed the crate door and followed Ray to the shower.

Chapter 25

Ray

Ray's first stop Thursday morning was at the Plateau Cafe, where, as he had hoped, the table of five flagged him over.

As he passed the counter, Elma May lifted a coffee cup and nodded in his direction. Ray responded with a smile and nod of his own. "In a to-go cup." He spied a plate filled with pastry under a domed-glass cover. "And one of those caramel rolls to go with it, please." He'd sampled a pastry before. It had been homemade and delicious.

Ray greeted the men, grabbed the empty chair facing the front window and Silken's store across the street. He joined in the casual conversation, waiting to see if anyone would broach the subject of the failed raid.

Mayor Archie Bib was first to acknowledge the dead possum sitting in the middle of the table. "We hear y'all tried another raid that flopped."

"We did, but we got some information out of the deal."

"Such as?" Bib said.

"I'm sorry, Archie, I really can't discuss an ongoing investigation."

"Why not? Everyone in town is talking about it, probably at this very moment."

"That's a good thing. We asked the guys to chat it up, hoping the information in its varying forms reaches the right

IMPERFECT ESCAPE

ears. However, that doesn't apply to everything we learned. I'm sure the chief will be happy to give you more in private." He cast his eyes around the table. "Sorry, gentlemen."

"Ah," Bib said.

The men nodded, and a couple muttered. One said, "Hadn't thought of that."

Elma May delivered Ray's coffee and paper-wrapped pastry.

John Johnson leaned forward. "Now that you mention it, I thought it was odd Jimmy called when he finished his shift last night and wanted to talk about the raid. He's usually secretive about what goes on, especially when it involves the sheriff."

"Good to know." Ray took a sip of his coffee, then snapped a plastic lid on the cup. "In any event, we'd appreciate it if you'd discuss the *failed raid* aspect around town and add a little self-righteous disappointment to your comments."

After the five men agreed, Ray left and headed to the department. While at the table, he'd seen no activity at Silken's store and not even a drive by from Deputy Sheriff Krantz. Maybe Krantz had smartened up and was staying clear of his uncle, Ray thought.

Ray's cell rang as he pulled into the lot. "Stone."

"Hey, Stone. Shim, here. I heard your raid was a bust."

"Yup, just like we all figured it would be. We're on to step two in a few minutes."

"I'd love to watch." Shim chuckled.

Ray laughed. "Have you seen your good buddy Krantz this morning?"

"Actually, I did. He was in here a few minutes ago. That's why I called. He's hopping mad *you* excluded him from the raid team, since he lives in the area and all."

"Lives—but no longer works—here."

"That sticks in his gullet, too. He claims he has to leave home an hour early to begin his shift," Shim said, then chuckled.

"The son of a bitch should have thought of that earlier.

By the way, I suspect Krantz watched the raid from a distance. I overheard him yapping on his cell about you and the deputies finding an open door."

"Truer words. Gotta go." Shim disconnected, which had Ray wondering what was happening in the big town and why Shim had called.

Ray stepped into the squad room, saw Ope at his dispatch station, and raised a hand in greeting.

"Good to see you, Stone." Ope pushed a button and answered a call.

Ray wondered if it was real or a play-acted excuse to avoid conversation. He would know soon enough. Relief had been scheduled for Ope without his knowledge. When the lady arrived, the interrogation of Ope would begin.

***

Hearing a tap on his office doorjamb, Ray quit keying the failed raid report into the system.

The chief stepped inside and pulled the door closed, leaving his hand on the knob. "The relief dispatcher will be here in five minutes or so, I expect. I think we'll talk to Ope in the conference room—start off friendly-like. I take no pleasure in what we have to do." Mullins studied his hands for a moment.

"Neither do I. It's always tough when it's an officer—"

"Former officer. But I take your meaning. You take the lead."

"Can do." Ray took a deep breath, exhaled, saved the report on his computer, and stood. He'd been involved with questioning police officers in the past and dreaded repeating the experience.

Mullins opened the door and stepped out.

Ray followed. He looked toward the dispatch desk in the corner of the squad when Ted Ope said, "Netty, what are you doing here? You're not due until five this afternoon."

"The chief asked me to come in and relieve you for a

IMPERFECT ESCAPE

spell."

Ope's expression changed from one of wide-eyed curiosity to the pinched face of fear. He removed his headset, neatly coiled the cords, and put it in the desk drawer that served as his locker. Standing, he reached for his walker, which was folded and leaning against the desk, slowly opened it, then walked to the chief.

"Ted," Chief Mullins said.

"I'm assuming we need to talk."

"In the conference room. Stone and I will join you shortly."

"It's like that, is it?" Ope's voice was soft, almost childlike.

"Afraid so."

Through the open door, Ray and the chief watched Ope as he settled in a comfortable chair, then folded his walker and set it aside.

"We may as well get this over with." Ray led the way into the room. "Ted, can I bring you a cup of coffee before we get started?"

"Cream and one sugar." Ope scowled. "What's this all about?"

"All in good time, my friend." Ray left and returned with three cups of coffee. He'd taken his time. He placed Ope's coffee on the table in front of him, handed a cup to the chief, who'd selected a chair near the end of the table, then sat directly opposite Ope. Ray took a minute to settle, put a file with notes on the table next to his coffee, then removed a digital recorder from his shirt pocket, and placed it in front of Ted.

"Stone, are you ready yet?" Ope's voice was streaked with tension.

Ray switched on the recorder and recited the date, time, and location. "Detective Ray Stone and Chief Marvin Mullins interviewing Ted Ope on the matter of obstruction of justice in the failed meth lab raid on One Cherry Lane last night."

"That's ridiculous," Ope growled. "How the hell did you get that idea?"

"Back off, Ope. I'm not finished. You have the right to remain silent." Ray continued with the revised Miranda. He knew it from memory, but he read from a card, wanting to be sure each word was correct. "Do you wish to call an attorney or shall we continue?"

"Ask your damn questions. I have nothing to hide."

"We have cause to believe you alerted the people operating the meth lab at One Cherry Lane about the raid planned for last evening. Why'd you do that, Ted?"

"I didn't, and you can't prove I did. I wouldn't do a thing like that."

"I'm thinkin' you did," Ray said, rubbing his goatee.

Ope glared at Ray.

"You were the only one who had access to the information. We designed it that way. You were here when we had the planning meeting. You were caught on camera entering this room and going through the materials."

"Camera, what camera?" Ope's voice cracked.

Ray pointed to the fish-eye lens in the corner of the ceiling. "New addition."

"I was curious, is all. I didn't tell anyone."

"Actually, my friend, I believe you did," Ray said.

"You can't prove anything."

The conversation continued in a similar vein for an hour.

"Ope, it's obvious you won't fess up out of a sense of honor. So, let me tell you a few facts. We know Deputy Krantz had inside information on numerous raids, showing up to help when he wasn't part of the team. A witness will testify that in several of those instances he saw you talking to Krantz after the planning, but before the raid. This time, we have the call log from the dispatch phone showing you called Krantz after reviewing the materials in the conference room." Ray laid several documents on the table in front of Ope.

"I want a lawyer."

"Fine." He shoved the landline over to Ope, stood, and left the room with Mullins following. "I was hoping to not have to reveal so much to get his attention."

IMPERFECT ESCAPE

"Especially because the part about the testifying witness isn't true." Mullins chuckled.

"There is that."

Ray and Mullins returned to their offices, leaving Ope alone.

The lawyer appeared two hours later. Holly Aster, a woman of about thirty, wore a conservative black suit, white blouse, and two-inch heels—courtroom clothes. She asked to meet with her client.

At one o'clock in the afternoon, they reassembled, this time with Aster also in attendance.

She said, "I've counseled Mr. Ope to cooperate with you on the condition he does no jail time for his involvement."

Mullins nodded. "Could be our recommendation, given he helps us resolve this situation."

"Anything you want, Chief," Ope said. "Anything. I'd be a dead man in lockup."

"Mr. Ope," Aster said, "please let me do the talking. We need a commitment, Chief, not just a maybe."

"Fine. Ms. Aster will you join us, please." Mullins stood and left the room, followed by Ray and Ms. Aster.

Five minutes later they returned.

Ray said, "Ted, the DA has committed to no jail time, providing you do what we ask."

Aster nodded. "Go ahead with your questions. We'll see where they lead."

"I've carried this with me for a long time. Now is the time to get shed of it."

"First," Mullins said, "I want to know why you went over to the other side. I trusted you."

"Krantz has something on me, and he threatened to tell." The old man looked pale. His hands shook until he grasped them together.

"What?" Mullins voice was forceful, though quiet.

Ope shook his head.

"We'll find out from Krantz anyway when we bring him in and charge him with his part in this fiasco. If you want our cooperation and leniency, then you have to be up front, Ted. Totally."

Ope rolled his head back and exhaled. "When I was on the force, I'm sorry to say, I strong-armed Clarence Jasper. Old Jasper was growing weed in his barn at the time, so he had no choice but to pay me. Problem was, Krantz knew about the weed, too, and was poking around. He overheard the conversation and has been dogging me ever since."

"Is he still calling you for information now that he's on the west side of the county?" Ray said.

"Every damn day. And every other damn day he threatens to reveal my secret."

"Why did you care?" Mullins said.

"Because my family lives in this town. I don't want them to know. They've always admired my place on the force." He looked down, studying his hands.

Mullins exhaled. "Stone, continue."

"We want you to wear a wire when the time is right." Ray leaned forward, crowding the old man and hoping he was up to the task. "Meanwhile, you'll keep doing dispatch and carry on with business as usual. Be sure to keep telling Krantz little bits of information, which I, by the way, will supply. After we've dealt with Krantz and his meth lab connections, you will quietly resign, never to grace these premises again."

"No charges?" Ope said.

"We'll arrange with the District Attorney for you to plead no contest and receive a suspended sentence," Mullins said.

"That's the best you can do?"

"That's the best I'm willing to do," Mullins said.

"Now," Ray said, "What can you tell me about Hinter?"

Chapter 26

Ray

Ray drove down the crowded Interstate towards Crestville and the county jail while mulling over the meeting with Ope. The former officer had looked like a broken man, shuffling as he clung to his walker on the way to his desk. Gone was the bravado. Ray didn't feel sorry for Ope—the man had brought his troubles on himself—but he sensed Ope's remorse for his actions was heartfelt.

Ray's cell buzzed—he'd silenced the ring during the interview. He glanced at the screen, then hit speaker. Sophie. "Hey, sweetheart. What's up?" He glanced in his mirrors, pulled into the left lane, accelerated, and bypassed an eighteen-wheeler, ending up behind a string of slow-moving cars. As a whiff of diesel fuel entered the Taurus, a vista of tree-covered hills appeared to the right, only to be blocked by another huge truck.

"I thought you might like to know the doctor discharged Bubba Flocker to county custody a few minutes ago. A couple of deputies brought him out through the ED."

"I thought that happened on Monday." Ray glanced at the time while looking for a way to move quicker.

"It was supposed to, then the doc decided to hold him for a couple of days."

"How'd he look today?" He moved right and bypassed

part of the jam, then found himself behind another truck.

"Like he could breathe better. He gave me a big thumbs up and thanked me for saving his ass."

"More than his ass, I'd say."

"Whatever. The nurses upstairs said he was a model patient and prisoner. So much so, the deputy left his station for a few minutes this morning to flirt with one of the staff."

"And?" Ray paused. "I feel like there's more." A sign announced the first Crestville exit. He stayed in the right lane.

"Yup. While he was unguarded, his mama dropped in to see him."

"No one called the deputy?" He didn't like the breach of protocol.

"No. They said it was his mama. The problem with all that is I heard a couple ranting in the cafeteria about how the deputy allowed the mama to visit, but he always went into the room with her. They thought that was an invasion."

Ray fumed. "I've forgotten how folks in the south think, I suppose." Ray exited the highway and stopped at the sign at the end of the ramp. "What do you want to do for dinner? I was thinking we could try the new Cuban place in Crossville."

"Sounds good. First one home feeds Mischief and takes her out."

"I'm at the Sheriff's now. Maybe I'll track down Flocker while I'm here. Just to be social."

"Right. Mr. Ambassador himself."

Ray laughed. "Love you." He disconnected, parked, and made his way inside.

The department had interview rooms on the second floor. He found Detective Shim, who agreed to show him the ropes on how to have a prisoner brought upstairs to interview. As it turned out, due to budget deficiencies, there weren't enough jail deputies available to deliver Hinter. Shim slipped on his sport coat and led the way to retrieve the prisoner. A well-muscled, male deputy—guard—met them at the door on the second floor of the department and escorted them to the minimum-security cellblock.

IMPERFECT ESCAPE

The aging facility, which was painted ugly beige with poop-brown trim, was much too small for the population. Ray learned it had a capacity of around two-fifty and today held nearly four hundred inmates. The deputy escorting them explained two things were in play. First, funding for expansion was limited, as was money for staffing. Second, the county was forced by state law to accommodate overflow from the prison system. The state also required them to keep some of their own prisoners beyond the customary one-year county jail maximum. They even had a *lifer* in the maximum-security section, which Ray found disconcerting.

Ray stroked his goatee and peered through the windows into the various cell blocks. Men played cards and paced in circles in the crowded enclosures. Mattresses covered much of the floor space and others were rolled and shoved against the wall. The interior of the no-privacy bathroom was partially visible from the window. Flashing to the cleaner and more humane facilities in Coral Bay, Florida, where he last worked, he was shocked by the comparison.

He spotted Hinter talking to Flocker on the far side of the room. "That's him. Why isn't Flocker in sick bay?"

"There weren't room, so we put him here." The guard shrugged.

"Is the sheriff willing to accept the liability? The man was on a ventilator a couple of days ago."

"Sheriff accepts worse. If Flocker weren't okay to be here, the doc shouldn't have sent him." The guard opened the door and waited.

Ray and Shim entered the cell block.

The smell of unbathed bodies engulfed Ray. He ignored the stench and approached Flocker. "Sophia said you'd been discharged from the hospital today. Glad to see you've recovered."

"Fine woman you have there, Stone." Flocker snickered and stepped away, putting several feet between himself and the detectives.

Ray thought to pursue the comment, noting a hint of

threat in Flocker's soft voice. He mentally filed it next to Sophia's report of her ED conversation with the man.

Rather than take Hinter back to the detective division, Ray and Shim escorted Hinter into one of the interview rooms in central booking, cuffed him to the chair, stepped outside, and left him alone.

"You might want to hang around if you have time." Ray said. "Hinter sells the majority of his shit within my city limits, but he ventures out into the county, too. I have reason to believe he may be one of the biggest dealers outside of Silken's network."

After Shim raised a questioning brow, Ray repeated Ope's response to his question about Hinter. "That's what I'm here to pursue."

Shim nodded and followed Ray into the room, taking a chair next to the table in the center of the room.

Ray sat across from Hinter and surveyed the small space. The unadorned ugly beige box held a bolted-down, battered metal table and four unmatched chairs. Once settled, he poked at Hinter with loaded questions suggested by Ope's comments.

"Listen, man," Hinter whined, "I admitted I use the stuff. I admitted I stole the stuff off Silky. You confiscated the goods from the store. That's the whole deal. Now, take me back to my cell and leave me the hell alone."

Ray nodded to Shim, and they both left the interview room.

"I suggest you call the prosecutor," Shim said. "Maybe we can get a deal for him to flip. If what Ope told you is true, Hinter has inside information on the meth trade in the county." After telling the guard they were leaving Hinter alone to cook, Shim led the way upstairs to his desk.

Ten minutes later, Ray had secured the DA's promise to not prosecute Hinter with any crimes he might confess to in the course of the interview. The charges for theft of the appliances and possession of methamphetamine would stand. Hinter needed to plead guilty to those and accept the standard sentence or risk additional charges and jail time.

IMPERFECT ESCAPE

Shim pushed back his chair. "I'll hang around until you're done downstairs."

"Good." Ray called Holly Aster, the public defender assigned to Hinter, who agreed to come right over from the courthouse next door when she finished a hearing. "I'll meet you downstairs in the lobby and update you on what's happening." He waited for about thirty minutes near the Sheriff's Department rear door, using the time to review the case and his suspicion Hinter was in up to his scrungy hair.

When Ray saw her approach, he extended his hand. "Twice in one day."

"Hello again, Detective."

"Do you think you have a conflict representing both Hinter and Ope?" While it was possible to do so without conflict, it was, he believed, difficult to walk on both sides of the same fence with objectivity.

"No. I'm court appointed for Hinter. If the lawyers in town didn't represent more than one person charged with drug related crimes at the same time, we'd need to quadruple the number of practicing attorneys in town, which isn't going to happen."

"Point taken."

"Trust me, I can keep their concerns separate. If there's a problem, I'll go to the court and ask to be replaced."

"I suppose that's fair." Ray took a moment to update Aster on the proposed deal with Hinter, then waved in the direction of lockup.

"You'll give me a few minutes with my client," she said, "then we'll go from there."

Once back in the jail, another deputy—this one a short, plump female—opened the door to Hinter's room for Aster and Ray.

Hinter reared back in his chair and likely would have stood but for the restraints. "What the hell is she doing here? You have no right."

"Mr. Hinter," Aster said, "I assure you he does have a right. You were read your rights at booking, and you asked for counsel. We met, we talked, and I told you at the time not to discuss your case with the detectives without me present. Now, you and I need to talk about what is going down here. You have some important decisions to make."

Hinter glared at Ray. The befuddled-druggie persona gone. Hinter jerked his head, signaling the lawyer he'd talk with her.

She stepped into the interview room and pulled the door closed behind her. A few minutes later, she reappeared. "Let's get this over with."

Ray entered and took the chair across the small, square table from Hinter and motioned Aster to another. As Ray had suspected, Hinter was smarter than he acted, playing the part of the confused—hick meth head. "So, Hinter, I've been led to believe you haven't been forthcoming."

"Who says?"

"We're asking the questions." Ray took his time removing a sheet of paper from his pocket and laying it on the table. "I know Ms. Aster explained it, but here's the deal. In exchange for your truthful testimony, the DA will not press additional charges. If, on the other hand, we find you were less than truthful, we will throw out the deal and charge you with every crime you've committed."

"That's what my lawyer said."

She nodded.

"What's your decision?"

"I'll go along to get along." His tone remained in control, the meth head gone.

"We know you've been dealing meth," Ray said, leaning closer. "Who's your supplier?"

"More like, who was my supplier. I got the goods from LeRoy Vast."

"I thought LeRoy cooked for Silken? At least, that's the word on the street."

"Oh, he did. But he made a lot more meth than he sent up the line to Silken. Me, and some other boys, worked for Vast. Ran his product all over the county." Hinter laughed.

IMPERFECT ESCAPE

"Drives Silken friggin' nuts. Can't figure out who his competition is."

"How did you explain your activity to Silken?"

"Didn't. I sell for him, too. Yeah, I swiped the appliances, but I didn't steal product. I stop down there, and he hands the stuff to me. That way he knows I'm selling. He just don't know how much shit I got moving."

"What do you know about the explosion at Vast's?"

"Nothing, man. That's the God's honest truth." Hinter slipped back into his meth-head persona. "I think Silky's behind it, though. Maybe someone ratted on us."

"Who else was selling for Vast?"

"Can't say." Hinter stiffened. "I gots to live here for a spell. I don't want to end up dead."

Ray stood. "We'll give some thought to whether you're living up to your end of the agreement. We'll have more questions later. This interview is over."

"Ms. Aster, let's go." He led the way upstairs to the detective suite and held the door for the lawyer.

Aster stopped near Shim's desk and faced Ray. "He was forthcoming. Do I have your commitment to the deal?"

"Actually, ma'am, I think he left out a load of stuff. Why else would he have said he felt threatened and then clammed up? There's more for your client to say on the matter."

"Be sure I'm there for the whole conversation next time, whether he wants me there or not. Or, next time we'll be talking to the judge." She scowled and clenched her jaw.

"Of course." Ray turned away.

After a miffed Aster left the office, Ray said, "If Hinter agrees to testify against Silken—and Vast, when we find him—I'm inclined to take the deal. There is still a missing piece. I'm sure of that, but I don't think we'll get it from Hinter."

"Let me run the agreement and Hinter's statement past the sheriff first. But, I think he'll be good with it. You'll be able to bag Hinter again when he's back on the street. He never behaves for very long."

Chapter 27

Ray

Following the less than satisfying jailhouse interview with Ken Hinter, Ray headed up the mountain to Plateauville. A quick check of traffic conditions on I-40 confirmed the minor eastbound backup earlier that morning was now a major jam, thanks to the scheduled road repair.

He opted for US-70N, the original highway crossing the state. Built on the Avery Trace, it led pioneers to that section of Tennessee land the government said they could own if they farmed it, resulting in the area being dubbed *The Promised Land*.

He needed to think, and the two-lane road would provide the opportunity, along with lush trees, the occasional sharp drop off, and a scattering of well-maintained farms, little white churches, and homes in every state of repair. That particular stretch of US-70N reminded him of the road outside his hometown in Virginia. It brought back memories—some of them pleasant. Others, like the death of his first wife and the unlawful behavior of his former chief, caused him to shudder and redirect his thoughts to the criminals in Plateauville.

The road east of Crestville began with a gentle slope. Ray sped up to sixty, a smidge over the limit, and settled back to enjoy the drive, knowing he'd be slowing down numerous times for tiny residential areas and curves severe enough to warrant yellow, rectangular warning signs.

IMPERFECT ESCAPE

Checking his mirrors, he noted a white SUV about fifty yards back. From a distance, it looked like a sheriff's vehicle—the department had opted to replace aging vehicles with powerful Ford Interceptor SUVs. He slowed to the posted limit of fifty-five. While he doubted he'd be ticketed, there was no reason to encourage an encounter.

Over the next few miles, the Ford closed the following distance, allowing Ray to ascertain the vehicle was an Explorer, and not an official ride. The dotted, white center lines on the upcoming stretch of road indicated a brief passing zone. He slowed a bit more and edged toward the right, encouraging the driver to go around him.

Instead, the driver lurched forward to within inches of Ray's bumper, then dropped away.

Ray lowered the driver's side window to better hear engine sounds from the outside—but he only heard wind.

The terrain on both sides of the road was rough, and there hadn't been any buildings since before the last big curve. The left shoulder was edged by irregular concrete barricades and gave way to a steep, wooded two-hundred-foot drop. The other shoulder widened, abutting a gradual incline.

In the rearview mirror, the driver, a stocky-appearing male, wore a dark brown shirt. Ray got the notion it was Krantz in his personal vehicle. In an earlier conversation, Krantz had commented about his wife driving a white Ford Explorer that was similar to the new department Interceptors. The similarity worked to Krantz's advantage as he pursued his activities on his Uncle Silky's behalf.

Again, behaving aggressively, the man—maybe Krantz—revved his engine and encroached further before swinging a few degrees left into the oncoming lane and accelerating.

Ray surged forward in an effort to stay ahead of the SUV and avoid the maneuver he suspected was coming. The trailing driver kept pace, stifling Ray's plan.

Ray slowed—a move mimicked by his tormentor. A slower speed would lessen the effect of a collision. He hit his radio to call for assistance. "I'm on 70 N. About eight miles out. Someone is trying to run me off the road."

The driver continued to keep pace, expertly adjusting his vehicle's position.

Ope, the dispatcher in Plateauville PD, said, "I'll—"

Ray felt a slam to the Taurus's left rear. Feeling the spin to the left, he attempted to steer in that direction, but the hit was strong enough his vehicle lost partial contact with the pavement and spun out of control.

Still in the process of spinning, Ray's Taurus cleared the barricade and rolled.

Once.

Twice.

Three times.

It crashed, upside down, with the passenger side against a huge oak in the gulley at the bottom of the hill.

Ray fought to stay conscious in the overturned car. First, he moved his extremities. The left leg hurt like a demon, but wasn't stuck. His head felt as if it were split open. He turned it from side to side and heard no crunching in his neck.

He braced his left forearm against the crushed ceiling, then released his seatbelt, thanking God it had held tight. He marveled that none of the air bags had deployed.

The strong odor of spilling fuel filled the passenger compartment.

Switching forearms on the ceiling, Ray moved his left hand to the window controls on the door, fumbling to open the window. Then he remembered having opened it earlier. There was no broken glass in front of the opening, and the area looked clear. He needed to summon the strength to ease out.

As the smell of gas increased, he grabbed the doorframe with both hands and squeezed himself halfway through the bent window opening, stopping to rest and clear his head for a moment.

Focusing all of his efforts into his arms and right leg, he slid onto the ground, then rolled away. The pain in his left leg and head escalated with each movement. He came to rest near

IMPERFECT ESCAPE

a massive fallen tree, which blocked his forward progress.

With great effort, he crawled over the tree and dropped to the moss-covered ground on the far side.

He felt the ground vibrate and a flash of heat, then heard a boom.

Chapter 28

Sophia

Sophia heard the radio transmission signal an incoming ambulance with an escort from the Sheriff's Department. The victim, a law enforcement officer, was unconscious following a rollover motor vehicle accident involving an explosion. The estimated time of arrival was under ten minutes. She felt the same surge of adrenalin that pushed her through many a trauma alert.

Sophia's co-worker in the ED's trauma rooms for the day was Ricky Tondo, who'd left for lunch ten minutes earlier. She leaned over the nursing station counter and spoke to the secretary. "Page Ricky and ask him to head back STAT, please."

Dr. Gold perched on a stool near the radio. Based on his conversation with the paramedics, he'd ordered the OR to hold an open room. Radiology, laboratory, and respiratory technicians were standing by. Gold would decide about the need to call the trauma surgeon when he saw the victim.

Sophia surveyed her assigned trauma room to assure its readiness, pulled a couple of bags of IV solution off the shelf, and positioned them on the counter near the stretcher. She pulled the code cart a few inches away from the wall so she could move it without interference if required and went out to the ambulance entrance canopy to await the arrival of her next patient.

IMPERFECT ESCAPE

The ambulance swept in, and the paramedics pushed the door open.

Stretching tall on her toes, she noted the patient inside was breathing on his own and had not been intubated. An IV line ran into the victim's left arm.

Familiar-looking shoes poked from beneath the thin blanket. She thought the man was Ray. Her gaze jumped to his face.

"I can do this," she said, her quiet whisper shaky.

The two paramedics—Shelly, a tall, middle-aged female and John, a short, beefy younger male—eased the stretcher from the ambulance.

Shelly said, "MVA victim is Ray Stone."

"I know. He's my fiancée." Sophia's voice cracked.

"You have someone to take this for you?"

"Not at this moment. I'll get help as soon as we move him inside."

"Okay," Shelly said, "Vitals are stable. He was unconscious at the scene and has a small laceration and large hematoma over his left ear. The situation at the scene suggested he crawled from his overturned vehicle and pulled himself to safety, avoiding the explosion."

"Anything else?" Sophia glanced down the hall hoping to see Ricky. She'd do what needed to be done in the meantime.

"We saw no burns or other injuries except for a four-inch gash above his left ankle," John said.

"Broken?"

"Don't know."

As Shelly and John continued their report, Sophia helped guide the stretcher into the trauma bay. She saw Ricky trot down the hallway in Dr. Gold's wake.

"Ricky, thank God you're here," she said. "The victim is my Ray. Please take over. I'll help." She fought to still the shaking in her hands and the dread in her heart.

"Fine." Ricky hurried into position and helped transfer Ray to the hospital gurney. He eased Sophia aside and continued providing care. "Stand away. I'll handle it."

"But, I—" she said, her voice breaking.

"Lady, I'll take care of him. Move." Ricky used the voice he reserved for out-of-control patients and visitors.

Sophia moved. She struggled to maintain her professional composure, knowing if she didn't, she'd be asked to leave the room.

An hour later, various physicians and techs had examined, x-rayed, and scanned Ray. He was restless and beginning to waken.

Sophia remained at his side.

Dr. Gold said, "He suffered a severe concussion, but there's no bleeding inside the skull." He pointed to an image of the inside of Ray's head on the bedside computer screen. "This is limited and will resolve. As soon as he wakes up fully and can lie still, I'll suture his leg wound." He touched the computer screen, bringing up an x-ray image of Ray's leg. "There's no fracture. He's a lucky man. From what Shelly and John said, if he hadn't pulled himself out of the vehicle, he'd be dead."

"What happens next?" Sophia asked, an unusual question for a nurse to be sure, but she wasn't feeling as much a nurse as a family member.

"Dr. Clark is on his way in."

"Neurosurgeon? I thought you said there was no bleeding inside the skull."

"I don't see any evidence on the film and neither did the radiologist who read it. But, given the severity of the accident—the medics think he rolled three times—I want another opinion. Clark will, no doubt, admit him for a couple of days."

"Sophie," Ray said, his voice soft, the bass notes rumbling.

"Hi, baby. How do you feel?" She stroked his face, stopping at the edge of his goatee. Tears welled in her eyes.

"Like I was run off the road."

"Good thing you got out of the car."

He drifted off for a moment, then opened his eyes. He said, "I think whoever ran me off the road. Maybe Krantz.

IMPERFECT ESCAPE

Looked like Krantz . . ." Ray dozed. He awoke with a start and continued telling Sophia about the incident and the Ford Explorer, then he went back to sleep.

Sophia faced Ricky. "I put out a suture tray. Meanwhile, if it's okay with you, I'm going to find Sarah and ask to go off duty."

"Fine by me."

Sophia found her manager, clocked out, and returned to the trauma room. As she walked, she answered a call from Jimmy Johnson on her personal cell phone. He asked about Ray's condition.

"Concussion. He'll be in here a couple of days, I think. Are you handling the investigation?"

"No, it's a sheriff's case because it happened in the county. Ray said he was being forced off the road when he made his distress call."

"That's what he told me a few minutes ago."

"He's awake?"

"Was. Fell back to sleep. Just as well. His head has to hurt like a sucker." She paused. "He said some other things, too." She repeated the conversation.

"Sophia, if you need anything, I'm here for you. Keep me posted. I'll relay the information to the chief."

"Thanks, Jimmy. Let me know if you hear anything, please."

She stepped into the room and found a tall, slim, grey-suited black man watching Ray snooze.

He stuck out his hand. "Sophia, I'm Erik Shim." The gold badge on his belt indicated he was a deputy. "I'm the sheriff's investigator working with Ray."

"On the exploded meth labs, I assume. Ray said you're another South Florida transplant."

Shim nodded. "I lived there a few years. I'm closer to home now."

"You'll find the bastard who ran him off the road?"

"What makes you say it's deliberate?" Shim raised a brow.

"He told me before he passed out again." For the second

time, she repeated Ray's earlier comments. "He also said his airbags didn't deploy. He suspects someone disabled them while the car sat in the PD lot in Plateauville."

Shim stepped away from the stretcher. "Well, the skid marks at the scene suggest he was, indeed, forced off the road. I'm hoping he comes around and can answer a few questions."

Chapter 29

Sophia

On Friday, Sophia went through her morning routine with Ray on her mind. She'd stayed at the hospital with him until almost eight the previous evening but had to go home to feed and walk Mischief. By then, Ray had been awake for several hours and had moved past the crisis.

After taking Mischief into the yard for her morning outing, she called Ray's room at the hospital. When he answered, she said, "Mornin', sweetheart, how y'all doin'?"

In a deep, sleepy voice he replied, "Soundin' mighty Southern." He chuckled. "I'm fine, I think. The doctor wants me to stay one more day and repeat a couple of the scans to make sure there is no bleeding and that my brain cells aren't too rattled."

"I told him your head was hard enough to protect you."

"Don't make me laugh. It gives me a headache."

"Oops."

"How was Mischief when you got home?"

"Upset, hungry, but she didn't have an accident. Good puppy. She slept in the bed with me."

"Doesn't she always when I'm not around?"

Sophia laughed.

"What's your plan for the day?" Ray said.

"I need to do a couple loads of laundry before heading in

to you."

"You're off today. I forgot."

"The beauty of working three twelves."

They chatted awhile longer, then Sophia grabbed the basket, the dog, and her purse. The morning was cool, as usual on *the mountain*. It would warm up later—she'd heard to the high eighties—but by then she planned to be in air-conditioning.

Somewhere in the night, she'd remembered her conversation with the ladies while doing her wash in Crossville and their scathing comments about Jasper, the attendant at the Plateauville laundry. Maybe he would give her more information about meth.

The drive from the Cove into the main part of town took ten minutes. She parked in front of the door and looked inside. As the ladies at the Crossville laundry had described, the laundromat was grungy and in general disrepair. Several broken machines sat in the back near a pool table.

Sophia grabbed her basket and Mischief's leash and made her way inside. She half expected to be told dogs weren't allowed, but a scruffy-looking man in the office nodded a greeting and went back to scratching at his beard.

She piled her clothes into two adjacent machines. The task was complicated since Mischief jumped at every sock, succeeded in capturing one, and attempted to kill it. Sophia rolled a large wire cart over to her spot and put her basket in it. Then she moved to a row of chairs, sat, and pulled out her iPhone. Mischief settled in at her feet, accepting a chicken flavored chewy in lieu of Ray's smelly sock.

A few minutes later, the man from the office wandered over, his gait unsteady. He was boney and bent a bit at the waist. "Good morning, ma'am. I haven't seen you in here before." With shaking hand, he petted Mischief, who licked his fingers and returned to chewing. "I had a Boston Terrier when I was a kid."

The man had no trace of a Southern accent.

"My name's Sophia." She extended a hand.

IMPERFECT ESCAPE

"Jasper. Donald Jasper. But here, I'm just Jasper." He looked at her hand but didn't offer his. "Mind if I sit here and pet your pup?"

"Her name is Mischief. Be my guest."

Jasper sat a chair away.

"I'm surprised you don't have an accent," Sophia said.

"You don't either."

"I was born in North Dakota, ended up in Florida. Now I'm here, working at the hospital in Crestville. I'm an emergency department nurse."

"Why'd you move here?"

"My fiancé's job." She decided to lie about the job, if asked, but he didn't. "How'd you get here, if you don't mind my asking?"

"I was in the Marines in Afghanistan. Got back. Couldn't get a job. Ended up here. Saw a sign advertising for an attendant. Took the job. Stayed on."

"Sounds very cut and dried."

"Ma'am, the details aren't relevant anymore." They met eyes for the first time.

"Seems sad."

Jasper shrugged.

They chatted while he rubbed the dog's head.

Mischief abandoned her chewy for the attention.

"It's none of my business, but as a nurse I like to know details. Will you tell me about your meth habit?"

Jasper shook his head as if shocked, then looked thoughtful. "Why not? It's obvious the stuff will be the death of me. Fact is, the doctor said if I don't give it up, it'll kill me within the year."

Sophia waited for him to continue. Her heart pounded in anticipation.

"You can see the condition I'm in. I have no real reason to quit using, so I won't."

"Suicide by drug of choice."

"You could say that."

"Where do you get your supply?"

"Why would you want to know?" Jasper said. "You don't look like the usin' type to me."

"I'm not, but I'd still like to know."

"It's a bit complicated." He shifted in his seat. "I sell a bit out of here for the man."

"Who is?"

"Carl Silken, himself. He owns this place—secretly, I'm told. Pays me minimum wage and supplements that with product if I continue to deal for him. I buy a bit extra from a dude named Hinter. Silky keeps a close inventory, and I don't want him to know how much I'm using. Need the job for a while yet."

"Okay. You're giving me a lot of free information. Why?"

"Well, I know your fiancé is the new detective in town. He hasn't been around to see me yet, so I figure I'd pass on the information through you. I'm a dead man walking, but I was honorable earlier in my life. Got a Silver Star and a couple of commendations. Want to die honorable, I suppose."

Sophia wondered why Jasper pretended not to know who she was at first. She decided to let it pass but to poke a bit and see what he knew. "Do you know anything about the fire and explosion at Vast's lab?"

"No."

"How about the attempt on Bubba Flocker's life?"

"Not that either. I do know there is someone in the area, other than Vast that is, who is trying to take Silky's place as king on this mountain. Seems to me one step in that process would be to cut off Silky's main lab, and that would have been Vast's. Flocker was cooking for Silky, too, but acting all sweet and innocent about the deal. Krantz, his dutiful nephew, drops by all the time trying to find out if I've heard anything. Several of the local users and lab employees—if you can call them that—hang out here. They talk, you know."

"Have you heard anything?"

"No, but I have some ideas."

"Which are?"

"I don't think you need to know that. Perhaps you'll send

IMPERFECT ESCAPE

your detective-honey around, and I'll tell him—for a consideration."

"I'll pass it on. He's in the hospital, though. Someone ran him off the road."

"Heard that."

"Do you know anything about it?"

"Not really. But I do know it wasn't Krantz, even though it was his vehicle." Jasper gave Mischief a final pat, stood, and shuffled away. "I was honorable once."

***

Sophia finished her laundry, took the pup home, grabbed a tote bag she'd prepared for Ray, and headed into Crestville. The day was already warm and humid, with rain in the forecast. She hoped to be inside the hospital before a deluge hit. Meanwhile, the sunshine and thick greenery on both sides of the highway down the mountain pleased her and lightened her mood.

Growing up in North Dakota, she'd learned that trees grew either in straight lines—shelter belts—or along river beds. In Florida, palm trees and carefully groomed tropical foliage surrounded her. The Tennessee woods were thick, lush, and a thousand shades of green.

She parked, ran through rain drops to the ED employee entrance, and sought out Ricky Tondo. Sometime during the last month they'd bonded. Maybe it was because she'd earned her place. Maybe it was because she didn't care he was gay. Maybe because he had awesome ED skills, and she respected him. Or, maybe because she simply wouldn't put up with his verbal shit.

She found him in the back of the main nursing station doing his charting. "Hey, Ricky. Got a second?"

"Sure." He tapped a key to blank out the computer screen and stood. "I heard your man is doing okay. In fact, I wandered over to the scan center and checked on his films a bit ago."

"And?"

"The radiologist told me there is no bleeding," Ricky said.

"The benefit of a good thick skull."

"Your words, not mine."

"Have you heard anything more from the paramedics or cops about the accident?" Sophia said.

"Not from the medics. They haven't been around. But a couple of deputies were in this morning, headed up to your man's room. I overheard them say the skid marks look like he was hit using a PIT."

"Which is?"

"A pursuit intervention technique. I know about it from going to auto races. I saw a whole TV segment on it before one of the big NASCAR events, too."

"Tell me more."

"The pursuing driver slaps his right front fender into the left rear of the forward car. From what I understand, it's a precise movement, a quarter turn of the wheel. That striking force lifts the target vehicle slightly and spins it to the left. The rear car skids to the right. So, in a racing situation, it looks like an accident, and the attacking driver apologizes. Meanwhile, he's forced the leading car off the road, or possibly into other cars."

"You think a race car driver attacked Ray?"

"No, baby, no. The cops adopted and learned the technique. Changed the name to PIT, though it is known by several others like *pit block*, *pit stop*, and *blocking*."

"Ah, shit."

"The deputies suspect the location of the attack was selected because it promised maximum damage to Ray's vehicle and a safe shoulder for the attacker."

"Attempted murder."

"Sounds like it." Ricky glanced down the hall. "Gotta go. When's your next shift?"

"Monday. I have the weekend off." Sophia watched Ricky trot down the hall and into a room with a blinking call light.

She left the ED, rode the elevator to Ray's floor, and found him in a patient gown, sitting in a bedside chair with a sheet over his knees, and watching CSI on TV. After kissing him

IMPERFECT ESCAPE

hello and examining the wound on the side of his head—it didn't have a bandage—she handed him the tote she carried. "I brought your stuff."

"Such as?" He peered into the bag.

"Underwear, lounging pants, tee shirts, and clothes to go home."

"Thanks, sweetheart." He stood and held onto the back of the chair for a moment. "Dizzy." He limped toward the bathroom with his butt showing through the opening in the back of the gown, reappearing in a couple of minutes dressed in the things from home.

"Better?" she said.

"Much. Those stupid gowns y'all force patients to wear don't cut it—leaves my ass out in the cold."

"*Au contraire*, my good man. The gowns provide us access to all the parts."

"Yeah." He scratched his head, staying clear of the sutures. "Sit."

"Arf." She giggled, pulled over a chair, and sat. "How does your left leg feel?"

"Like it was slashed with a dull knife, then sutured with a dull needle."

"Did they change the dressing this morning?"

"They did. Said the wound is clean."

"Good." Sophia told Ray about her conversation with Jasper.

"I'll take Jasper up on his invitation as soon as I'm out of here." He took a sip of water from an insulated cup on his overbed table. "Two interesting things. One, my attacker was not Krantz. His wife reported their SUV stolen that morning. Johnson, in fact, handled the call. Shim confirmed Krantz was working a traffic stop in Baxter—on the other side of the county—at the time."

"Makes you wonder if it was a carefully planned alibi."

"Sophie, you're jumping to conclusions. We know Krantz is a problem. We know he does things for his uncle. We suspect he tips off the meth labs to planned raids. But, there is no evidence he's a killer—or, in this case, an attempted killer."

"I guess you're right. You do know a special maneuver was used to force you off the road?"

"Heard about it this morning."

"We sure jumped from the stewpot into the fire pit, didn't we?"

"This too shall pass, my love."

Sophia sat with Ray for most of the afternoon, reading a mystery on her iPad while he watched the Red Sox-Yankee game. After dietary staff served his dinner tray, she headed back up the mountain, promising to return early in the morning so he could make his escape.

She pulled her MINI in behind Ray's Ram—Johnson had delivered the truck while she was gone. He said he'd put the keys under the mat, which she found as promised. As she stood to close the door, she heard someone speak her name.

Turning in the direction of the voice, she saw Deputy Krantz. "What can I do for you, Deputy?" She kept her hand on the open truck door, thinking it might be a convenient escape route.

Krantz took a few steps closer, stopping about five feet away.

With haste, she climbed into the Ram. Pulled the door closed. Turned the ignition. Cracked the window.

"What's wrong? You scared?"

"Uncomfortable would be the word. Now, what do you want?" She slipped her hand into her purse and grasped her weapon.

Krantz advanced a step. "What I want, little lady, is for you to quit poking around and asking questions."

"Or?"

"Hope that mutt of yours doesn't get eaten by a coyote—or something. Take it for what it's worth." He backed off, walked down the drive to his car, and left.

Sophia climbed out of the Ram, locked it up, and went into the house and, with shaking hands, dialed Johnson. "No

IMPERFECT ESCAPE

one is going to hurt my puppy," she said as the phone rang. She'd learned her lesson about going too far afield on her own.

Chapter 30

Sophia

On Saturday morning, Mischief's frantic licks on her face brought Sophia to consciousness. Her cell phone buzzed and vibrated on the bedside table. She grabbed the offending device, put the dog on the floor, and answered the call—the screen showed Ray's picture.

"Hey, baby," she said. "What's up? It's seven o'clock, for God's sake."

"The doctor just left. He said I can get out of here as soon as I have transportation." His voice was clear with no hint of slurring.

"Have you been out of bed? Are you still dizzy?"

"I'm dressed. The dizziness is gone, for the most part, unless I move suddenly. The doc said it would pass."

"When did he say you can go back to work?"

"Next week . . ." His voice dropped an octave and trailed off. "He told me to take it easy."

"And?"

"And I was thinking you can drive me around while I check on a few things."

"Don't think you should go to work, sweetheart. You need to heal." She didn't try to soften the edge in her voice.

"I'm doing a couple of things today, with or without your help."

IMPERFECT ESCAPE

"Men." She exhaled in exasperation, knowing arguing was futile and refusing would destroy their *working* relationship—meaning he wouldn't include her in his work when he could. "Fine. They'll serve breakfast in about thirty minutes, I think. I'll tend to Mischief, take her on a long walk, then head into town."

"Make sure you're carrying," Ray said.

Damn, she thought, he was going to be back on her case about carrying her Sig. "Yes, sir."

"Did Johnson bring my truck home?"

"He did."

"Drive that, please." He paused. "Did he put my equipment in it?"

"He said he did. And he brought your badge and weapon here last night after I called him."

"Hold that thought for a minute." Ray continued talking. His voice was audible, but muffled, as if he were talking to someone in the room. Then he said, "I just told the chief I'd use my personal vehicle for a couple of weeks, rather than a patrol car. Resources are limited. He's trying to find a replacement from one of the other PDs in the area. There's a town just north of us that downsized recently, so they might have an available vehicle." After another pause for a side conversation, he continued, "Why did you call Johnson last night?"

"Because Krantz stopped by and told me to quit poking around."

Ray cursed. "See you in a bit." The line went dead,

Sophia redirected her attention to Mischief, who was scratching and whining at the door. She took the dog out for a brief walk in the front yard, then washed and pulled on jeans and a tee. While Mischief scarfed her food, she grabbed a muffin. Breakfast was done in three minutes for both of them. She hooked on Mischief's leash and headed out for a longer walk. The puppy—because she still was a puppy—would be incarcerated in her crate for most of the day.

The walk around the golf course's lake was beautiful, as

usual. Sophia kept an eye out for golfers, but it was early and none had reached the hole skirting the water yet. She took her time, trudged around the back behind the dam and the water pump, and through a break in the trees. When she returned to the little house, the dog was panting, and Sophia felt energized. She crated Mischief and headed into Crestville.

After parking the Ram in front of the hospital, she called Ray to say she was there and went in through the front door. The lobby was deserted except for the information desk volunteer. Sophia nodded a greeting as she passed by on her way to the elevators.

Ray, favoring his left leg, stood near the fourth-floor elevator, his belongings in a clear plastic bag labeled *CMCC Patient Belongings*.

Sophia stretched on her toes to plant a kiss on Ray's lips, then went to the desk. "Okay if I walk him down?" she said to the charge nurse.

"Go for it." The harried looking, young nurse nodded toward Ray. "We couldn't get him to sit in a wheelchair while he waited. I doubt he'd cooperate with a chariot ride to the exit."

"For sure," Sophia said. "Anything I need to know?"

"We gave Detective Stone written directions. He asked for the dressing to cover the stitches over his ear. You can remove it whenever you like. The dressing on his ankle can be removed tomorrow for a shower and then left off. He's supposed to rest for the week and see the doctor on Friday."

"For all the good it will do." Sophia smiled, then moved to join Ray. "Let's go."

When they reached the parking lot, Sophia climbed into the Ram, using the handhold over the door to pull herself up. "Where to, master?" She giggled.

"Give me a minute. Where's my gear?"

"Under your seat."

She waited while Ray clipped his badge to the left side of his belt, his service weapon holster to the right, and his smaller personal weapon to his uninjured right ankle. Then she eased

IMPERFECT ESCAPE

out of the parking lot. "Where to?"

"Take 70N to Plateauville. I want to see the site where that ass forced me off the road."

"Don't you mean the scene of the attempt on your life?"

"When we figure out who it was, that's what he'll be charged with."

Sophia headed east, taking the route Ray traveled two days earlier.

"The chief didn't like the idea of you driving me around," Ray said, "but there is no one available to do it until Monday—unless Johnson decides he wants to work tomorrow. You're on an official ride-along. We'll stop by the station later, and you can sign the release. I also need to get a portable light bar for the dash and a radio."

"Really? I have to sign a friggin' release?"

"Yup. Direct orders, in fact."

They traveled east for several minutes on the scenic drive. Sophia saw the concrete barricades on the left.

"Pull over to the right here," he said.

Sophia parked on the side of the road, turned on the four-way flashers, and climbed down from the truck. It was already nine o'clock, and the day was warm, though it wasn't uncomfortably hot yet. The humidity hit her in the face.

Ray inspected what was left of the skid marks. The previous day's rain never became more than a drizzle, and traffic stayed light on the road unless I-40 was clogged.

"What do you think?"

He pointed to the marks. "The driver was skilled. It wasn't his first assault on a moving vehicle. I'm still surprised he hit me going that fast."

She followed him to the barricades. Two of them were knocked over, and several small trees lay on the ground. She pointed to a large charred tree. "The tree that saved your life, I presume."

Two things occurred to Sophia. One, it was lucky the explosion hadn't ignited a fire in the trees, and two, there was no doubt the attacker had intended to take Ray's life. Only by luck had he crashed into the huge tree.

***

Sophia pulled the Ram into one of the five vacant spaces directly in front of the laundromat. She pointed to the window of a small side room. "That's Jasper sitting in his little office."

"You can come in with me if you want, but do me a favor and don't participate in the conversation."

"Not even an introduction?"

"Not even." He rubbed the small bandage on his head then exited the truck. He waited for Sophia to join him on the sidewalk and held the door to the laundromat open for her.

"Thanks."

Motioning to her to stay back, Ray went into Jasper's office.

Sophia moved to an angle where she could see into the office and hear the conversation without being front and center.

Ray extended his badge. "Detective Stone, Plateauville PD."

"Glad you could stop by, Detective. I'm also, by the way, happy to see that son of a bitch didn't kill you." Jasper sat straighter in his chair and motioned to one in the corner. "Have a seat."

Ray pulled the chair closer to the battered desk and sat. He tipped his head in Sophia's direction. "She told me you were willing to talk—for a consideration. Which would be?"

Jasper looked thoughtful. "You know, Detective, I was a Marine. Semper fi. Proud to serve my country. Came home and things didn't go well. My fault, you understand. I could have stayed in the service."

Ray didn't say anything.

After several moments, Jasper said, "Anyway, your lady," he motioned toward Sophia, "was in here yesterday asking questions. I talked a bit, then she wanted more information. The thing is, she treated me like a person, not a meth head."

IMPERFECT ESCAPE

He paused. "I got to thinking about my telling her I had no reason to quit using meth. I have no family, no hope for one, no career, and basically no life. Maybe I can recapture the honor I had as a Marine. No quid pro quo. Ask your questions, sir."

Ray thought Jasper's words had the ring of truth. "It's my understanding that your pool table over there is a favorite for local users and meth lab workers."

"It is. Some come in to buy what I sell."

"Who do you sell for?"

"Silky. He owns this place as well."

"Sophia told me. Tell me what you hear from the pool players."

"I hear there's a war brewing." Jasper laughed. "Someone—I'm not sure who, but I have a suspicion—is looking to take over Silky's piece of the pie. Don't know quite how that works out, since Silky is the one with the connections to South Florida for both the supply chain and product sale."

What Sophia was hearing at that moment didn't jibe with her impression of Jasper and his station in life. She leaned closer, straining to hear every word.

"Who do you think wants Silken's turf?" Ray said.

"Maybe Flocker is moving out on his own?"

"I heard that as well."

"He pretended like Silken forced him to cook meth, but he'd been cooking it all along."

"Is he pushing into Silken's business?"

"Some. Silken knows. Flocker needs to watch his back. In jail, he's a sitting duck in a pond full of decoys."

"Anything else?"

"Yup. Krantz was in here last night. He wanted to know what your lady was asking me about. I'm sorry to say I was a little wired, you know what I mean, and I told him."

"Which explains the visit she received last night."

"I suppose it does."

The men talked awhile longer. When Ray asked, Jasper volunteered he had been a lieutenant in the Marine Corps.

Gregg E. Brickman

Ray stood, easing his weight onto his left leg. "Stay safe, Jasper. If I can do anything to give you a hand, let me know."

"Just keep your little lady safe—and her pup, too."

"I shall." Ray left Jasper's office and motioned to Sophia to join him.

They stepped out into the searing mid-July heat.

"No matter how hot it gets, I can always look at my phone and see that it's hotter in Florida," she said.

"It's a small reward." Ray wiped his brow. "Next stop, Silken's Dry Goods Store."

They climbed into the truck, and Sophia started the engine and turned the air-conditioning to max.

"Can I come in and listen?"

"No."

Sophia stuck her tongue out at him, then drove down the street, around the corner, and turned right at the light. The drive to the store took all of two minutes, including waiting at the red light. She sat in the truck pouting, playing with her phone, and watching Ray at work.

He returned to the truck ten minutes later. "That bastard delivers heating oil in the middle of July—for all the good it did to question him."

"What did he say?" Sophia said.

"That he is an upstanding citizen, doesn't have anything to do with the meth trade, and if I don't quit harassing him, his friend the Judge will see to it that I never work in this county again."

"I know you didn't expect a confession."

"No, I didn't. What I hope to do is provoke some thoughtless action on his part."

"Like trying to kill you again?" she said.

"Wasn't Silken and not on his orders. I believe it was a setup, pure and simple. Someone trying to throw the blame on Krantz and Silken by association. It was Krantz's usual off-duty day, but the lieutenant called him in to work at the last minute because of staffing."

"Hence, he has a perfect alibi."

IMPERFECT ESCAPE

"That he does. And his wife noticed the Suburban was stolen and reported it early. The frame-up didn't work."

"However, the killing almost did." Sophia started the truck.

"You're right. My head hurts." He patted the bandage on the side of his head. "I want to stop by the station next."

"No, dear. You're going home. It's time. We can sign papers and get the lights another day."

"But..."

Sophia glared at him, popped the Ram into reverse, and backed into the street. "Going *home*."

After about three minutes, Ray said, "You're off tomorrow. Right?"

"Yes."

"I'd like you to drive out and visit Kelly Ann Vast."

"I can do that," Sophia said. "Why?"

"You have a good rapport with her. I'm convinced LeRoy is hiding, hurt, and in danger. Find out where he is."

Chapter 31

Sophia

Sophia slipped out of bed on Sunday, making a special effort not to disturb Ray. It was his habit to be up early, and most of the time she'd find him reading at the kitchen table, having already taken Mischief for a walk. But he'd had a restless night, complaining of both headache and leg pain. She'd checked his pupils and balance—which was iffy—then decided he'd done too much during the day.

After starting coffee, she released Mischief from her crate and went for a walk. When she returned, Ray was in the kitchen sipping from his extra-large mug. He looked pale and in pain. His hair needed combing and his goatee needed a trim.

"How do you feel?"

"Run over by a truck."

She exhaled in a huff. "What did you expect? You ignored doctor's orders. You should have come right home."

"I had things to do." The edge in his voice conveyed both annoyance and frustration.

"Right. Think you'll be able to do them if you're back in the hospital?"

He extended his arms, inviting a hug. "Let's not fight. It makes my head hurt."

She moved into his embrace. "I think you need to stay put for a couple of days and rest. There is nothing to be gained by

IMPERFECT ESCAPE

rushing back to work."

"Maybe so. I'll tell you what. I'll rest today, while you track down Kelly Ann. I don't foresee you getting into much trouble. Then, we'll decide about tomorrow, tomorrow."

Sophia nodded. It was a compromise of sorts, but she hadn't expected him to lay low for very long. Once she left the house on Monday morning, he'd go to work anyway.

They ate scrambled eggs and English muffins for breakfast and talked about her plans for the day.

"The first thing I have to do is call the hospital and see if the baby has been discharged," Sophia said. "I checked on her Friday, and the nursery told me she was about ready to go home. I also learned that Kelly Ann's mother spent most of every day at the hospital with the baby."

Sophia called the hospital and discovered that baby Vast had been discharged the previous evening. The babe's mother, grandmother, and grandfather had picked her up.

"I'll bet they've left the friend's house and gone back to the mother's house in Lebanon, which is this side of Nashville, I think."

"It is." Ray scowled. "I don't think that will keep Krantz and whoever else is after LeRoy out of her hair. Seems a simple matter to find her."

"Kelly Ann told me she grew up on a farm north of Lebanon. But, she also said her mother remarried after Kelly Ann left home and now lived in another place. New name, new farm."

"Sweetheart," Ray said in a tolerant tone of voice, "don't ever think Krantz is dumb. Misguided perhaps, rogue possibly, stupid no."

"Can't you guys do something about him? I mean really." She rolled her eyes.

"First we would have to prove he's done something wrong. Visiting his uncle and showing up at raids isn't illegal."

"How about threatening Kelly Ann?"

"Her word—and that's the word of the wife of a meth producer—against his. He's allowed to visit his aunt and his

Gregg E. Brickman

uncle for that matter. If people in the police and Sheriff's Department were expelled because of their relatives' behavior, we'd have no one in law enforcement. Me included, I might add."

Sophia laughed. Point taken. "So, how do I find Kelly Ann?"

"Try the cell number she gave you to give me."

"Duh." Sophia did, and had Kelly Ann on the phone a moment later. "Kelly Ann, I'd like to come over and talk to you, if I may."

"What about?"

"We shouldn't discuss it on the phone. My fiancé suggested I come to you. Did you know he was run off the road the other day?"

"I saw it in the Crestville paper. Was it Krantz's doing?"

"Not directly, no. Where are you? I'll take a road trip, and it will give me a chance to meet Keri Lynn, too."

"Hang on a minute." There were voices in the background, then Kelly Ann came back on the line. "This is the address." She gave the address and general directions. "Call me before you turn up the drive. My stepfather has a couple of things set up to deter intruders. Plan to get here in late afternoon. They're going to church, then they have a lunch thing. I want them here."

"Okay." Sophia thought for a moment. "I'll leave here about three o'clock. I guess it'll take me about an hour and a half to get there."

"Probably two. Come alone or you won't get on the property," Kelly Ann said, then hung up without saying goodbye.

Sophia repeated the conversation to Ray.

"I'm having second thoughts about sending you alone."

"You have no choice."

"I could ask Johnson to go with you."

"If I show up with a cop, that'll be a huge breach of trust—what little she has."

Ray looked thoughtful. "I suppose, you're right. She would

IMPERFECT ESCAPE

never have told me where she is. Make sure you take your weapon."

"Of course."

Several hours later, Sophia grabbed her purse, showed Ray the gun stowed inside, then kissed him and patted Mischief goodbye.

Ten minutes after that, she rolled onto I-40, headed west to Lebanon. Traffic was light, and she zipped along, admiring the pines and oaks, which shimmered in the sunlight. The drive to the Lebanon exit took an hour. Then the GPS gave three wrong turns and led her into a dead end. She laughed at the sign that read *GPS Wrong, No Outlet,* cursed under her breath, and turned around. After stopping and asking directions at a service station, she found the address, having extended her travel time by an exhausting hour.

The location was a ranch, with a fancy, dark-stained, four-rail fence bordering the property. The fence seemed to go on forever, turning the corner and continuing along the intersecting road. She pulled over and called Kelly Ann as directed, receiving a go-ahead to enter the property.

Sophia slowed and drove until she found the entrance, then made her way to the two-story, brick farmhouse, parking in the circular driveway in front of the door.

Kelly Ann appeared and greeted her. "Hi, Sophia."

"Sorry I'm late. I had quite the GPS guided tour, but it was hard to miss the place once I found the right road." She waved her hand at the expanse of land. Black Angus cattle dotted the pastures on both sides. Three horses stood in a paddock behind the house. Barns and outbuildings sat toward the back. Sophia noted other smaller houses within the fencing. Employees or family? she wondered.

"My stepfather—his name is Warren—done well. Oops, my stepfather has done well. Mama wants me to talk some better. To talk better."

"You're looking good," Sophia said. Kelly Ann appeared well-groomed and healthy. Her jeans and overblouse looked new and fit her post-baby chubbiness. Sophia imagined she was normally slender. The most striking difference was Kelly Ann's hair was washed, cut, and colored, and light makeup concealed the trace of pock marks from teenage acne along her jaw.

"Come inside." Kelly Ann stepped away from the door and disappeared into the next room, reappearing a moment later with the baby in her arms.

Sophia glanced around the home. It looked comfortable with wood floors, leather sofas, and heavy wooden tables. Then she raised her arms and accepted the baby from Kelly Ann.

"She's beautiful. I can see she's gaining weight."

"Mama took breast milk to the hospital every day. Now that she's here, she's taken to the breast like one of Warren's piglets."

Sophia laughed.

Kelly Ann led the way to the living room and sat in a worn-looking recliner.

Sophia followed, baby in arms, selecting the chair next to Kelly Ann. "What are your plans, may I ask?"

"I don't know for sure. I can stay here for now, forever, Warren says."

"What about LeRoy?"

"He's still alive."

"That's why I'm here. Ray needs to track him down and get his side of the story."

"Will he arrest him?"

"I suppose he will, but he'll also make sure he gets medical attention. At the moment, the police don't know if LeRoy is an arsonist or a victim."

"LeRoy isn't a killer. All he did was cook the meth and deliver it to Silken. He's hurt bad."

"When was the last time you saw him?"

"Yesterday. Warren drove me there. Drove."

"And?"

"LeRoy's arm is infected. It looked green to me. We changed the dressing and left him with plenty of food and water."

"Kelly Ann, LeRoy will die of gangrene and infection if

IMPERFECT ESCAPE

he doesn't get medical treatment. Tell me where he is, and Ray will see he gets care."

Warren and Ella Hogarth stepped in from a side room.

"Honey," Ella said, "tell her. You don't want your child's father to die. It'll be okay in the end."

"And when LeRoy gets released from prison, we'll help him get a fresh start, too," Warren said.

Chapter 32

Ray

Ray awoke when he heard Sophia return from Lebanon late Sunday afternoon. Mischief, who had been nestled in the crook of his arm, jumped off the bed. Though Ray's dizziness had passed a couple of hours earlier, he still felt out of sorts. He hoped he didn't have to retrieve Vast right away.

"Hey, sweetheart," he said when she entered the room, "what did you learn?"

She grinned. "I learned Kelly Ann Vast has a beautiful baby, wonderful parents, and she isn't as dumb as she acts."

"Nice to know. Did she tell you where her husband is?"

"She did. He's hiding in a cabin a couple of miles past the main house on a friend's property." She held up a slip of paper with the address. "She saw him yesterday, and he looked awful. The arm is infected, and he was feverish."

"Charming." Ray moved the dog, then sat on the side of the bed. His head didn't spin. "What's he doing for it?"

"Kelly Ann and her stepfather took him dressings, antibiotic ointment, and food. From her description, he's fading." She went on to relay the remainder of the details she'd learned at the farm, including the fact Kelly Ann's stepfather would visit Vast, who is armed by the way, at his hideout in the morning.

Ray grabbed his phone and called Johnson. "Vast is hiding

IMPERFECT ESCAPE

in a cabin behind the house Fred Jones owns out on Dripping Springs."

Johnson said, "You want to head out there tonight?" Ray heard the sounds of a baseball game in the background.

"No, tomorrow. Kelly Ann thinks LeRoy isn't thinking clearly. The stepfather will pave the way for a peaceful surrender."

"Here's hopes," Johnson said. "I'll pick you up at eight." Ray disconnected the call and stood. "How about I help you get dinner ready? I need to do something. I just can't stay in bed."

"Point taken. I started the chicken and dumplings before I took my field trip. You can take Mischief for a little walk around the yard and then make a salad—if you want."

"I want." He stood, verified his balance was intact, then slipped on his shoes. "Come on, puppy. Time to go out."

Sophia watched as he crossed the room. "Your gait is normal. That's good. How do you feel?"

"Not bad, now that I'm off the bed. By tomorrow, I should be good to go out and get the son of a bitch."

***

Steady, light rain fell, cooling the July morning. Ray stood outside their little house on the covered porch waiting for Johnson. He wore a baseball cap to cover the small bandage on his head and a reinforced dressing Sophia had provided on his leg. Still, he hoped they didn't have to hike to the cabin.

After they were underway, Ray said, "I think we should play this low key. If Sophia is right, Vast will be expecting us and, hopefully, be ready to end this."

Johnson took the long, rutted road to the Jones's house at a slow speed. He avoided the bumps, kept out of the larger puddles, and didn't bottom out his patrol vehicle. The gravel proved to be thick and the mud minimal. The rain, however, was a downpour.

The house, atypical for the neighborhood, was a modern

log cabin with a wrap-around porch and several matching outbuildings. The land beyond the house opened into a pasture for a small herd of cattle. A field of corn flanked one side of the pasture and, what looked like bean plants, hugged the other side.

Fred Jones stepped through the front door, coffee cup in hand. "Busy place today. I reckon you're here to visit the cabin."

"Yes, sir." Johnson exited the car and approached the man. Rain pounded his hat and cascaded down the back of his department-issued slicker.

Ray rolled down the window to hear the conversation.

"Detective Stone—" he motioned to Ray, "and I are here for LeRoy."

Jones nodded. "That's what Warren said when he was here an hour or so ago."

"You know Warren Hogarth?" Johnson said.

"I do at that. We served in the Army together many years ago, but we've kept in touch. I offered the cabin until they could figure out what to do with the kid."

The explanation answered several questions. Ray thought for a moment about the numerous laws the man broke and the possibility of pressing charges. Then, he shoved the notion aside. Go along to get along.

"Can I get to the cabin in the vehicle?"

"No, Jim, you can't, especially in the rain. The road isn't anything more than a mud trail now. I'll take you and the detective in my Land Rover." He stepped off the porch and approached Ray's open window. "I heard you were forced off the road, Detective. I'm glad to see you're okay."

"Coming along." He slid out of the car and turned his collar up against the rain. A wave of dizziness overtook him, and he grabbed the roof of the car for support. After the spell passed, he offered his hand to Jones. "Thank you for assisting us."

"It's the right thing to do." He headed in the direction of an outbuilding that looked like a freestanding garage.

IMPERFECT ESCAPE

"You sure you're okay for this?" Johnson said. "I saw you almost keel over a moment ago. I can call for a sheriff's deputy to help."

"I'm fine. Let's get to it."

Ray and Johnson sloshed through the mud, following the path Jones had taken, and soon they were in the Land Rover—Ray riding shotgun and Johnson in the back seat—bouncing over the raw terrain to the left of the house. After a few hundred yards, Jones turned toward the back of the property and found a well-worn trail, just wide enough for the Land Rover.

Jones maneuvered the vehicle with expertise, keeping its tires on the grassy hump in the center of the trail and the leaf-covered edge to the right until he slipped off and into the mud-filled ruts.

"Damn," Jones said.

The rain grew heavier, sheeting off the windshield and hood of the Land Rover.

Jones backed a few feet, then eased forward. The vehicle dug further into the muck. A front tire found solid ground, and Jones eased back onto the elevations in the center and on the side of the trail.

"Close one," Ray said.

"Even with the four-wheel drive, I've gotten stuck out here. Today we were lucky."

Several minutes later, Jones stopped in front of a weathered, though solid-looking, log cabin. "Wife and I lived here while the house was being built. At the time, there was a decent driveway, but I covered it with crops. I planned to let the old place fall apart, but it's sturdier than I thought."

Ray felt as if he'd stepped about one hundred and fifty years back. The cabin was in decent repair and had pristine window frames. Otherwise, it all looked original.

"I'll wait here." Jones settled in his seat. "Oh, there's a back door, by the way."

"Thanks." Ray climbed out and pulled up the collar of his windbreaker. Rain pelted him in the face. He waded through ankle-deep mud to the half-open door, standing on the porch and to the side of the door frame. "No time like the present." He motioned to Johnson to head to the right.

Johnson made his way around to the back of the cabin.

Ray unsnapped his holster strap and rested his hand on the butt of his Glock. He knocked on the doorjamb. "Police. Vast, are you in there?"

A weak male voice responded. "Come in, Detective. I've been expecting you."

Ray found Vast propped against a pillow on one of the two single beds in the one-room cabin. The bandages on his left hand were clean and intact, though applied without obvious skill. His rifle lay close, but Vast made no move to grab it. A wood stove, dry sink, and fireplace occupied the far wall. Several boxes of ready-to-eat foods filled the middle of a small table. A couple packages were open, though there were no visible plates or utensils.

Ray approached Vast, moved the gun out of reach, then secured his own weapon. "Johnson, come in," he said in a loud voice, then softer, "LeRoy, you're under arrest for manufacturing and distributing methamphetamine."

Vast nodded, then closed his eyes.

Johnson moved to Ray's side.

"Johnson, read him his rights. Vast open your eyes."

Vast mumbled, "Yes, sir."

When Johnson finished, Ray stepped closer to the bed. "The first thing we're going to do is haul you into the hospital. I think we'll do that in Jones' Land Rover and Johnson's patrol vehicle, if you think you can handle the ride. It'll be faster than calling an ambulance."

"Ah hell, man. No ambulance could get here anyway." Vast closed his eyes and appeared to drift off for a moment. "A police car is fine. I've lasted this long. I'll last another hour."

Johnson fashioned a sling from a roll of gauze, helped Vast to a sitting position, then assisted him to stand. Vast's legs collapsed under him. Johnson supported the weight while Ray grabbed the blanket from the bed and wrapped it around the

IMPERFECT ESCAPE

man's shoulders.

With Ray on one side and Johnson on the other, they half-carried, half-dragged Vast out the door and through the downpour and mud to the Land Rover, then lifted him into the back seat. Johnson climbed in next to him.

Vast passed out before Jones started the vehicle.

Johnson said, "Hope he doesn't die before we get to Crestville."

"Hope not, too. We need him alive and talking."

Chapter 33

Sophia

Sophia peered through the glass doors at the deluge threatening to flood the ambulance entrance portico. Huge portions of the emergency department's parking lot were submerged as Tennessee's infamous ponding claimed the immediate area. The mid-morning storm raged and blew. She hoped it would soon be over. Even so, it would take hours for the flooding to disappear.

A phone call a few minutes earlier from Ray had alerted her to his and Johnson's impending arrival with LeRoy Vast. The usual, heavy truck traffic on I-40 meant the trip down the mountain in the storm would be tricky.

Nerves on edge, she watched until a Plateauville patrol car pulled into the ambulance entrance. Ray, driving the Ram, slid in behind. He slid out and opened the driver's side, back door of Johnson's vehicle. Rain whipped around him. A puddle of water splashed against his calves.

"Hey Ricky," Sophia said, motioning for him to join her. "Let's go out and help get LeRoy Vast in here."

Ricky Tondo laughed, pointing to the foggy window and the blowing rain. "Good eyes, girl."

"Nah, Ray called me on his way in. He knew I was working trauma today."

She snagged a wheelchair and headed out. Ricky followed.

IMPERFECT ESCAPE

"Hi," she said, touching Ray's shoulder. "How you doing?"

"Head's fine, but I suspect my leg dressing is soaked. Vast needs some attention first." He leaned into the driver's window. "Johnson, I'll stay here. You can head back up the mountain. Give the chief an update when you get there."

"Will do," Johnson said.

"Ricky and I can handle it, Ray. Go inside so that leg doesn't get even wetter. We'll be going into Room One. You can wait there." She slipped around Ray and leaned into the car. A faint, foul odor of gangrene drifted toward her. "Mr. Vast, slide over this way if you can."

Vast edged toward the door. The stink intensified.

Sophia and Ricky helped Vast turn in the seat. He stood, then collapsed into the car. Trying again, they eased Vast out—one nurse on each side—and into the wheelchair. After pushing him into the ED, they helped him onto the stretcher.

Vast closed his eyes.

"Mr. Vast, I'm Sophia." She tipped her head in Ricky's direction. "That's Ricky. We need you to stay awake for a few minutes and give us some information so we can take care of your arm. Ricky, get the physician, please."

"I aim to serve." Ricky scowled and left the room.

Vast opened his eyes. "Are you the Sophia my wife talked about?"

"Yes, that's me. We want to get you taken care of and on the road to recovery."

"Don't you mean on the road to the jail?"

Sophia took his vital signs, performed a quick exam, and asked Vast the essential questions about his health history and allergies. "How long have you had a fever?"

"A few days."

"Tell me how you lost your left hand."

Vast glanced in Ray's direction, shuddered, then seemed to drift off.

"Mr. Vast, tell me about your hand." She donned gloves and a mask, placed a linen protector under the wounded arm, and began to remove the tape holding his bandage together.

She gasped at the stench, then held her breath.

"I was outside the lab, you know, where we cooked the meth. It exploded. Somebody torched it." Vast mumbled other things for a few words, but his speech was incoherent. Then, "I ran. Figured someone wanted me dead. I'm always in the lab, but this time I was out back because I had to take a leak."

Sophia turned her head away and grabbed a breath. "So, how did your hand get amputated?" She continued pulling tape and snipping at dressings with her bandage scissors, finding it necessary to breathe and smell while doing so.

"I figured I'd fake that I died in the fire. Who'd know? I could see through the window that my cousin Richie was a goner. I mean I could see him burning. He'd been standing close to the product. We look a lot alike. So, I ran off into the trees."

"Then what happened?"

"I went to the old cabin on my property and cut off my hand."

"Were you high at the time?" She snuck another almost-clean breath, cringing at the thought of what Vast had done.

"Higher than a kite. I did some product before I took a leak. Then I did some more before I cut myself." He paused. "I tied my belt around my arm and took the hand with me to Kelly Ann. I burned it some, then made her throw it in the trees at the park. I wanted someone to find it and believe it was all that was left of me."

Sophia continued removing the bandages from Vast's left arm. She was getting closer to the wound.

He cried out in pain.

"Sorry." She kept working on the arm. "Did you see who started the fire?"

"I think it was the devil."

Ray made a little spinning motion with his finger, signaling her to keep asking questions.

"Did you see him do it?"

"Hell no, but he threatened me, said he was going to blow me the hell up and take all my business."

IMPERFECT ESCAPE

"Wow. You don't really think it was the devil, do you?"

"No, a man, but the devil anyway. Evil."

"Did you recognize him? Does he have a name?"

Looking at her with a puzzled expression, Vast muttered, "He wants to be the man. He says he's going to put Silky out of business and be king." He closed his eyes.

"I'm going to remove the last of the gauze. It looks like it might stick a bit."

Vast didn't reply.

Sophia continued, being as gentle as possible, while Vast moaned. The foul smell was close to unbearable. Thick brown puss oozed from the infected stump. Red, swollen, angry flesh framed the jagged amputation wound. She glanced at Ray. "Gangrene."

After taking a culture of the drainage, she cleaned the wound. It appeared the infection, though well-established, was confined to the immediate area. She loosely covered the stump. "We need to wait for the doctor, now."

Sophia pulled a stool over and perched on it, being careful to be upwind in the draft created by the air conditioner. She removed the mask. "What else can you tell us about this guy who wants to take over?"

"Be king, you mean," Vast said. "King of the county, maybe. Where am I?"

"You're in the hospital. Detective Stone and Officer Johnson brought you here."

"What day?"

"Monday," Sophia said.

"Did you take care of my cousin Richie?"

"No, LeRoy. You told me you saw him get killed."

"Ah, I guess so." He muttered several incoherent sentences, then slurred his words as he continued. "The devil blew up my lab. Said he had a load of stuff out in the hills, that he was cooking there, too. Said he had enough to supply the whole damn county, maybe the whole state."

"Did he tell you where this place is?"

"No, he's the devil, but he's not stupid." Vast closed his eyes.

Chapter 34

Ray

The next morning Ray called Sophia at work.

"Do you have time for a coffee break?" he said, his voice soft and deep.

"Give me a minute to check with the charge nurse."

While he waited, he reviewed what he wanted to accomplish with his bedside interview of Vast. The meth cooker had alleged his lab was torched but never gave up the name of the perp—the perp who Ray wanted to arrest for arson and multiple murders.

Sophia came back on the line. "When you getting here?"

"In five minutes."

"I'll be in the cafeteria," Sophia said. "It's looks like a good time for my break. I'll get you coffee and a Danish or something."

"Nice. Can you get me the scoop on Vast's condition before then?"

"Ah."

"He's in police custody," he said. "It isn't a breach of confidentiality."

"Right. Yes, I'll check the notes in the system. Meet you in ten minutes then."

They disconnected, and Ray took the Willow exit off I-40. Willow was a mishmash of old and new businesses and reminded him of streets in South Florida, 441 in particular. He hit a couple of red lights and a small Crestview-style traffic jam, all of which delayed him enough to arrive at the cafeteria as Sophia entered. The combined smells of coffee and frying bacon filled the entry foyer. He joined her in line to get coffee, snagged a sweet roll for each of them, and paid the cashier.

He sat across from her at the table she chose near the window. "Thanks for meeting me, sweetheart." He prepared his Danish and took a big bite. "What do you know about our friend Vast?"

"Nothing like getting right down to business." She paused. "His surgery finished around eight last night. The surgeon took off another couple of inches of his left arm and was able to get a clean wound closure. At least, she thinks it's clean. Time will tell. He's on intravenous antibiotics and heavy-duty pain medication, but the nurses' notes said he was oriented times three."

"Which means?"

"Oh, to person, place, and time."

"Better than yesterday, I suppose."

"Hey, with all due respect, the man had reason to be confused." Her voice rang with sass.

He scowled, then sipped his beverage and took a bite of his Danish. "Anything else?"

"Kelly Ann and her mom were in to see him late last night. The deputy let them in. Rumor has it she brought the baby, too. It was the first time LeRoy saw his daughter."

Ray shook his head. "So much for police hold, no visitors." The interpretation of the rules and the lenient enforcement amazed him. The department he had worked for in Florida followed regulations.

"Honey, it didn't do any harm. LeRoy isn't going to escape. He doesn't have the strength, and given he was a target for murder, I'd guess he doesn't have the inclination either. He's safe at the moment."

After they finished their snack, Sophia headed to the ED, and Ray took an elevator to Vast's floor. He stopped at the

IMPERFECT ESCAPE

nursing station and learned Vast had not been medicated for pain for the last three hours. Then he signed in with the deputy sitting at the door, noted there had been no visitors other than Kelly Ann and her mother, and went into the room.

The head of the bed was elevated, Vast's eyes were open, and he looked alert. The room smelled clean. No gangrene odor. A sling suspended his left arm from an IV pole. On the right side, a couple bags of fluid ran into an IV pump. The tubing connected to the back of his right hand.

"Remember me?" Ray said.

"Who the hell are you?"

"I'm Detective Stone from Plateauville PD. We saved your ass yesterday." Ray removed a digital recorder from his shirt pocket and held it for Vast to see, then turned it on. "I'll be recording this interview."

Vast nodded.

"Please don't nod, speak."

"Okay."

"I'm recording this interview. Are you aware of that?" Ray said.

"Yes, sir."

"Please state your full name."

"LeRoy Vast."

Ray proceeded through the preliminaries, getting Vast's address, date and time, and the location of the interview on the record.

"The nurse said you haven't had pain medication since eight this morning. Is that true?"

"Yas'ir, it's true. I could use some more of that medication now. Damn hand hurts like the devil."

"It'll have to wait until we're done." Ray chose not to remind him that he didn't have the hand. "When we picked you up yesterday, we read you your rights. Do you remember?"

"No. I don't remember a whole hell of a lot about yesterday to tell you'uns the truth."

"Okay. I'll read them again." Ray did. "Do you understand?"

"I do." Vast grimaced and shifted his arm a bit in the sling. "Damn thing hurts."

"I'm sure."

"What exactly am I arrested for?"

"For now—running a meth lab, selling meth, suspicion of murder, and anything else I can think of."

"You lying son of a bitch, I didn't kill nobody. I'm the victim here."

Ray thought Vast was the victim of his own stupidity but didn't say so. "I advise you to keep this polite." He paused. "Explain how you're a victim?"

"Someone blew up my lab."

"Just to be clear, what were you doing in your lab, Vast?"

"Ah shit, you'uns know all about it. I was cooking meth for that bastard Silky."

"Do you think it was Silken who ordered the hit on your lab?"

Vast scratched the side of his neck with his right hand, then bit his lip. "I don't rightly know. Maybe. I know Silky don't do the job hisself, but he has ways. People he pays to do his dirty work. The thing is, there was just two of us cooking for him. Me and Flocker. I made way more product than Bubba, and Silky said mine was better crank. So, I don't get why he'd want to blow me up."

"Point taken. You told the nurse in the ED that you saw the devil set the fire."

"Man, I was crazy out of my mind. I don't remember. I must have dreamt it."

"Did you see who blew up your lab?"

"No. I saw someone running away, I think." Vast looked confused. "But, I didn't see his face."

The interview continued for a few more minutes. Then Vast said, "Man, I got me a new baby and a nice wife. I want to do right by them."

Ray paused as if thinking. "Explain yourself."

"Can we make a deal?"

"What is it you have in mind?" Ray said.

IMPERFECT ESCAPE

"Just give me probation or somethin', man."

"Vast, I can't offer that."

"Maybe keep me out of jail or at least put me in a cell by myself. If I go to jail, someone will kill me for sure. If it was Silky who tried to kill me, his guys are everywhere. If it wasn't Silky, then I don't know who to watch even."

"What is it you can give me? We know Silken is top dog in the county, but we don't have proof. Your word in court won't be credible. I need you to help set up Silken. If that goes well, I'll talk to the assistant DA for you."

"I might could do that. What do you want me to do?"

***

Thirty minutes later, Ray said to Vast, "Do you have a cell phone here?"

"Kelly Ann left me one. It's in the cabinet." Vast pointed toward the bottom drawer of the bedside table, which was out of his reach. "The deputy didn't want me to use it, but I asked him to leave it here in case Kelly Ann calls. He stuck it there. Said he'd get it if it rang."

"Nice of him." Ray shook his head. Another leniency. This one he'd take advantage of.

"He's my cousin, twice removed—or somethin' like that. You know how it is in these here parts. We're all related somewhere along the line."

Ray resisted the urge to do a Sophie-style eye roll. He retrieved the device and put it on the overbed table. "I want you to call Krantz, put the phone on speaker."

"He'll object."

"Tell him you can't hold it. IV in one hand, bandage on the other."

"Right."

Ray set the recorder, which was still recording, next to the cell phone. "What's Krantz's cell number?"

Vast recited it—which gave Ray another piece of information about the ongoing communication between Vast and Krantz.

Krantz answered on the first ring. "Yeah."

"This is LeRoy."

"What you calling me for, scum?"

"Listen Bobby, I need some cash—to take care of Kelly Ann and the baby and to help them get out of the county."

Ray thought it was a nice misleading bit of information for Vast to throw in. At least some of his brain cells were working.

"You on speaker? It sounds like it. Who else is in the room?"

"No one, man. I can't hold the phone, I'm in the hospital, and both hands are taped up, you know."

Krantz said, "Why should I care if you need cash? You're nothing. A goner."

"I need to talk to Silky. I have a stash, you know, that I need to unload." Vast's voice shook slightly. Ray thought it gave him more credibility as he told his lies.

"How can that be? You blew your damn operation to bits, along with your helpers."

"First, you son of a bitch, I didn't blow up my own friggin' lab. Second, I need to deal with Silky, not you. You're just the damn messenger. Like always. Acting high and mighty over the rest of us. You just walk out of your house and grab your share."

"I'm the one taking the biggest risks, you son of a bitch." Krantz was quiet for a moment. "Where'd you get the product?"

"Ah." Vast drew out the word, sounding unsure of himself.

"I'm not going to help you if you don't tell me. What I'll do instead is come over and shove the phone up your ass."

Ray nodded.

"I have another lab. It's working just fine, turnin' out product. Good stuff, too."

"How do you know your people didn't rip you off?" Krantz said.

IMPERFECT ESCAPE

"I was hidin' there, man. They took care of me 'til I got real sick. Then on a morning, they took me to the cabin and called the cops to pick me up. I needed to get to the hospital, you know."

"I'll call my uncle." Krantz disconnected.

Ray turned off the recorder. "Now we wait." He stepped out to speak to the deputy guarding the door. "I need to change my sign in time and sign out for two hours ago." He reached for the clipboard.

Deputy Smith, who was an older man on the verge of retirement, said, "Not unless you tell me what's going on."

Ray didn't see he had a choice. "I'm expecting Deputy Krantz to show up in a little while. When he does, I'm going to hide in the bathroom so I can overhear his conversation with Vast."

Smith nodded.

"I'm going to shut the door. When you see him coming, tap twice."

"I'll do that."

"For the record, if you tip him off, I'll see your ass fried as an accessory."

"No need to threaten me, buddy. Truth is, there's no love lost between Krantz and any of us. Dirty deputy contaminates us all."

Ray went back into the room, hoping the guard wouldn't alert Krantz.

They didn't have long to wait. Thirty minutes later, Ray heard two faint taps on the door. He turned the recorder back on and stuffed it into Vast's sling.

Then, "Hey, Smitty, I want to see the prisoner."

"How ya doin', Krantz? I don't see you on my list."

"Smitty, you know how it is. Vast is from Plateauville. I've known him for years. Thought he could use a little support."

"You have a point. Just sign the log," Deputy Smith said.

"Rather not. I'll be out in a few minutes."

Ray stepped into the bathroom and pulled the door shut.

Krantz said, "My uncle told me to come by and get the

information about your product."

"I'd rather talk to the man, himself. He can call me. I'll recognize his voice."

"Not how this works. You know better, you stupid ass."

Ray heard footsteps.

"Hey, Krantz. Keep your filthy hands off my arm."

"LeRoy, old friend. I just want to see your boo boo."

"Nah, man. It hurts a lot, and the doc says we need to be real careful with it."

There was a rattling sound. Ray imagined Krantz was shaking the IV pole suspending Vast's injured arm. He hoped the recorder wouldn't fall out.

Vast yelled, "Ouch. Leave it alone." Then in a quieter voice, he said, "I'll tell you, just leave it alone."

"Thought you'd see it my way. Now, where is the stash."

"Down Dripping Springs Drive, all the ways to the end. Then, go right for about two miles. Maybe more."

"There's no road," Krantz said.

"I know, man. You gotta hike. Take the trail."

"Then what?"

"Turn onto another trail, can't see it good, but it's up in them trees. Gotta cross the creek. Go up the hill for about a mile. Cabin's set back."

"And you think Silken is going to go get the product?" Krantz said.

"Nah, man. I don't. But, I think you will. Or else you'll have Silken call me, and I'll have one of my boys deliver."

"If you're lying to me, Vast, you'll suffer the consequences when you get into lock up."

"So, you say," Vast said.

Ray heard footsteps again, then the sound of the door latch opening.

Vast said, "He's gone."

Ray stepped out of the bathroom. "You did good." He collected his recorder, being careful not to jar the arm, and left, stopping to tell the nurse Vast needed pain medication. Next, he had to coordinate the steps of his plan.

Chapter 35

Ray

Late Tuesday afternoon, Ray finished updating Chief Mullins—who had been out of town for a couple of days for a family emergency—on his interactions with Vast, then Vast and Krantz. He also laid out his plan to stage a fake raid. "I'm thinking Krantz and Silken will want to rip off the stash before the raid starts."

Outside, the rain slammed against the window. Bolts of lightning brightened the dreary sky and heralded the rolls of thunder, prompting Ray to think God was coming to the mountain.

"Why don't you think he'll just go out there today, find nothing, then blow it off?"

Ray laughed and pointed to the window behind the chief's desk. "It's raining so hard the sky might fall, and it has been for days. You've been lucky enough to be east of the weather. The directions Vast gave Krantz make the roads and paths to the cabin impassable until it dries up. Then, he'd have to take a long hike to go check the place out."

"This is good for us, why?"

"Because there's a more direct back route in. It's obvious Krantz is clueless about it—but Johnson knows. Meanwhile, I contacted the DEA. Smith and Custer are assigned. I met them in Nashville during the training. They are eager to help for a share in the action. So, right now they are setting up a fake operation, fake stash of product, everything. They'll lock it down, then reappear when we schedule the sting."

Mullins nodded. "I hate calling them in, but they have the capability to make it look real."

"The DEA wants Silken because of the finished product he moves to Florida. And they are considering the whole *lock him up* scenario if Krantz—or Silken for that matter—is dumb enough to assault federal agents."

Mullins looked skeptical. "Is there already a cabin on site? Sometimes not being born in the area is a handicap."

"It's an old log building, which belonged to Vast's ancestors. His parents used it as a hunting and fishing cabin back in the day. Smith and Custer checked it out and said they could run a gravity feed from the creek above the cabin to provide potable water. They'll bring in everything else. I'm hoping it will keep raining today."

"What does Vast get out of all this?"

"The DA has agreed to no jail time and extended probation— if, and only if, Vast continues to cooperate with us. I figure Krantz will visit Vast at least once more. He'll want to verify the directions to the cabin. Vast will tell him there is another way. That should suck him into the trap and tip us off to him taking the bait. Silken will want him—or someone—to steal the product. At the moment, both of Silken's labs are gone, which puts him out of business and in trouble with his bosses down south."

The chief shook his head. "Lots of ifs and buts in this plan." He sat for several moments, appearing lost in thought. "Well, it's in motion. Iffy, but in my opinion, it may work. I'll go along with it because I think it's the only way we'll put a dent in the meth business in this town. The object of all this must be taking Silken out of the picture. There are so many underemployed young men around, he'll have no problem setting up another lab and picking up where he left off."

"He may have already started," Ray said. "I heard something about it from one of the deputies in the jail. He

IMPERFECT ESCAPE

overheard an inmate bragging he would be working for Silken when he's released next week."

"Any mention of the location?" the chief said.

"No, but the deputy thinks it's out of our jurisdiction. He's alerted the sheriff."

"What's your next step?"

"We need to get Ope in here."

Mullins looked at his watch. "Let's do it. I'll have him transfer his calls to county dispatch." He stood, stepped around his desk, and left the office, returning a few minutes later.

Ope followed, pushing his walker into the room. Then he stood as if waiting for direction, holding on with one hand and running the other through his grey hair.

"Have a seat, Ope," Mullins said.

"Yes, sir." Ope sat, his tenor voice shaking. "What's happening?"

Ray thought the stress of being caught, then being forced to relay planted information was taking a toll on Ope's health. Gone was his cavalier refusal to use his walker around the office. He looked bent and ten years older.

Mullins said, "Ray, it's your show."

Ray filled Ope in. "What we need you to do is contact Krantz. Tell him we're scheduling a raid on Vast's personal lab for tomorrow."

Ope nodded. "Okay."

"I want you to do it now. Use your personal cell phone and put it on speaker."

"Krantz won't want to talk on speaker." Ope spoke in a whisper.

"Don't tell him. Just tell him the connection is bad, has been all day."

"I can try." Ope extracted his phone from his pants pocket and placed it on the desk.

Meanwhile, Ray stood, closed the door, removed the recorder from his shirt pocket and turned it on, and placed it next to the phone.

"Is that necessary?" Ope said.

"It is," Ray said, his voice commanding. "We're building a case against Krantz and will need all we can get to put him where he belongs. Call him. Call him now." Ray didn't like being aggressive to the former cop, now a broken old man. However, Ope needed to cooperate if he was going to stay out of jail.

Ope found Krantz's number on his favorites list and touched the number.

Krantz answered on the second ring. "What's up?"

"Ah, I just heard them planning a raid on Vast's other lab." Krantz said, "Am I on speaker?"

"No. My service has been patchy all day because of the storms."

"Mine hasn't been so hot either." Krantz cleared his throat. "I just heard about the lab yesterday. When are they hitting it?"

"Tomorrow afternoon."

"They'll never get there with all the rain. I drove out to the end of the road this morning, and the trail is over a foot deep in mud."

"There's another way into the cabin."

"Is there now? Where?"

"I don't know for sure. I only know that Stone and Mullins were talking about going in tomorrow by an alternate route."

"Do you know anything else?" Krantz said.

"No. You want me to report it all to Silky? I can walk over there on my break."

"Don't bother, Ope. I'm headed into Plateauville now, so I'll stop by and tell him."

Ray smiled. The plan would work out fine if they could get the timing right.

***

Ray's cell vibrated at a few minutes before nine on Wednesday morning. He expected the call and reviewed paperwork at his

IMPERFECT ESCAPE

desk in the PD while he waited. The rain had stopped, and the day was bright, sunny, and hot. It wouldn't take long for the trails and roads to the Vast family's cabin to dry.

He activated his recorder then tapped the answer icon. "Stone."

"This is LeRoy. I just had a visit from Dep-u-ty Krantz."

"Did you? What was on the deputy's mind?"

"He wanted to know the other route to the cabin. He said he was out that way this mornin' and the mud along the trail is knee deep in some places. Said he made it about a hundred yards before he had to turn back."

"What did you tell him?"

"What we agreed. There's a two-rut trail from the other side, but he'd have to cross Old Man Janus's pasture, and he might not take kindly to it, him hating the sheriff and all."

"Did Krantz mention Silken?"

"Yup. Said he'd tell Silken on a morning, the same one where hell freezes over. He said, too, he'd make sure I get my percentage of the take when he unloaded the product. I told him good. I needed the money for my lawyerin' and stuff."

"Anything else?"

"Yup. He wanted specifics about how much I was cookin', what my market was, and who was a-helpin' me."

"What did you say?"

"I told him it wasn't his damn business. He threatened to hurt me some, so I told him I have a couple of kilos of product under a certain floorboard, and some more stashed in a hidey hole under the foundation on the left side. Then I pretended to drift off. He woked me again, so I acted confused and asked him for my pain shot. He got frustrated and left."

"Sounds like you did a good job." Ray paused. "I'll remember and be sure to tell the DA."

Ray disconnected, called DEA agents Smith and Custer to alert them, then stepped into the next office to tell Mullins the plan was in motion.

"The good thing is, Old Man Janus doesn't much like the sheriff, but he likes the locals just fine. Have Johnson give him a call and tell him to move Tornado into the pasture between the road and the trail." Mullins laughed. "I'm told he's the meanest bull in Middle Tennessee, and we've got a bunch."

Ray had Ope put a call out to Johnson with the prearranged signal to meet Ray at the department. Knowing Krantz routinely monitored the channel, they wanted to use the message to assure he continued to believe the raid was planned for late in the evening.

Thirty minutes later, Ray met Johnson in the parking lot and headed out to Janus's place. Though it was early, the day felt warm and humid from all the rain. Ray cranked up the air-conditioning.

"Smith and Custer are at the cabin," Ray said. "And, they have cell service. Amazing. Said the road was solid enough for hiking, but too soft for their vehicles. Janus is waiting for us to cross the pasture, then he'll close the gate and release Tornado."

"Why are we puttin' the bull in Krantz's way? I mean, we want to get him to the cabin, then catch him in the act of robbin' the place. Right?" Johnson said.

"We do. But we want to make sure it looks like the real thing and assure he isn't tipped off. If there was always clear access to the back road, there would be no reason to ever use the trails."

"You're right." Johnson pointed. "The turn is up there on the right. Are you sure he didn't bring Silken in on the deal?"

"To a degree. The feds have Silken under surveillance. Krantz hasn't been near the store or the house. There haven't been any phone calls either."

"They could be usin' burners."

"True, but they haven't in the past, so there is no reason to suspect they would now." Ray turned into the drive leading to Janus's farm. A sprawling, ranch-style home faced the main road. A big red barn sat to the left. Beyond, a lush green pasture, surrounded by a sturdy wood fence, stretched to the trees in the rear of the property.

Janus stood near the barn door. He waved them closer,

IMPERFECT ESCAPE

then approached the Ram on the driver's side.

Ray rolled down the window. "Hello, Mr. Janus. Thanks for the hand today." The man's appearance was in direct contrast to his well-maintained property. Though he wasn't really old—fifty perhaps—he was balding, sported a ragged white beard and weather-beaten face, and wore coveralls with numerous patches and tears.

"No problem." Janus said, his voice sounding youthful. "Tornado hasn't had any sport in a while. He'll enjoy this." He opened a gate next to the barn. "Leave your truck in there." He pointed to a weathered shed. "Go across the field, then through the gate on the other side. Be sure to lock it. I've already hidden my truck, and the wife is in Charleston visiting the girls. I'll be watching from the back of the barn." He smiled and waved them through.

Ray eased the Ram over the cattle guard—a grid of steel pipes designed to keep the animals inside—and into the pasture, then pulled into the storage building next to the feds' vehicle and a ten-foot high stack of hay bales. "Looks like this is the event of the century for Janus." He stepped out.

Johnson laughed as he climbed down from the truck. "A couple of years ago, Krantz had it in his head he was goin' to bust Janus for havin' a still out back." He pointed to a second gate on the far right side of the pasture. "It's in the trees."

"Mullins knows?"

"Sure. We all do. We don't bother with it. He makes shine for personal use and for his friends. Really good stuff, too. I've had it a few times."

"Part of the letting some slide to get the job done, I suppose."

"Yup." Johnson laughed again. "Mullins is a wise man. He knows how to gain cooperation in these here parts, even if he is an outsider."

Ray shook his head. There were too many moving parts in the plan. And, a bull named Tornado, of all things, had the opportunity to screw it all up.

Chapter 36

Ray

Ray and Johnson trudged across the pasture, exited on the other side, and secured the gate. They watched as Old Man Janus opened the back door of the barn and released Tornado.

Janus gave the big brown bull a pat, then removed the lead from his halter. He waved to Ray and Johnson and disappeared into the barn, closing the door behind him.

Ray was puzzled. "I don't understand why Mullins wanted the bull outside. Looks like he's a manageable critter."

Johnson laughed. "First off, Tornado is only manageable to Janus and his wife. Everyone else, including you and me, are the enemy." Johnson laughed again. "Allowing Janus to have some fun at Krantz's expense is Mullins' reward for the old man cooperating, I expect."

"But Janus let the feds through without a problem?"

"He did. The Vast and the Janus families go way back. In fact, Janus bought this stretch of land from the Vasts. Part of the deal was access to the cabin. Then Janus married one of the Vast cousins and sealed it proper."

Ray chuckled. "Everyone related to everyone else once again. Gotta love it."

Ray and Johnson backed into the trees to watch and wait, making themselves comfortable on a couple of old logs hidden behind a stand of prickly blackberry bushes.

IMPERFECT ESCAPE

As Ray rolled the course of events around in his mind, he realized, yet again, how long, if ever, it would take him to become a part of the Plateauville community. Perhaps it was a good thing in the long run. It would lend him objectivity. Still, he was happy to have Johnson, who seemed to know everyone and everything about the people and the area, with him and on his side.

Fifteen minutes later, an older-model Jeep pulled up to the far gate and Krantz emerged wearing black boots, cargo pants, and a faded tee shirt with the Sheriff's Office logo. His Glock was strapped to his hip. He stood behind the fence staring in Tornado's direction, probably deciding how to cross the pasture. He couldn't go around.

Krantz backed away from the fence and approached the house. He knocked on the door and waited for a minute before returning to the gate, which he opened. He eased the Jeep over the cattle guard and didn't bother to close the gate behind him.

"Son of a bitch," Johnson said. "That's irresponsible, even for him."

"It's a good thing Janus has both the cattle guard and the gate," Ray said.

"He had a problem a couple of years back with kids wantin' to go cow tippin' and leavin' the gate open. First, he put in the guard, then he moved the cows to the side pasture away from the house and the road and put Tornado in here. Problem solved."

Ray shook his head. "Things must get boring around here if kids are still pushing cows over for the fun of it. I tried it once. It isn't as easy as it sounds."

Krantz proceeded at a slow pace.

Ray elbowed Johnson. "Watch. The show starts now." He'd seen bulls in action before and had a sense of what was about to happen.

Tornado dipped his huge head almost to the ground and shifted his weight side-to-side, snorting and pawing the ground.

Krantz crept along, a few feet at a time.

Gregg E. Brickman

Tornado charged and nailed the Jeep mid-grill. The grill dented inward and water shot from the radiator. Tornado twisted his head from side to side before extracting his horns.

"Holy shit." Ray contained a laugh.

Though he had the presence of mind to continue toward the exit, Krantz looked shaken.

Tornado moved to the driver's side of the Jeep and continued poking at it with his horns. Then he backed up and slammed into the Jeep at full speed, lifting it up on two wheels.

Krantz yelled a string of obscenities at the bull, who seemed to take it as an insult.

"Now he gone and done it," Johnson whispered, chuckling under his breath.

Tornado's next run flattened the left-rear tire. As Krantz eased the vehicle forward, the massive creature moved to the rear, dug his horn into the spare tire, then ripped it from the rack.

Krantz pulled tight to the rear gate, opened the sunroof, crawled out, and stepped to the hood.

After pausing for a moment to shake his head, Tornado lined up his attack and rammed the Jeep hard enough to turn it onto its side.

With a look of pure panic on his face, Krantz propelled himself over the gate, landing on his face in the mud.

Tornado, apparently bored with the game, returned to the other side of the pasture. He looked back over his shoulder several times as if monitoring his quarry.

Ray and Johnson, both struggling to contain themselves, made their way up the hill toward the cabin with Johnson in the lead. They were careful to remain out of sight, but still reached the cabin minutes before Krantz.

The one-room rough-log cabin looked sturdy, but weathered and battered. The windows on the front lacked glass, and two out of three steps pitched to the left. A large blue vinyl tarp covered the roof and was tied in place with ropes attached to tent stakes.

"Not a bad job for a short day's work." Ray poked at his

IMPERFECT ESCAPE

cell phone then put it back in his pocket. He motioned toward the cabin. "My cell won't work. Go around back and alert the agents the plan is in play."

Johnson crept off, keeping well inside the tree line.

A few moments later, long, lean, dark-skinned Smith and short, thin, light-skinned Custer followed Johnson around to the front. Both agents looked unkempt, like average meth lab workers. But, Ray knew, they cleaned up well.

"The plan is to let the suspect enter the cabin and lay claim to the methamphetamine. Then we'll all move in and make the collar," Ray said.

"Is Krantz armed?" Custer asked.

"He's carrying his Glock," Johnson said.

"Fan out." Ray pointed in several directions. "We'll come at him from all sides. Be ready to move in fast."

"I agree." Custer crept to the left, slipping into the woods.

The others moved out of sight as well.

Krantz, still covered in mud, approached the cabin, looking side to side. "Hello. Anybody here?" He listened, then drew his weapon, approached with apparent caution, and disappeared inside.

Ray heard the banging and scraping as Krantz moved things and conducted his search. Five minutes later, he appeared carrying a large canvas tote and a small cardboard box. While the two DEA agents and Ray, all with weapons drawn, surrounded him, Johnson captured the events with his cell phone video.

Custer flashed his credentials and motioned to Smith, who did the same.

"DEA. Drop the stuff and with two fingers, toss your gun over here," Smith said.

"Screw you." Krantz dropped the items, pulled out his gun, and pointed it at Ray. "You bastard, Stone. You're an outsider. I knew you weren't one of us."

Custer moved in from the left, his weapon trained on Krantz. "You can't hope to win this. Drop your weapon."

"What's going on here? I'm confiscating these drugs. Back

away and allow me to do my job." Krantz backed up three steps but didn't lower his weapon. "I'm not letting you grab my case. For all I know, you'll have this stuff on the market tomorrow."

"Krantz, put down your weapon. It's over," Ray said.

"This is a big mistake you know, Stone. You set me up." He swung his Glock toward Custer.

Custer, sounding reasonable, said, "Lower your gun, sir."

Krantz looked from man to man, then dropped the Glock to the ground.

Smith closed in on one side, Ray on the other.

With no further resistance from Krantz, Ray handcuffed him. "You have the right to remain silent . . ."

Chapter 37

Ray

"Thank you, gentlemen." Ray nodded to Custer and Smith.
"What am I being charged with?" Krantz said.
"It's a long list," Ray said. "Possession with intent to sell for starters, assaulting an officer, and assaulting federal officers. I'm sure we'll add charges as we go along. Let's go inside."
"So y'all can beat the crap out of me?," Krantz said, attempting to pull away.
"Not your decision." Ray shoved Krantz toward the cabin door. "It's time to talk."
"I want an attorney."
"Of course, you do. We talk. You listen," Ray said.
The DEA agents moved Krantz inside and sat him on a stained folding chair—the only chair—next to a tattered card table. Bottles of liquid and jars of powders littered a long counter next to a make-shift sink and a camp stove. The odors of the chemicals mixed with underlying mildew created a thick, nauseating stench.
Ray removed a folded paper from his back pocket and laid it on the table in front of Krantz. He put a pen next to it. "Johnson, move the former deputy's cuffs to the front, please, so he can sign the paper."
Johnson did as directed.
"I'm not signing anything." Krantz spat out the words as

if they tasted bad.

"Read it. It says you've been read your Miranda Rights and understand them."

"Okay." Krantz signed, then rubbed his face with his cuffed hands. "I'm listening."

Ray admired Krantz's illusion of control.

Agent Smith stepped forward, taking the lead. He laid out the details of the setup at length. "Detective Stone and Officer Johnson have a solid case on the local charges against you. You can't get around it." He motioned to the cell phone Johnson pointed in their direction. "Officer Johnson was kind enough to capture the whole event. He is continuing to record this interview. In fact, the whole process was recorded, including the call you received from Ope and your promise to talk to Silken. We've had the store under surveillance, and you never went to see him, nor did you call."

Krantz stared straight ahead.

"We'll get your Uncle Silky for interstate trafficking with or without your help. However, it's up to you whether you take the fall with him or not."

"How so?"

"We know you blackmailed Ope for information about planned drug raids and passed the information on to Silken, Vast, and Flocker," Smith said. "We can prove you've been an errand boy for Silken. And we can prove you acted as a shield between him and the Sheriff's Department until you were reassigned. If you cooperate, by that I mean tell us everything you know about Silken's operation and help us build a solid case, we will see to it you don't face federal charges or do any federal time. You know you won't get early release from a federal facility. If, on the other hand, you decide to stay quiet, we can and will take you down."

"What about the local charges?"

Ray stepped forward. "We can deal. You won't get off free. I can't make any promises on behalf of the DA, and you know he won't deal on any homicide charges. It all depends on you."

IMPERFECT ESCAPE

Krantz squinted. "Damn, Stone, I wish I'd gotten your job."

"It wasn't for lack of trying." Ray leaned close to Krantz. "What will it be? We can haul you into Crestville now for booking on the local charges and pending the federal arrest warrants, or you can decide to cooperate."

Krantz glared at Ray. "You son of a bitch, you leave me no choice."

Ray smiled. "A setup is about not having a choice."

"I'll talk."

"Good. Now, before we continue, do you waive your right to an attorney?"

"I do."

Ray produced a second form. "Sign here." He pointed.

Krantz signed the form waiving his right for counsel.

"How did you find out about this stash?" Ray said.

"I went to see Vast, and he told me. What's in it for him, by the way?"

"None of your concern." For the sake of the recording, Ray led Krantz through the events leading to his appearance at the cabin. "Why didn't you tell Silken about the stash?"

"I'm tired of being his boy. I thought I'd get the meth and do a little business. Vast is out of the way, and will be, probably, forever. Flocker, who you know is a major player in the whole local competition, is also out of the mix for a while. I thought I'd fill the void. Who would know? Certainly not my uncle, who relies on me for his local information."

Ray filed away the comment about Flocker for later use. He knew, of course, Flocker was involved in the meth trade. What he hadn't heard before was the term *major player* in reference to him.

Custer asked, "What do you know about Silken's business?"

Krantz paused, looking threatened for the first time. He took a deep breath and exhaled. "Silken was sent here by the powers in Miami. They wanted to expand their market and needed to assure a steady supply for the South Florida meth heads. Silken picked Plateauville because of my aunt's tie to the community. He knew he'd be able to establish himself as a legitimate businessman. His boss in Miami funded the store. Now the Miami people are threatening to kill him if he doesn't fix his production problems."

"What's his take on the lab explosions?" Ray said.

"The thing is, Silky doesn't know who's to blame. It's for sure he isn't. He had a nice operation going. Vast produced a huge amount of product. Flocker, too."

"Did he know both of them were dealing on the side?" Ray said.

"Sure, he did. In fact, I told him myself."

"And?"

"He said, 'Let them. They aren't taking much out of my pocket, and it gives them incentive to keep me supplied.' He had me keep track of their output and make sure he received his first."

"Were they aware Silken knew?" Ray said.

"I don't think so."

"You said you wanted to go into business for yourself. Did you blow up Vast's lab?"

"No. I'm not a killer. What I planned to do was make Vast supply me, too. My idea was to tell him that if he didn't I'd report all of his outside sales to Silken."

"You're a real scuz, you know?" Ray shook his head. He spent some time going over the details of the meth lab explosions and Krantz's alibis for the times in question. He felt somewhat certain Krantz told the truth.

"Why were you harassing Kelly Ann Vast? And my fiancée, for that matter?"

"Silken's orders. Nothing personal."

"Funny, they don't feel that way about it. Did you try to kill Flocker in the hospital?"

"No. I went to see him. I even threatened him."

"Why were your prints on his IV pole?"

Krantz looked like he was about to speak, then stopped. He clenched his brow. "Strange thing. He asked me to move it.

IMPERFECT ESCAPE

I didn't think much about it at the time."

"Did you touch it?"

"Yes. I did. He couldn't reach it, and he said he wanted to be able to move it around."

"Someone put an extra drug in his IV bag. Weren't you a medic? You know how to do it."

"I was a medic and know how. But, I didn't do it. Maybe Flocker did it himself. I wanted his product, too. Figured if I took some from Vast and some from Flocker, I'd be in good shape. Then Vast's lab blew. I tried to put the screws on Flocker. Then he blew up his own operation."

***

Late Wednesday afternoon, Ray, Johnson, and Custer gathered in the back of a white van they'd borrowed from Johnson's father and parked in front of Silken's Dry Goods. Smith sat in an old clunker behind the store near the back door.

Ray set up a feed from the video camera in Krantz's sunglasses to a monitor and digital recorder in the van. Keeping it on a need-to-know basis, the signal was also routed to Mullins in the Plateauville PD and Sheriff Foster and Detective Shim in Crestville. The sunglasses recording device was new for the Sheriff's Department and was something Krantz had not used before, preferring the model worn on the front of the shirt. Ray thought it a perfect setup.

Right on schedule, Krantz parked two spaces away from the van.

"Krantz, now is the time," Ray said.

Krantz nodded. In full uniform, with his earpiece in place and cam running, he exited his vehicle and stepped into Silken's Dry Goods. "Uncle Carl, you around?"

"I'm in the office. Come on back, Bobby."

The video showed the patron-free store and the narrow isle leading to the office. Silken sat behind a wooden desk in a cramped space, which was nothing more than a wide hallway with the alley exit on one end and the open door from the store on the other. The only items on the desk were a bottle of whiskey and a small revolver.

Krantz's hand waved in front of the camera. "What's all this, Uncle?"

"Bobby, Bobby. They're coming to kill me. You see, I haven't kept up with my production goals. Now, they've lost faith and . . . you get the picture."

"What would happen if you had a good haul of meth? Would that help?"

"Sure it would, but where am I going to get it? Vast and Flocker are both in custody and their labs are bust. I heard rumors of another lab close by, but I don't know where it is or who's running it. My sources seem to have dried up."

The view from the camera lowered as Krantz sat. Then Silken's image filled the monitor. "It's time to offer him the product," Ray said into the microphone connected to Krantz's standard-issue ear piece.

Krantz adjusted his sunglasses, a prearranged signal that he had the message.

Krantz said, "I heard about another lab out on Dripping Springs at the edge of the county."

Silken grabbed his gun and stood in one motion. "And you didn't tell me? You ungrateful bastard."

Krantz's hand, making a take-it-easy motion, came into view. "That's not how it is. Ope called me yesterday and told me about a raid on the lab scheduled for today. Mullins and Stone were playing it real close, didn't even tell Foster until the last minute."

Silken sat back down but kept his hand on his gun. "Is that the huge lab we've been hearing about?"

"I thought it might be. I tried to get out there yesterday afternoon to check it out, but the trails leading to the place are knee deep in mud. So, this morning I went to the hospital to see Vast."

"Wait a minute. I thought it was Flocker's lab." Silken's face reddened. "You better not be lying to me." Silken pointed the gun at Krantz, who didn't flinch.

IMPERFECT ESCAPE

In the van, Ray laughed. "The boy has bigger balls than I gave him credit for."

Shim's voice drifted over the wire from Crestville. "He should have used them to do his job."

"Put the gun down, Uncle Carl." Krantz's voice rang with authority. "If you kill me, you won't get the kilos of methamphetamine I have in the trunk of my patrol car. The county will just think I made an impromptu bust and scored big. You'll have nothing and get hit by your buddies from down south."

Silken laid the gun on his desk and leaned back in his chair. "I want the damn meth. It's what I need to stay alive and in business. Are you going to quit pissing around and give it to me, or not?"

"First let me show you a sample." Krantz laid a quart size bag filled with meth out of Silken's reach but on the desk. "This stuff is pure. Vast gave me directions to get to the lab through Old Jasper's place this morning. He's been running it on the side. But when he turned himself in to go to the hospital, his guys helped him hide the stuff. He told me where it was in the cabin."

"Why would he tell you?"

Krantz laughed, sounding sincere. "First, I roughed him up a bit, then I promised him a fair share. As if he can claim it from jail."

"You're sure he won't talk, maybe turn for a deal."

"Yeah. He has himself a new baby with that wife of his. I told him I'd get even, and he wouldn't have a family if and when he survived jail and walked out."

In the van, Custer said, "We need to wait for Silken to take possession of the package. Then we can move in."

"Right," Ray said. "Johnson, you stay here and monitor the feed. Tell us when he makes the touch."

"Okay," Johnson said, tapping the microphone. "Everyone hear me?"

A chorus of affirmative replies echoed through the van.

"I'm in position in back," Smith said.

Gregg E. Brickman

Ray and Custer climbed out of the van and assumed their positions near the front door, chatting and attempting to look casual. The plan was to draw as little attention to the bust as possible.

A Plateauville black and white pulled to the curb. "What's happening, guys?" the young officer said.

Ray took three quick steps toward the vehicle and leaned close to the driver's side window. "Drive on."

The officer frowned, said "Asshole," loud enough for all to hear, and sped away.

Ray returned to the front door, hoping their quarry hadn't heard the interruption.

Silken said, his voice demanding, "Give me the damned product."

"Here you go, Uncle."

Johnson's voice came through the earbuds. "Silken is handling the baggie."

Ray said, "On three. One. Two. Three."

Ray and Custer burst inside, weapons drawn. Smith appeared through the alley door.

Krantz grabbed Silken's gun.

Ray, Custer, and Smith rushed into the office and grabbed Silken.

Silken stood with his hands behind his back, facing his nephew, who had his service weapon pointed at him.

Ray cuffed Silken. "Stand down, Krantz."

Johnson entered the room.

"Cuff Krantz."

"Yes, sir," Johnson said.

"So, Bobby Boy, that's how it is, huh?" Silken sneered.

"I'm afraid it is. I didn't have a choice."

Custer and Smith pulled their federal badges, waved them at Silken.

"DEA." Custer went on to read Silken his rights.

"I want my lawyer."

"All in good time," Smith said.

Custer grabbed one of Silken's elbows, Smith the other.

IMPERFECT ESCAPE

They led him out the back of the store, where, Ray knew, an unmarked Federal SUV awaited.

Chapter 38

Sophia

On Thursday, Sophia drove into Crestville as the sun rose over the mountain and shone in her rearview mirror. The varying green of the trees, their leaves shimmering in the light, was interspersed with brown—trees that had fallen victim to some form of pestilence. She had grown to love Tennessee, but the woods reminded her of the evil that lived and died amongst the throngs of good folks.

The previous evening, Ray had updated her on the events of the day. The DEA had whisked Silken away to a place unknown, and for his protection, the county sheriff had transported Krantz to the lockup in Blount County, where he would be anonymous.

Two dead trees chopped from her world, but Ray had said there was more. The arson and murders at Vast's lab still lay on his desk as an open case.

She focused on the day to come with pleasant anticipation. Her assignment was the ED Trauma Unit.

She checked her mirrors and the road ahead for the Tennessee Highway Patrol, then increased her speed. A few minutes later, she parked the MINI in the employees' parking lot nearest the ED and entered the hospital.

The staff lounge was empty except for Ricky Tondo, who was busy making a fresh pot of bad coffee.

IMPERFECT ESCAPE

"Hey, Ricky. One of these days I'm going to bring in a bag of real coffee."

"You'll put everyone in shock. Then who will staff this hellhole?" Ricky frowned.

"My, my, aren't we negative today." She put her purse in her locker and removed the tools of the trade—stethoscope, bandage scissors, hemostat, pens, and her favorite calipers—placing them in the various pockets of her cargo pants. "Where are you assigned today? Do you know?"

"Trauma."

"Cool. Me, too. At least the time flies there."

"True." He replaced his frown with a scowl.

"Why the grumpy mood? Are you going to be like that all day? If you are, I'm going home. I feel a headache coming on." Sophia smiled to soften her words.

"Nah, I'll cheer up. Jonathan was on a roll this morning before I left for work. Not even a kiss goodbye. I'm sure it'll be fine when I get home." He removed the pot from the coffee maker, interrupting the flow of coffee, and poured two cups, handing one to Sophia. He sat at the table and motioned for her to do the same. "Which room do you want today?"

"How about I be primary on the first admission."

"Works."

Twenty minutes later they stood under the trauma entrance canopy watching an ambulance maneuver into position. The back door opened. Two deputy sheriffs emerged, followed by two paramedics handling a gurney containing Charles Flocker, a.k.a. Bubba.

Sophia moved to the head of the stretcher. "Mr. Flocker. We meet again."

"You know, sweet-ums, I was hopin' I'd have you today."

Sophia rolled her eyes. "You can tell me why after we get you inside and settled."

"I might could do that."

Sophia looked at the huge, female medic. "What's the story, Pepper?"

"Mr. Flocker got himself into a knife fight in the jail. The assailant stabbed him three times on his abdomen, another on his left arm, and another on his left leg. None of them appear critical." Pepper went on to recite Flocker's vital signs and other data.

"Let's put him in room one."

They rolled the stretcher into the room, parked it beside the hospital's gurney, adjusted the respective heights, and assisted the patient to move. Sophia and Ricky spent the next several minutes examining Flocker. The bleeding in the arm and leg lacerations had stopped. The same with two belly wounds. The third seeped bright red.

Dr. Gold came into the room, listened to their report, and examined the patient. After he'd probed the most severe abdominal wound, he packed it with gauze to staunch the bleeding. "I'll call the surgeon to be on standby, but I think we can handle this without the OR. Meanwhile, Mr. Flocker, you'll need a CT scan to see if there is internal damage. Sophia, cover all the wounds and start an IV of normal saline."

"Did that son of a bitch kill me, Doc?" Flocker's voice shook.

"No, but I'll need to spend some time sewing you up. One of the puncture wounds on your abdomen is deep, but I don't think it penetrated beyond the adipose tissue."

"Huh?" Flocker knitted his brow.

"The abdominal fat," Sophia said.

Flocker laughed. "Saved by my belly. No shit."

Sophia called for the CT scan, started the IV, and covered the wounds, then she pulled up a stool. "Now, Bubba, why were you glad to see me? One nurse is the same as another."

"Not really. You saved my life on a morning. I want to thank you." His grin was sheepish.

"You're welcome. Right time, right place." She looked him in the eye. "What else?"

"What else?"

"I can tell there is more." Sophia leaned closer so she would be able to hear Flocker's response but the deputy outside the door wouldn't.

IMPERFECT ESCAPE

"When Vast's lab went up, I saw—"

She looked up when Paul, a tech from the main ED, entered.

"Bubba," the tech said. "I haven't seen you in a spell."

"Nah, I've been busy."

"In jail, I hear."

"Yup."

Sophia looked from man to man. "You know each other?"

"Ah—" Flocker said.

"Sure. You didn't know Bubba used to work here? Fact is, he was in the same paramedic class as me."

A piece fell into place for Sophia. She kept her face neutral.

"Anyway," Paul said, "I wanted to say hello." He left.

"Now, where were we?" Sophia hoped Flocker would continue the conversation. "What did you see when Vast's lab exploded?"

Flocker exhaled in a rush, then surveyed the room, stopping when he was eye to eye with Sophia. "I misspoke. I didn't see nothing." He paused. "I know De-tec-tive Stone is your main squeeze. I want you to give him a message."

"Why? Just have the jail call him." She rolled the stool a few inches away from his stretcher.

"No, you see, if I stay there in the jail, I'm a dead man. Silken's crew is after my fat ass." Again, Flocker's gaze shifted about the room, stopping, this time, on the deputy outside the door. "They'll put me in sick bay for a few days. I'll be safe there, but then it'll be back to the cell. Then the clock be's tickin' on my days."

"So, let me get this right. You want to talk to Ray about making a deal so you don't have to go into the general population."

"Right. I knew you were smart, sweet'ums." Flocker grinned.

"I'll give him a call." Sophia thought, boy would she. She set up for suturing, notified the physician, and assisted.

Two hours later, transport arrived to move Flocker back

to sick bay in the jail.

Sophia called Ray. When he answered, she said, "Flocker just left the ED."

"No shit? Why was he there?"

She gave him the information. "I learned two things. First, he was an ED tech. He's one of the guys who finished paramedic school and ended up working in the ED because he couldn't get a position with Fire Rescue."

"I didn't know." Ray's bass voice slid across the airwaves.

"He had the knowledge to mess with his own IV. In fact, he'd know which drug to use. How much. How to get the timing right to look like an attempt on his life." She spoke rapid fire while trying to contain her excitement.

"Interesting. There is more, I can tell."

"Oh yeah. He said, 'When Vast's lab blew up, I saw—'"

"Saw what?"

"I don't know, we were interrupted. When I asked him what he saw, he said he misspoke. But it means he was there at the time, not riding over after the explosion?"

Chapter 39

Ray

Ray said goodbye to Sophia and disconnected. He remained at his desk, pondering what he'd heard. Flocker had fed him a load of crap, and done so with smoothness and expertise. Now, the task was to corner the fat man and drag a confession from his lying lips.

Ray grabbed the keys to his dented, unmarked Taurus, which the chief had acquired from a neighboring town. He stuck his head in Mullins' office, gave him a quick update, and headed out. He planned to interview Flocker again at the jail.

While on I-40, halfway down the hill to Crestville, his phone buzzed. The caller was Erik Shim.

"Shim, I am headed your way. I want to talk to Flocker."

"That's a problem, bud, and the reason I'm calling." Shim's slight lisp sounded pronounced, as it often did when he was stressed.

"Tell me."

"Flocker is brighter than we gave him credit for. About ten minutes ago, he overpowered the deputies doing the transport from the jail, grabbed one of their guns, forced them to uncuff him, then jumped out the back of the van. A Ford F-250 had been following—casual-like. He jumped into the passenger's seat, and the truck barrel-assed down Broad Street."

"Why am I not surprised?" Ray said.

"I don't know. Why are you not surprised?"

"He slipped and told Sophia, who was his nurse today at the ED, he saw Vast's lab blow. I'm thinking he blew it, and knows he's my perp for the murders." Ray paused. "I'll turn around and go back up the mountain." He exited I-40 and pulled to the side of the road.

"You need to know Flocker set up the fight and the knifing," Shim said.

"Extreme, but I figured. The truck, by the way, sounds like Flocker's. I saw it parked on his farm."

"Makes you wonder if his *invalid* mother was driving it," Shim said.

"The one who needs Flocker for everything?"

"Dear, sweet Mama." Shim cleared his throat. "The deputy driving the van pursued the Ford. The other deputy called it in, then ran the block to the department, hopped in his patrol vehicle, and gave chase. The van driver followed the truck east until it reached the other side of the highway, but he couldn't keep up. By the time dispatch sent another deputy to help look for the Ford, it was long gone."

"It's a big county east of Crestville." Ray waited for a car to pass, then made a U-turn, crossed the bridge spanning the Interstate, and drove east on US-70N. "Do you suppose he's stupid enough to go home?"

Shim laughed. "I'd bet he thinks we're stupid enough not to check, at least not right away. Besides, if he has a stash of cash, it'll be at the farm. He'll need it."

"I've turned around and am heading up 70N now."

"See to it someone doesn't force you off the road again." Shim laughed. "I'll send a couple of deputies out to the park near Dripping Springs Drive to meet you. I'm leaving here now. I'll get there as fast as I can."

"You're thinking we'll have trouble waiting for us at Flocker's house?"

"I am."

Ray disconnected. Fifteen minutes later, he pulled into

IMPERFECT ESCAPE

Bluff Overlook Park where he and Sophia hiked the day the bloody hand fell from a tree and slid down her back. Johnson, whom Ray called during his drive, waited in the parking area. Ten minutes later, three sheriff's deputies and Detective Shim arrived, followed by Mullins in his unmarked.

When the group assembled, Ray said, "Shim thinks there is the possibility of violence—if, in fact, Flocker is at his house. The plan is to approach and surround the house. I'll knock on the door, and, with luck, talk to the woman and find out where her son is hiding." He surveyed the group, discovering he, Shim, and Mullins were the only ones not wearing protective vests.

Two minutes later, they all wore vests and had fitted earpieces and positioned microphones. After removing the AR-15 assault rifles from the trunks, Ray and Mullins climbed into Johnson's Cruiser.

Shim joined one of the deputies. The other two deputies shared a car.

The ride to the house Flocker shared with his mother took ten minutes.

Ray didn't see Flocker's Ford. What appeared to be fresh tire tracks led to the double doors of the barn. Extra markings suggested someone drove the truck around the yard, stopping in front of the house, perhaps, and heading out to the main road.

Johnson parked several yards from the house's front door.

Both deputies positioned their cruisers to block the driveway and prevent an escape run.

Shim and one deputy checked the interior of the barn. After finding the F-250, they walked around to the back of the small, frame house to guard the only other exit.

Johnson, Mullins, and the other two deputies took protected positions behind the vehicles.

Ray approached the front door, stood to one side, and rapped. "Open up. Police."

There was no reply, but he smelled stew. He whispered into his mic, "I think someone is here. I smell food."

"A shadow moved past the window. Someone is moving around inside," Johnson said.

On either side of him, the crash of breaking glass shattered the calm. At first, Ray thought someone on his team was trigger happy, but he was wrong. Rifle barrels emerged from the living room and front bedroom windows.

A scratchy, screaming female voice said, "Stay away from my son. Get off my property."

A shot rang out, and Ray dropped to the deck and rolled off the porch. He screamed in pain as his injured leg hit the first step, but he had to continue the fight.

"Shim," Ray said, "What's the chance of going in?"

"Can't get close enough without getting shot." Shim's voice was loud in Ray's ear.

Ray signaled the men out front to begin shooting. "Keep 'em busy, but don't hit me."

Johnson laughed, then blasted out the top window pane in the bedroom. Mullins took out the one in the living room and the glass in the front door, impressing Ray with his shooting.

"Flocker, you are out-gunned and out-manned," Ray said. "Give it up."

"Go to hell," Flocker yelled, confirming his presence.

Both people inside fired again, but they had hunting rifles, not assault weapons. A volley of shots answered, punching holes in the house's siding and splintering the wood in the door.

"Hold up on the count of three," Ray said as he pulled two grenades from his pocket.

Another round of shots from the assault weapons hit the house, most of them going high.

"One. Two. Three." Ray stood and tossed the first grenade, which sailed through the broken pane in the living room, then hit the ground. The flashbang detonated in the house, illuminating the interior as if hit by lightning. "Resume fire."

Sporadic shots hit the house.

IMPERFECT ESCAPE

"Hold your fire on three." Ray counted, scrambled to his feet, and pitched the tear gas grenade through the same window.

The old lady screamed, then coughed.

"Mama, are you hurt?" Flocker said, choking out the words.

"No," Mrs. Flocker said, then continued hacking and rasping.

"Put your weapons down and come out with your hands up," Ray said.

The barrels withdrew into the house. A moment later, Flocker staggered through the remnants of the front door with his mother clinging to his arm. Both were red faced and coughing.

Chapter 40

Ray

Deputies transported Flocker and his mother to the jail in Crestville. By the time Ray, Mullins, and Shim collected their own vehicles and drove down the mountain, the prisoners were locked in separate interrogation rooms.

Shim headed upstairs to check on Bubba Flocker—who was, in theory, fanning his temper in the interrogation room in the detective unit. Mullins elected to accompany Ray to interview the mother—who they found in a similar room in the women's section of the jail.

The shriveled old woman sat shivering in the too-warm room. She stared at them, not bothering to wipe away the tears streaming down her face.

"Give me a minute." Ray stepped out, returning a moment later with a tattered blanket, which he laid over Mrs. Flocker's shoulders. "Mrs. Flocker, I need to read you your rights." When he finished, he said, "Do you understand?"

"I do."

"Knowing and understanding your rights as I have read them to you, are you willing to speak with me now without an attorney present?"

"Yes, I am."

"Tell me what happened today?"

"Charles's friend called me from the hospital and said

IMPERFECT ESCAPE

deputies were comin' to move my son back to the jail. He wanted me to come to the hospital in his truck. He told me to follow the van real close."

"Did you?" Mullins said.

"I sure did."

"Then what happened?" Ray said.

"The back doors of the van opened, and my Charles jumped out. He climbed in the truck, and I speeded off."

"Are you aware what you did was illegal?" Ray said, keeping his voice gentle.

"I suppose. He's my son. He said he'd get killed in jail. Can't expect me to let you'uns kill my son."

"Do you know what your son planned to do after he escaped?"

"He said he was goin' to run. Wanted to take me along real bad, but I'm too sick. I told him I'd make him a meal first. I thought it would be the last one I ever made for him." She used a corner of the blanket to wipe her tears. "I'm thinkin' I was right."

"What happened at the house when we arrived?"

Mrs. Flocker sobbed. "I'm so sorry. I didn't have no choice when he handed me the gun and told me to shoot. I fired over you'uns heads on purpose. Sweet Jesus, I'm not a bad person."

Ray continued questioning her about the incident at the house. When he was satisfied, he moved on. "Do you know who forced me off the road last week?"

"I think it was the man Charles made to stay with me in the house. He was from Knoxville. Told me hisself, he was a cop there but got hisself fired. The man went out one morning and came back in a white SUV. Then, that same day, Charles called and told me, 'Tell him to do his job now.'"

"Mrs. Flocker," Mullins said, "You've been very forthcoming. Why is that?"

"My Charles told me when we was riding into the jail to tell the truth. He don't want me gettin' more upset."

"I need you to sign a search waiver allowing us to search the house and property again." Ray handed her a sheet of paper to sign, which she did.

***

The upstairs tan-painted room was devoid of adornments and contained a table and four chairs. The deputies had cuffed Flocker's hands to a bolted-down chair and positioned him facing the camera on the wall.

Ray, Mullins, and Shim peered in through the one-way window in the door.

"What did the old woman say?" Shim said.

Ray updated Shim on the interview. "Flocker has a friend in the emergency room who was happy to do him a favor and call her. She and Flocker went to the farm. He was going to take off for parts unknown after a meal." Ray laughed. "Fat stomachs are dangerous." Something Sophia would say, he thought.

"Did Mrs. Flocker say what gun she used?" Shim said.

"Yes. The one with the carving on the butt," Mullins said.

"Then, the ballistics can tell us if it's true," Ray said. "I'll go out there when we're done here and collect the slugs and casings."

"No need. The DA called Nashville. TBI's crime scene techs are on their way. I notified the deputy who's guarding the scene."

"Good," Ray said.

"Oh, by the way, I received a call that Ashley Beach died this morning," Mullins said.

"Too bad. The last I heard she was doing well, and they were planning to take her off the vent." Ray thought a moment. "That makes Flocker's tally two charges of arson and three murders—Ashley Beach, Vast's cousin Harold Kramer, and Vast's double-first cousin Richie Vast. Plus, two attempted murders—LeRoy Vast and me—and multiple charges from today." Ray put his hand on the door to the holding room. "Now's the time. Wish us luck."

Flocker scowled when Ray and Mullins walked into the

IMPERFECT ESCAPE

room. "Made me wait long enough. Think it's going to soften me up?"

"First things first." Ray read Flocker his rights.

"I don't need to wait on my stupid-ass attorney."

"We're only too happy to wait," Mullins said.

"No. Let's do it. Where's Ma?"

"She's being processed downstairs," Ray said. "You dragged her into a mess of trouble."

"That's the thing, Stone. She went and done those things because I made her. She's a good God-fearin' woman."

Ray nodded. "With the list of charges, she's likely to die in jail. Thanks to her loving son."

"Stone, can't you do something to help her? I mean, what if I come clean with you? Can you cut her some slack?"

"Explain to me why we should?"

"She really is sick. She has the cancer, and it's spreading. That's why I had to go off on my own and make more money. The insurance didn't cover the cost of the treatment to keep her alive. All I wanted to do was make some money for Ma."

Ray thought Flocker had put an interesting spin on his story, but it was something to work with. "Flocker, I don't see why we should deal."

"Then get my lawyer."

Ray and Mullins left the room and called the lawyer, who was, again, Holly Aster. She happened to be in the jail meeting with another client, so was available within the hour.

After speaking with Ray and Mullins, Aster met with her client, then asked the detectives to come into the room.

"Lay out what you have for my client, please."

Ray went through the litany of charges, giving specific details and incarceration times for each.

Flocker laughed. "You can't prove anything. Just because I misspoke to that-there nurse of yours, doesn't mean I blew up Vast's lab. I already admitted to blowing mine. And, you done got me solid for today's *Bonnie and Clyde* run, but I didn't do no murders."

"You remember Ashley Beach?" Ray said.

Flocker stared at the table. "No."

"She's one of the people you critically injured when you blew up Vast's lab."

"I told you I didn't blow his friggin' lab. Besides, she's on a ventilator and can't talk no more."

"For your information, Ashley Beach is alive, well, and talking." Ray leaned across the table until he was about twelve inches from Flocker's face. "She saw you torch the place, and she'll testify at your trial." Ray leaned a couple of inches closer. "We'll get you on all the charges, lock you up, and wait for the hangman to come. Tennessee is a capital punishment state, you know. Then we'll get your mother, too. First, she'll know her son is on death row, then she'll die in prison."

Flocker motioned to Aster, who leaned in close to listen.

Epilogue

Sophia

Sophia poured another full glass of Chianti for herself and Ray, then snuggled beside him on the sofa. She settled Mischief on her lap, where the dog closed her eyes and commenced snoring.

"I don't get how she is awake one minute, down for the night the next."

"She's a pup." Ray kissed Sophia on the forehead. "The officers in town and the deputies who helped on the Flocker takedown took me out for a beer today."

"Oh?"

"Johnson said, and I quote, 'You proved you're one of us. We're happy to have you on the team.'"

"Wonderful. I know you've felt like an outsider."

"It does make me feel good. Like, maybe, we made the right decision to come here." He kissed her again, this time on the lips.

Sophia sipped. "You haven't said anything about the case in a couple of days. Is the end result Flocker did it all?"

"Not all, but enough to put him away forever."

"Is it true that he wanted to take over the whole meth trade in the area? Put Silken out of business?"

"He says it is. Turns out he really does—make that did, because the DEA went there today—have a huge operation out in the hills. Thank heavens it's out of *my town*."

"Where did Krantz fit in?"

Ray thought a moment. "I'd say he wanted a bigger slice of his uncle's profits, not Flocker's. Flocker didn't know and decided he'd try to take Krantz down along with Silken."

"So, he set up Krantz with the IV thing?" Sophia said.

"Yup. It would have worked, too, if you hadn't connected the dots when he had the visitor in the ED."

"I feel bad about the old lady. She tried to help her son, and now she's sitting in jail," Sophia said.

"I think his mother's circumstance is what moved Flocker off the mark. He agreed to talk if we went lightly on his ma and took the death penalty off the table for him."

"There is some good in the guy," she said.

"There is some good in most everyone, though in this case, I think he was self-serving." Ray sipped his wine. "The DA talked to Mrs. Flocker's doctor. She's dying of cancer, doesn't have but six months to live. I spoke with the DA and convinced him nothing would be accomplished by her incarceration. So, after the arraignment, they released her on her own recognizance and gave permission to travel to Kentucky to stay with her daughter. The trial date is already set for nine months from now."

"Will she live that long?"

"Doubtful. And if she is still alive, chances are they'll delay it further."

"That's good," she said, snuggling closer. "See, I am useful. I helped." She smiled.

"Never said you weren't. In fact, Mullins wants to put you on the payroll—occasional part-time for when your input would be useful. It will also serve to cover us legally when you get involved."

"Hot damn."

The End

ACKNOWLEDGMENTS

Writing this story has been an adventure. When we moved to Middle Tennessee, I took Sophia Burgess and Ray Stone along. Here I faced a new culture, new language, Tennessee laws and rural policing, different weather and terrain, animals of all manner, mountains and rivers, and not a palm tree in sight. My learning curve was huge, hence the long interval between releases.

I wish to thank:

Shannon Lee, Office Manager, Putnam County Sheriff's Department, for answering my questions and selecting me for the Sheriff's Citizen's Academy. The Academy brought me up to speed on many differences in law enforcement.

Cookeville Creative Writer's Association for help with my Tennessee Southern.

Carpenter extraordinaire, Ed Miller, and hair dresser supreme, Lisa Harvey, for giving me many Tennessee-isms and explaining the usage.

My Florida Critique Group—Randy Rawls, Stephanie Saxon Levine, Ann Meier, Bob White, and Victoria Landis.

My new Cumberland Cove Group—Jeffrey Philips, Beth Nelson, and Eric Beaty.

Retired police officer Tim Schmidt for help with the pit maneuver scene.

My new friends and neighbors who have tirelessly answered my questions, sometimes without laughing. I hope they forgive the liberties I took with the names and descriptions of towns and cities in Middle Tennessee.

The unnamed contributors who are unaware I wrote down their words and phrases, some of which made it into the book.

Beta Readers—Steve Brickman, Stephanie Saxon Levine, Jennifer Samuels, Janet Portnow, Joy Heit, and Katherine Capotosto.

I appreciate every contribution. Mistakes, as always, are mine alone.

ABOUT THE AUTHOR

Gregg E. Brickman was born in North Dakota. She completed her education in Florida and embarked on a varied career in clinical, administrative, and academic nursing.

Credits include *Imperfect Defense, Illegal Intent, She Learned to Die, Plan to Kill, Imperfect Daddy, Imperfect Contract, Illegally Dead,* Chapter 14 of *Naked Came the Flamingo*, a Murder on the Beach progressive novella edited by Barbara Parker and Joan Mickelson, and *On the Edge*, a short story [MiamiARTzine.com]. The Writers' Network of South Florida recognized On the Edge among the finalists in their Seventh Annual Short Story Contest.

Gregg has been active in MWA since 1999. She co-chaired SleuthFest in 2001, coordinated the moderators for several years, served on various committees, and was the Florida chapter treasurer and photographer in 2014 and 2015. She has also been an active speaker in the community, attending book fairs, signings, and other events.

Gregg resides with her husband, Steve, on the Northern Cumberland Plateau in Middle Tennessee.

Made in the USA
Columbia, SC
23 October 2023